DEAD ON TARGET

A Further Thornton King Adventure

DEAD ON TARGET

By
GLYN IDRIS JONES

DCG
Publications

First Published in Greece 2010

© Glyn Jones 2009

The author's moral rights have been asserted.

DCG Publications
www.dcgmediagroup.com

ISBN 978-960-98418-4-9

10 9 8 7 6 5 4 3 2 1

Typeset by
DCG Publications

Printed in England by
Lightening Source.

www.glynjones.net

CHAPTER ONE

Thornton had a client. He was at his desk busily sorting through a mound of invoices and dividing them into neat piles of urgent, not so urgent, not nearly so urgent and bloody hell, if I don't pay this by tomorrow I'm in deepest shit, when there was a knock on the door and she followed it up by entering without waiting for a response. It was a miracle she had made it up the narrow wooden nineteenth century staircase in this almost condemned building, or didn't bring the doorjamb into the room with her, dry rot and all, but she was obviously used to manoeuvring her way through, onto, up, down, around, into, and out of tight spaces.

Thornton honestly believed himself under any circumstances to be a cool customer and he didn't mean to show surprise but his eyes opened very wide at the sight of her, probably a reaction she was quite used to because she didn't seem to be unduly affected by it. To put it bluntly she was, huge, enormous, gigantic, three Amazons all rolled into one. She had more meat on her than a Sumo wrestler, and a Victorian lady novelist (of either sex) would have rated her at a million shekels or more in any Sultan's harem. At a cannibal feast, Thornton thought, she would have satisfied the appetites of forty covers; that is if they had a pot big enough to cook her in. Alternatively she could always have been spit-roasted.

Her name was Aurora Margarita Pemberton, known to her friends as Rory she informed him, proffering an all encompassing fist. Of course at school she was nicknamed "Amp" and when a teacher questioned this as being short for "Ample" with a real adult concern regarding bullying by those in her charge, the rejoinder with wide innocent eyes was, 'Oh, no, Miss! It's because she's so full of life, Miss. It's short for "Ampere", miss because she's so electrifying. A real spark. She is, miss, honest.' Which was a load of old codswallop

1

if ever there was but invariably raised a giggle and settled the matter. Rory of course knew different but didn't seem to mind, Amy for amiable could have been her middle name.

'How do you do?' Thornton responded wondering if he was ever going to get his hand back and feeling mightily embarrassed that neither of his two rickety second-hand chairs seemed large enough to encase her bulk; and they could hardly conduct an interview standing up. There was also the distinct potential, if she did decide to sit down, of splintering wood and an unfortunate, ungainly, and undignified collapse with the possibility of damages both physical (current) and legal (future) that, considering the unpaid bills on his desk, would be catastrophic. Admittedly he had a diamond in his pocket but he didn't want to get rid of that until he was really in trouble, that is the bailiffs were battering down his door. He believed they could strip him of all his possessions bar his bed and the tools of his trade, but tools of his trade had he none, unless an ancient Smith Corona typewriter that had seen better days, was missing the letter F and badly needed servicing could be considered a tool worth talking about.

There was also a further worry, the fact that the office temperature seemed to be hovering just a mite above zero, as was pretty obvious by the fact it was almost lunchtime and Thornton was still in his overcoat and you could see his breath as he exhaled. Freezing cold would increase the danger of painful injury. Bones, no matter how well padded, become brittle in freezing conditions.

'Miss Pemberton...'

'Rory,' she corrected him with a smile.

'Oh yes, of course, Rory. I presume you have come seeking my assistance in some confidential matter and I am sorry to say, thoughtless of me not to collect some on my way in, but I have run out of shillings for the meter and as it would hardly be conducive to an intelligent conversation with chattering teeth, quivering lips, and frozen fingers...' He paused momentarily to wonder what frozen fingers had to do with it... 'and considering the hour of the day,' he looked at his watch, 'may I suggest we move on to enjoy the warmth of my local which is situated conveniently just around the corner. Well nearly,' he added as an afterthought, as around the corner was a good two blocks away, and why was he uttering these entirely unnatural and stilted phrases? Perhaps it was because Miss Pemberton with any luck was going to be his very first genuine client and he badly wanted to impress. But not being himself was not going to impress except badly and he mentally kicked himself for being an ass. Part of his problem could be put down to the fact that she was a most impressive young lady and not just because of her size. She quite obviously never had to or never would have to put shillings in a meter. Her couture was of the highest quality, the string of pearls nestling on the pale blue angora was of the finest, her accessories the most expensive Bond Street could provide, her manner the surest and everything was in the best of all possible taste. This was ex-Swiss finishing school and no mistake and, were it still in existence, she would have been a debutante making her curtsy at Buck House, no argument.

'That's a jolly good idea,' Rory quickly agreed to his suggestion of moving out as the chill was already beginning to seep into her bones. She could feel her teeth beginning to chatter and her chilblains to itch. She had been quite warm on entering the building as the cab that deposited her on the doorstep had been well heated.

'Will we need an umbrella?' Thornton asked as he reached for his hat lying next to the tea tray on top of the filing cabinet. His coat stand having lost one of its three legs was leaning against the wall in danger of falling over at any moment.

'I think not,' she replied. 'Clear blue skies when I came in, which is probably why it is so cold.'

Thornton had the distinct impression there was an adjective missing before the word cold. He was certainly glad though not to have to share his umbrella. Old it might be, well used against England's inclement weather, a little on the shabby and faded side but still the best there was from James Smith of New Oxford Street, hardly large enough though to accommodate the two of them and, in playing the gallant, sure as God made little apples as his mother would say, he would be the one whose shoulder was rained upon.

'Shall we go then?' He put on one of his meant to be charming smiles, which sometimes turned out to be more of a lopsided smirk, but she responded to it in kindly fashion as he held the door open for her.

'Thank you,' she said as she squeezed her way through at an

oblique angle. Good, he thought, by the very nature of her gracious acknowledgement she was obviously not one of the how dare you treat me like a helpless little woman when I am as good as you are sort, and the whiff of her very pleasant and obviously expensive perfume as she passed by seemed to reassure him that neither was she one of the burn the bra ladies who, though he hadn't actually come into contact with any of them he usually, because of television coverage, associated them with greasy anoraks and sou'westers, marching in teeming rain and, he was quite certain the smell of wet, and camping stoves from stopping now and again to brew tea in blackened billycans. Thornton did have a sneaky admiration for them though, at the same time, he wondered how anyone with brains could imagine their actions had the slightest effect on stuffed shirt politicians and world affairs. The bomb was exploded, the moving hand moves on, the clock does not go backwards and you cannot practically alter history, only in history books.

Thornton had distinctly old-fashioned, pre-women's lib ideas. He liked his ladies to be feminine, even ladies as large as Rory, and why not indeed? He had no objection to a girl being joli laid. Often that was sexier, more attractive than a vapid plastic pin up with everything the right size, shape, colour, and all in the right place, and he sometimes wondered if there were some homoerotic tendencies lurking somewhere in his nature when he found himself wistfully dreaming of the twenties when the girls had bobbed hair, flat chests, and called each other chaps. Thornton was definitely not into boobs. Pin-ups could boast them but large boobs were off the menu: small was the order of the day; petite, just enough to cup in the hand and why, he wondered, were humans beings the only mammals to develop breasts before lactation? Oh, yes, he knew all about sexual symbols and all that but it did seem a trifle odd if nothing else. Come to think of it though, (as he followed her down the corridor) did Rory actually wear a bra? And did she have them especially made in some East End or Far East sweatshop where questions as to size, reinforcement, and broken industrial sewing machine needles wouldn't necessarily come into it? But he was really letting his imagination run away with him.

*****

4

Some time previous to Thornton and Rory's coming together, in the boardroom of an office suite, this one in the heart of the city almost within spitting distance of St. Paul's: elegantly panelled, redolent of polish, old leather, and stale cigar smoke; an emergency meeting had been hurriedly called to discuss what seemed an almost intractable problem and the problem, as it turned out, was Miss Aurora Pemberton.

Word had got about that she was dissatisfied with the police investigation, undertaken by Detective Inspector Reg Venables and his squad, and dissatisfied more particularly with the coroner's resulting verdict of suicide while the balance of the mind etcetera; and she was seeking help in unravelling the mystery of her uncle's strange death.

'Evidently word has it,' the company chairman Sir Peter Wheeler, known as "Wheeler dealer Peter", a man of lean but impressive stature, steely determination and very little principle if any, barked once everyone had settled down around the table, 'she's after getting a private detective to look into her guardian's unfortunate death so I would appreciate suggestions please as to what we do about it.'

'Bump her off,' was the first laconic response after a short silence.

'Be serious, Trevor, old boy. How do you suggest we do that? And you don't think it would look highly suspicious coming so soon after Sir Roger's unfortunate demise?'

'Not at all actually,' a cut glass voice broke in. 'She commits suicide because she just cannot accept her beloved guardian's death. Poor little thing… '

'Little?' queried a voice from lower down the table followed by a general all round sniggering.

'I was referring to her femininity and emotional state. She was, after all, very fond of him.'

'And he of her,' another voice added, a remark that caused a further bout of chuckling.

'Now don't be like that please, Jack. Rumours, nothing but rumours.'

'Well he was an eccentric old bird, Sir Roger Pemberton, and we all know about the proclivities of certain bachelor uncles with their nephews and nieces, don't we? So who knows what took his fancy?'

'If he were still alive he could sue you for those remarks.'

'Just as well he's dead then,' another voice piped up.

'Look,' the chairman butted in, beginning to show signs of irritability and before they could all start voicing an opinion, 'we are not here to discuss the sex life of the late Sir Roger Pemberton, real or imagined, but what we are going to do about his ward who is going to be, stating it quite plainly, a right pain in the arse, or worse. Maurice, we haven't heard from you. Any suggestions?'

'Yes,' Maurice drawled. 'Run her over.'

'What?'

'Run her over, old boy.'

Wheeler Dealer bridled a little at being addressed as "old boy", a somewhat undignified and uncalled for way of addressing the chairman of the board, major shareholder and guiding light of an old established company he had more than once pulled safely through the most difficult of times.

'She'd make a splendid target you have to admit,' Maurice continued, unabashed by the change of expression on Sir Peter's face. 'Couldn't hardly miss her, could you?'

'Right. Fine. Yes. Anybody second the motion? I take it, Maurice, you are volunteering to undertake, if you'll pardon the rather doleful expression, no pun intended, this course of action?'

'Certainly not. I never drive. Chauffeur does it all for me. And I certainly wouldn't direct him to knock her over. Think of the damage to the car. A tiny scratch on a Rolls costs an absolute mint to cover up don't you know and the insurance premiums would rocket. No, it needs someone who's never taken a driving test, is therefore without a licence, uninsured, preferably behind the wheel of a stolen vehicle and who won't mind, for a fee of course, going down in the Scrubs or Wandsworth for a spell on a driving without due care and attention charge and causing death by misadventure or whatever the current legal jargon is. With the way things are going these days it probably won't be more than a slap on the wrist anyway and an admonition not to be a naughty boy and never to do it again.' Maurice was obviously one of the hang 'em, flog 'em or lock 'em up and throw away the key brigade though of course it would never apply to himself or any of his own.

'And where do you suggest we find this person?'

'Oh,' there're plenty around. If you were to ask me there's psychopaths virtually on every street corner these days. Turn over a stone and you'll find one. I put it down to the goggle box disturbing weak brains, not just because of the programmes you understand but I'm sure the rays have a terrible effect on brain cells. Addles them completely in my opinion. Never watch the damn thing myself.'

Sir Peter coughed to stop the flow.

'Yes, well just put out the word and, if there is a large enough reward, they'll come running.' Maurice looked around the table, well satisfied with his input.

'And what if he botches it? What if she isn't killed but only injured?'

'It will have put the frighteners on her, won't it? She'll know we've got her in our sights and she had better behave or else.' He waved an admonishing finger as though Rory were in front of him to take notice.

'We had hoped for that before with her uncle, if you remember, which unfortunately is why we are here at the moment.'

There was a silence whilst the board members ruminated on this. Obviously it was a plan with faults and they did not take kindly to plans that weren't considered a hundred percent foolproof, as if such a thing even existed. Many a dictator has ended his life wondering exactly where his plans went wrong. The first thing to worry about with this particular plan was that the person hired could blab and they'd all be well and truly up shit creek without a paddle. They had imagined their plan regarding Sir Roger to be foolproof and had just been painfully reminded by their chairman that it had most definitely gone wrong and they had been lucky in that the day of the inquest the coroner had missed his breakfast, had a terrible journey from East Croyden, standing all the way, was hungry enough to eat a horse and wanted his lunch. They hadn't reckoned on Miss Aurora's interference after the event though. Man proposes, God disposes, though in this case it seemed Miss Pemberton was going to do the disposing unless a solid means was found to dispose of her first.

'Why don't we just buy her off?' someone suggested.

The chairman glared down the table at the member who had come up with this one. Obviously the man was brain-dead. How did he ever get elected to the board? The sooner he was dispatched the better. He could turn out to be a distinct liability.

'Sir Roger might have been amusing himself with his test tubes and what have you down at the docks or wherever,' the chairman sneered, 'but he hardly died penniless and Miss Pemberton I believe is his sole heir. With what had you in mind to pay her off?' Sir Peter's glare became almost unbearable and in its light the miscreant shrivelled visibly. But worse was to come; everyone turned to look at the unfortunate who had opened his big mouth and the man blushed scarlet, recognising his stupidity if not his temerity, but he was fairly new to this game and consequently unaware of its pitfalls. His name was Wilkins, known from bathroom observations as "Wee Willy", and Wee Willy realised he was now in a dangerous situation.

'I do beg the board's pardon,' he whined, almost wondering if pushing back his chair and going down on his knees would help. 'I wasn't thinking clearly.'

'You weren't thinking at all,' the chairman snarled, showing nicotine-stained teeth that gave his dentist nightmares twice a year.

Wilkins, starting to sweat profusely, cowering in his chair to which the seat of his pants was beginning to stick rather uncomfortably but, fortunately, attention was diverted when another voice in self-assured tones piped up with, 'Why not let her go ahead and have her private detective?'

All heads swivelled in the speaker's direction. 'But let's just make sure the person she chooses is a complete nincompoop who couldn't detect his way from his bedroom to the bathroom, remember why he went or find what he's looking for when he got there, so that eventually she gives up in disgust or is just too damn tired of the whole thing and pays him off with nothing accomplished.'

All heads now turned in the direction of the chairman for his reaction.

'Ye-es,' the chairman drawled, stroking his goatee as a sign of his own deep thought, (the beard he fondly believed gave him an air of distinction, a bit like one or two members of royalty who sported small amounts of facial hair) 'and who do you suggest points her in the right direction? I mean in the direction of a private eye who is such a totally hopeless case?'

'I do.'

'You are acquainted with Miss Pemberton?'

'She has... how shall I put this? She has made it quite clear she has an interest in me... as a man, you understand.'

There were murmurs; growls, and grunts of masculine comprehension during which someone trickled out a silent fart and hoped it wouldn't be noticed.

'Naturally that interest is not returned.'

Naturally. Miss Pemberton was hardly likely to ever grace a Pirelli calendar. More murmurs growls and grunts accompanied by the lighting of a number of Corona Coronas, possibly to help disguise the fart that had made its silent way across the table.

'I mean!' He looked around. Would he, with his known and acknowledged reputation as a lady-killer, be interested in someone so... so... to put it kindly... unsvelte?

Nods and sly glances were added to the murmurs, growls, grunts, and the blowing out of clouds of blue smoke. Even Wilkins, wanting to be part of this male bonding, gave a sickly grin, his stomach still churning over, at the memory of his recent faux pas, the seat of his trousers now firmly stuck with sweat to his leather chair, his wee willy practically nonexistent and his scrotum totally retracted and tight as a drum.

'We understand, Mike,' the chairman said with a knowing smile, revealing his yellow fangs. 'Do you know of someone you can recommend her to?'

Mike nodded. 'I know just the man,' he said.

'Then I am sure we can leave the suggested procedure in your capable hands? Would anyone like to propose the motion that Mike proceeds as planned?'

'Proposed.' A hand went up.

'Seconded.' Another hand went up.

'The motion is passed.'

There were gales of laughter at the double entendre before they moved on to any other business.

*****

'So then, who was it recommended me to you?' Thornton asked. 'Does it matter?'

'I suppose not,' as he lifted his mug. 'Idle curiosity really,' and took in a mouthful of bitter.

'Mike Aliff.'

Thornton nearly choked on his beer. Coughing and spluttering he put down his mug so fast he almost sent it toppling sideway to spill a fair amount in her direction across the small dimpled pewter tabletop before he recovered it. He hoped none had splashed over her or that could be the end of a beautiful and rewarding relationship before it even got started.

'I'm sorry,' he spluttered, adding unnecessarily, 'accident.' He started to get to his feet. 'I'll get a cloth.'

'Don't worry,' Rory said, 'no damage done. Sit down.'

He sat down.

'Why the melodramatic reaction?' She asked.

'Mike Aliff recommended you come to me?'

'That's what I said.'

Thornton shook his head, frowning. 'Why I wonder.'

'Because he says you're the best, that's why.'

'There's madness in his method I warrant you, as that old geyser Polonius would have said, and I remember someone else saying that to me not so long ago, those very words in fact, and it nearly led to my early demise. What is he up to I wonder?'

'I don't believe he's up to anything except that he... well... this is a bit tricky...'

'Then let me say it for you, he's been trying, using an American expression I heard, to jump your bones.'

'There you are, you see. He's right. You are good.'

'Not at all. I just happen to be aware of the man's priapic nature. Who could miss it? If he saw a field of daffodils he would still walk about in a cloud of masturbatory fantasy. He's the kind of man who spent all his pay visiting brothels and buying dirty pictures in Port Said during the war. I'm also well aware that he'll maintain all the attraction comes from your side. That way when he's rebuffed his ego won't suffer any damage. What a toad. No, that's most unfair on the poor old toad. Well, well, well.' Thornton shook his head.

'What?'

'There's something very fishy about this. Mike Aliff and I... well... this is a bit tricky...'

'Then let me say it for you, you hate his guts.'

'Normally I'm not the hating type but yes, though I'm sure I don't hate his guts half as much as he hates mine, you're dead on target.'

'Hmn.'

'Have I said something wrong?'

'You know why I've come to see you.'

'As I said, I can only presume it's to do with the death of Sir Roger Pemberton, yes?'

'What do you know about it?'

'Only what I read in the papers, saw on the news. Oh!'

'Yes.' She looked down and ran a finger around the rim of her glass before looking back at him. She was obviously holding in the tears and Thornton could have bitten his lip for being so crass. She had remarkably deep blue eyes. 'So you know what killed him.'

'Yes. I'm so sorry. That was a bit off-colour, that remark about being dead on… yes, well.'

The barman approached their table with a damp not too clean looking cloth and gave the surface a quick wipe down before turning to go.

'Thank you,' Rory said, looking up with a beaming smile.

'What's your name?' Thornton asked.

'Ross.'

'Irish?'

'Yes.'

'What happened to Sean?'

'Sean?'

'The last one who was here.'

Ross shrugged, shook his head, and continued on his way back to the bar.

'This pub seems to have a new barman every other week. What happens to them all?'

'They go back to the Emerald Isle,' she said and then, after a pause, 'or to a better class of pub.'

'Yes, I agree, it is a bit dingy, but it's handy.'

They were both somewhat grateful for Ross's appearance that had given Rory time to recover and Thornton time to think of a better way of phrasing things in future.

'Do you believe it could have been suicide? As you know, that was the coroner's verdict. Do you believe it?'

'I couldn't possibly commit myself on that one unless I saw the police findings and the coroner's report, and analyse how he came to that conclusion.'

'No, Thornton... I may call you Thornton?'

'Of course.'

'You don't need the police report, or the coroner's. I've given it a great deal of thought and I simply cannot believe anyone, least of all my guardian, would commit suicide with a crossbow bolt. If you're going to stab yourself in the heart or anywhere else for that matter with a sharp instrument you use a kitchen knife. There are plenty of large sharp knives in our kitchen where he was supposed to have killed himself. Why a crossbow bolt? No, I cannot imagine for one moment a man like my uncle who, by the way, was rather squeamish when it came to pain, would stand there thrusting a thing like a crossbow bolt under his ribs. His pain threshold was so low removing the tiniest splinter from a finger made him react as though it were major surgery without an anaesthetic.'

'Removing a splinter from a finger, or anywhere else for that matter, can be extremely painful,' Thornton contradicted her.

'Maybe for you men. It's a well known fact that women can stand much more pain but, to get back to what happened, I simply can't see him pushing the thing up at an angle. Surely, if he did use it, he would have pushed it straight in?'

'An angle?'

'Yes, according to the autopsy the thing went in from below the ribs and moved upwards. Maybe it was an accident. You know of course that he was a very important scientist with a top secret naval research establishment, as a long shot... damn it, now it's my turn...' She stopped and Thornton waited for her to regain her composure. 'I believe there is an old Chinese proverb,' she murmured, 'that says we will always talk of feet in front of a cripple.'

'There's another Chinese proverb which goes, "I complained because I had no shoes until I saw a man who had no feet."'

She gave a wan little smile and took a sip of her Martini Rosso before going on. 'Could he have been conducting an experiment in ballistics that went wrong do you think? After all the power of steam was discovered in a kitchen.'

'Was the crossbow still there when you found him? I believe it was you who discovered…'

'Yes,' she nodded, 'on the floor just outside the pantry door but quite a way from his body, or the body was lying quite a way from it, and there was nothing attached to the bow that could have been used as a trigger so he didn't use it to shoot himself. No, accident is out as well which leaves only one alternative, murder. That should have been the coroner's verdict, murder by person or persons unknown.' There was another pause and then, 'So, will you take the job?'

'Of course.'

'In that case, if we're going to continue our discussion, may I suggest we move on to somewhere more congenial for a spot of lunch? The snacks in here don't look all that exciting, do they?'

'I don't know,' Thornton said, 'they serve a good scampi in the basket.' He was partial to a bit of scampi but Rory was already out of her seat and on her way. He looked at Ross, busy wiping glasses and Ross gave a nod. Thornton gave a wave and followed his new client to the door.

François saw them enter and rushed across the restaurant to greet them. Admittedly he didn't have far to travel, L'eminence Grise not being the Savoy or the Ritz, and he didn't actually pant, jump up and down, or roll on his back and pee himself with excitement, but his effusiveness gave all the indications of a puppy whose mistress had gone to the corner shop for a bottle of milk or a packet of fags and had been away seemingly for months.

'Miss Pemberton, how delightful! How wonderful! How unexpected!'

'I know, François. Naughty of me just to drop in like this,' she almost simpered in girlie fashion, 'but you might just possibly be able to squeeze me in somewhere?'

It would be a tight squeeze whichever way you looked at it but he would manage it somehow. His waiters were adept at manoeuvring between tables seemingly no more than a couple of feet apart. The whole restaurant, packed with diners, though no one fortunately waiting for a table, seemed to be in mid-air fork suspension mode as they concentrated on just how easy it was going to be for François to squeeze in Aurora and her escort. One bean-pole unmannerly woman with teeth and a rather scraggy neck, staring hard at

Aurora, giggled loudly and received in return a withering glare from Thornton, which unfortunately made her giggle even more. Aurora though seemed oblivious to it as they made their way to the small table François had brought out of hiding for just this sort of occasion and which was being busily set by one of the minions who greeted Aurora with many a smile and a bow. She was obviously a very popular patron, probably a generous tipper.

François, having placed a chair to seat Rory, now seemed to recognise for the first time that she had a companion and, remembering the previous visit Thornton had made to his august establishment, pulled himself up slightly and with rather a fixed smile said, 'And you, Mister King. Very nice to see you again.' He was not going to admit that the incident during Thornton's previous visit, if incident it could be called, had made his restaurant the most talked about, written about and *the* in place to dine so that it was booked solid for months, especially after Duncan Devonport Fawcett wrote it all up in the glossy magazine that hired him. Despite its popularity François didn't allow standards to drop but if anything grew even more imaginative in his culinary inventions and, being a good businessman as well as a cordon bleu chef, he did use the opportunity to discreetly raise his prices. Not that his well-heeled clientele would have noticed and, with inflation what it was, prices were rising all the time anyway.

He allowed Thornton to pull in his own chair and seat himself whilst he held Aurora's folded napkin high and dramatically flipped it open before laying it across her lap whilst Thornton dramatically flipped open and laid down his own.

'And how have you been keeping, François?' Thornton enquired with an engaging smile.

'Very well, thank you, Mister King. Very well.' He managed to go so far as to turn over both their wine glasses though his attitude was still just a little on the frosty side as though it was all Thornton's fault that old Shoggi had snuffed it in so undignified a fashion in his establishment and that he had lost an excellent customer with the demise of the Princess Spitskaya.

'What do you recommend today, François?' Rory asked and, before he could reply, 'What do you fancy, Thornton?' She opened her menu.

Thornton, who was only too aware of François' prices even before they were raised, was a little hesitant in replying.

'Lunch is on me,' Rory said as if reading his thoughts. 'Don't hold back though personally I am going to have something ever so light.'

'On a day like this?' François was horrified. 'Mais non! No no no! Forgive me, my dear Miss Pemberton, but on a day like this you need something to keep out the cold. May I recommend the stuffed fillet of sole? Or perhaps the Paupiettes de veau Perigourdine. The veal is so tender it melts in the mouth.'

'Sold. How about you, Thornton?'

'I'll take the same.' He closed his own menu without even having looked at it and held it up for the maitre to take.

'Bon.' François whisked the menus out of their hands and was gone.

'He's forgotten something,' Thornton murmured.

'What would that be?'

'The wine?' He leaned forward to whisper.

'Oh, no, he knows exactly what wine to bring. Oh, I'm sorry! You're my guest and I didn't even think to ask you what you would like. How remiss of me.'

'Absolutely no problem,' Thornton said gallantly. 'I'm not a great connoisseur, I'll knock back whatever plonk comes along.'

It was her turn to lean forward across the table as far as she was able. 'Whisper it who dares,' she said, 'but the truth is, I prefer Italian wines to the French. Il vino amabile, and you will have noticed François' wine list is all French he's such a patriot. So he keeps a bottle or two of my favourites just for me but you will see when the waiter brings it the label will be well hidden. The other problem I have is I suffer a terrible feeling of guilt whenever I order veal. Those poor little things to be born to such a short and sad life. Human beings really are monsters. I find it hard to believe those farmers who raise them and those butchers who slaughter them can sleep peacefully in their beds of a night. And their poor mothers, the calves' mothers I mean, not the butchers. How they must suffer having their babies taken away from them so young.'

Thornton was finding it a little difficult to believe he was actually hearing this but he chipped in with, 'I wouldn't let your conscience bother you too much, Aurora...'.

'Rory.' She smiled sweetly and raised an admonishing finger.

'Rory. After all nature is even more cruel, red in tooth and claw as the saying has it. Eat or be eaten. One of those sweet little calves probably wouldn't last three minutes in the wild before being torn to pieces. I can never understand vegetarians who use the cruelty to animals argument as their reason for not eating meat. If, like me, they had first-hand experience of African wildlife they would realise how much more cruel nature is. Even those little circus charmers, the chimpanzees occasionally feel the need for meat and in a pack can hunt down and tear to pieces a screaming terrified monkey.'

Rory shuddered visibly at the thought and laid a spread of chubby fingers on her pearls just as their waiter appeared with the wine, the label discreetly hidden by the napkin.

'Perhaps we should have had a white,' Rory said, the wine being the colour of blood, 'Of course we should have had a white! Who on earth drinks red wine with veal? Take it away, take it away!' Her voice had risen somewhat and she was making shooing gestures with both hands.

'What does it matter?' Thornton asked. 'The only good wine is the wine you like.'

The giggler started up again only now the giggle turned into the kind of laugh that requires a huge noisy adenoidal intake of breath between each guffaw. It was a bit like the braying of an ass, which was more than likely appropriate. Her companion looked rather embarrassed. If he was her husband, Thornton thought, casting a mean look in their direction, she was heading for a divorce and how on earth did he get to marry her in the first place? If they weren't married she would not be asked to lunch ever again. He decided they had to be brother and sister and the brother was performing a fraternal duty. She was down from the country for the day and as soon as he had seen her on the train and on her way home, he would rush into the nearest bar for a good stiff drink. How else to explain it? She was noticeably no oil painting, what with the teeth and the flat chest that was most definitely not sexy, so maybe her reaction to Rory was some sort of transference, a defence mechanism.

'Is something wrong?' François was immediately beside the table.

'Oh, François, you've sent a red wine instead of a white. Now that is not like you to defy convention.'

François leaned closer so that he could lower his voice almost to a whisper.

'Miss Pemberton, it is with much regret I have to inform you, at the moment I have no Italian whites in the restaurant. If I had known you were coming... I will send someone out for a bottle immediately. What would be your preference?'

'Oh, never mind.' And then to the waiter still hovering, bottle in hand. 'Pour.' An imperious gesture nearly knocked over a wine glass, rescued by François in the nick of time just as the food arrived.

For someone who felt so dreadfully sorry for the poor calves, Rory tucked into her veal with abandon and the fact that a red rather than a white accompanied it didn't seem to diminish her enjoyment one iota. For a while, between mouthfuls, she babbled away about nothing in particular, mainly complaints about London, how it was getting filthier and noisier by the day, the traffic was appalling, crime was rampant and there were so many immigrants you could stand in Leicester Square all day and play spot the Englishman. If you came up with more than six you would be lucky. Air travel had a good deal to answer for. It was only when she had demolished the food that she returned to the matter in hand.

'So, Thornton, how long have you been practicing?'

Thornton's fork was halfway to his mouth and remained there as he raised his eyes to meet hers. Practicing? Practicing? What a strange word to use. Do private eyes practice? Doctors have a practice, dentists practice, you reluctantly practice playing the piano or the violin when you're a kid and your parents are wasting their hard earned money paying for the lessons, but a private detective? He had never thought about it. He lowered his fork, mouthful still on it. Was this to be the beginning of the end? He could figuratively see those pound notes floating out the door before they even had a chance to discuss money.

'It depends,' he prevaricated, 'on exactly what your definition is of practice.'

'My definition of practice,' she said, obviously a pit peeved at the prevarication, 'is exactly what the word means. How long have you been a private detective?'

'Not very long.' He might as well be truthful. It will out in the end.

'And just how long is not very long?'

'Maybe a year? Maybe a bit longer?' He took another mouthful of food. He might as well finish it up before she finished with him and François was right, the veal really did melt in the mouth.

'And in that time you have earned a reputation for being the best in your field?'

'Not exactly.'

'And what exactly does not exactly mean?' She was obviously growing even more irritated and poured herself another glass of wine, splashing a few blood red drops on the snowy white linen.

'Look, what has Mike told you about me?'

'He couldn't praise your capabilities highly enough but he didn't exactly go into detail.' The word exactly was heavily accentuated.

'No, he wouldn't. Well, Rory, if you want my full CV I'm afraid you simply can't have it because it is virtually all top secret and filed away in the catacombs of Whitehall labelled not to be opened for fifty years, or something like that.'

'Really?' She was intrigued. 'Why is that?'

'Let's put it this way, if I were to write a book on my activities, the department would slap an immediate ban on it and I would probably be gaoled for treason. National security and all that.'

'But you can whisper it to me, can't you? After all I am employing you.'

He shook his head and put an index finger to his lips. She was hooked, but she wasn't going to admit it.

'Thornton,' she said, sounding the essence of patience, 'I know you come highly recommended but when I make a purchase in Harrods, despite the fact the store has a reputation for quality second to none and will always make an exchange should you not be completely satisfied, I do like to see what I am buying in the first place. Now you really are going to have to tell me just a little about yourself.'

Thornton heaved a sigh, reached in his pocket and withdrew a small stone he placed on the table in front of her plate. She looked at it for a while before picking it up.

'And what may this be exactly?' She turned it over between forefinger and thumb, held it up to the light, rolled it in the palm of her hand.

'That, my dear Rory, is an uncut diamond. Try biting it and you'll crack your teeth!'

Rory sniffed.

'I promise you, it may not look much at the moment but, cut, it could well be worth something like two thousand, maybe two and a half.'

She put the stone back on the table.

'Really. And why are you showing it to me?'

'Did you ever hear of a cult, an organisation, called The Army Of The Righteous?'

'I seem to recollect seeing some TV footage about it. Seemed a pretty harmless bit of foolishness to me. Just a collection of hippies carrying on in typical hippy fashion though the fashion for beads, bracelets, long hair, smoking pot, playing with crystals, taking LSD, and letting it all hang out must surely end soon, if it hasn't already.'

'Not harmless at all, Rory, highly subversive in fact and consequently dangerous.' He had lowered his voice now to almost a whisper, there seemed to be an awful lot of whispering going on at this luncheon, so that she had to lean forward to catch what he was saying. It was even less easy for her, the edge of the table pressing on a full stomach. The braying ass's ears nearby would develop a stitch or pop their gristle if they endeavoured to stretch any further as Thornton went on. 'Their leader had negotiated with an international thief, a South African I believe, I bumped into him very briefly and purely by accident at Heathrow Airport, strange little man, for the delivery of a whole sack full of these precious little beauties. We don't know what the final objective was when they were cashed in, what the funds where going to be used for, but even the CIA were anxious as to exactly what they were about and had put a man onto it. Well, I beat the CIA to it, thwarted the organisation's exchequer and their schemes by tracking the diamonds from the south of France to Sicily.'

'Why Sicily?'

'There was a young Italian involved, no more than a kid really, went by the name of Luigi. He suddenly upped and skedaddled one night with the diamonds so I figured, as he was Sicilian, Sicily was naturally where he would be heading. Maybe he wouldn't do anything with the diamonds immediately but gradually, in small drops, he could try to sell them in Messina where they deal in precious metals, gold, silver, and also of course diamonds, hoping not too many questions would be asked. So colleagues and myself hired a helicopter and got there first, waited for him at Palermo railway station. We'd tipped off the Italian police of course and he was nabbed as he got off the train. Not only that but they also arrested the organisation's leader who was obviously there to collect.'

'What happened to them?'

'They're both in jail in Italy as far as I know.'

'Sounds like James Bond,' Rory whispered, slightly awestruck.

Beneath the table Thornton crossed the fingers of one hand and hoped his story, which wasn't exactly the truth, the whole truth, and nothing but the truth, didn't have too many holes in it but words once issued cannot be reclaimed. Hopefully she would forget the awkward details.

It seemed she had. She picked up the stone once more and turned it over in her fingers.

'You tell me this is worth between two and two and a half thousand pounds?'

'Maybe even more. I'm not a diamond merchant and I've not been to Hatton Garden to have it valued so I couldn't say exactly but I don't think I'm too far off the mark.'

'What are you doing with it?'

Of all the questions she could have asked this was the one he had been dreading. He cleared his throat.

'Well, Rory, I have to admit here to a small misdemeanour. I kept this one as a sort of souvenir and something to put aside for that proverbial rainy day.'

'You mean you stole it.' She was looking him straight in the eye but he never flinched.

'Mea culpa. I'm afraid the temptation was too great and there were so many who would miss one small stone? Nobody. One teensy weensy diamond.' Thornton shrugged and finished his last forkful of food. 'After all,' he added, 'nobody knows just how many diamonds there were in the first place. I believe the original thief died of a heart attack at Heathrow airport but even he probably didn't know.'

He conveniently forgot to tell her they spilled from a wet carrier bag that split. It had contained oranges to cover the diamonds and were rolling with the stones all over the station platform creating a minor riot that took some time to bring under control.

'Where did the diamonds come from originally?'

'Hazarding a guess and knowing what I know about that part of the world I would say Sierra Leone.'

'And how did they get from Heathrow to the south of France?'

'In a suitcase with a false bottom.'

'And you suspected they were there? How clever of you.'

Thornton didn't contradict her but merely smiled modestly.

Aurora seemed fascinated and lost in thought as she fiddled with the stone. She pursed her lips and narrowed her eyelids.

'I tell you what, Thornton,' she said finally, looking up at him, 'I will give you a cheque for a thousand pounds now and, if you solve the case, a further thousand and a half plus all expenses. In the meantime I will keep this piece of stolen property and, if you don't come up with the goods as they say, well, it won't have been a dead loss would it? You will have made a thousand at least, plus expenses, and I will have this stone cut into a very nice ring for me.' She held it up to the light between thumb and forefinger as if she could already see its sparkling facets.

Lady Haw Haw was so totally fascinated her lower jaw was practically on the table. She couldn't take her eyes off them and her companion, first glancing around to see who else might be looking, coughed to remind her she was being just a wee bit obvious and whatever transaction was going on, it was no business of hers.

She turned back to look at him and whispered, 'I'm fascinated,' so that the whole restaurant could hear. He looked around again, smiling apologetically to the world in general. What a worm. She couldn't wait to tell her friends in the country what curious people she had come across in the big city.

'If you do solve the case,' Rory continued, 'to show my eternal gratitude, the stone will be returned to you and you will have made handsomely out of it, right? I might even take the trouble of having it cut for you, as an extra present. Agreed?'

Thornton had the feeling that somewhere down the line he was being done but he wasn't too sure, maths was never his forte, neither was logic which is a bit of a drawback for a private detective but the thought of that thousand pound cheque up front (wouldn't his supercilious bank manager raise his bushy eyebrows in surprise?) made him nod in agreement and she slipped the stone into her handbag just as François appeared once more to enquire as to whether or not they would like a dessert.

They decided on a chocolate, orange, and hazelnut mousse and, to round off the meal, coffee, accompanied by parfait amour for Rory, she obviously had a very sweet tooth, and a fine cognac for Thornton. He never could resist it. He rolled the balloon in his cupped fingers and sniffed the bouquet. He couldn't help feeling that, like coffee, sometimes the aroma was better than the taste but he lifted the glass to his mouth, took a sip and, as always, almost sighed with the physical pleasure of it, decided there and then he had better start practicing to be a detective.

'My turn to ask questions,' he said.

'Fire away.' She took a sip of her own sweet mauve liqueur.

'Right. Enemies.'

'What?'

'Did Sir Roger have any enemies that you are aware of?'

Rory shook her head. 'He simply was not the kind of man to make enemies. A milder, kinder gentleman would be hard to find.'

'Hmn... still waters run deep as the old saying has it.'

'Thornton, all he was interested in really, as far as I am aware, was his work, and I know nothing about that because, like yours used to be, it's a secret world, isn't it?'

'What do you do with yourself, Rory?'

'I beg your pardon!'

'Do you have a job? An occupation? Are you, as they say, in gainful employment?'

'Does this have any bearing on the case?'

'It helps to know exactly what the domestic set-up was. For example, do you have a nine to five, which means leaving the flat all day? Or do you have a job that takes in night shifts?'

'I don't have a job at all unless you call voluntary work for charity a job and that takes up a great deal of my time, fund raising, organising, travelling, both here and abroad. Yes, come to think of it, it is a full time job but I love it and I wouldn't do anything else.'

'Any help around the flat?'

'There's a daily, Mrs McIvor, a truly harmless old biddy. Well, not exactly old, middle-aged rather I suppose, she just gives the impression of being old.'

'You trust her?'

'Oh, completely! She's an absolute poppet.'

'So was Lizzie Borden.'

'Who?'

'Lizzie Borden, a supposedly completely inoffensive young lady in Massachusetts who allegedly murdered her parents with an axe. There was a rhyme written about it, "Lizzie Borden took an axe and gave her father forty whacks. When she saw what she had done she gave her mother forty-one." Maybe it was the other way round, mother first followed by father. Can't remember where I first heard that.'

'What happened to her?'

'Nothing was proved and she lived to a ripe old age in the very house where it happened. Isn't that macabre? Do you think the ghosts of her parents haunted the place? "Lizzie, dear Lizzie, why did you do it?" There is always the question of motive you see, and what possible motive could Lizzie, a demure and dutiful daughter living quietly in small town America, have had to murder her inoffensive old parents? Like Jack The Ripper, another mystery, another unsolved case. This Miss McIvor of yours...'

'Mrs.'

'Mrs. Married? Divorced? A widow?'

'I believe she has what she calls "her old man" who goes by the name of Jimmy, originally from Glasgow.'

'Do we know what he does for a living?'

'He's a mini-cab driver. I know that because he drops her off and picks her up every day and she's mentioned it, and I've seen him once or twice.'

'Capable of violence do you think?'

'I doubt it very much. Looking at him I wonder he has the strength to turn the steering wheel he's such a weed.'

'He doesn't have to be a muscular giant to be strong or dangerous. Dynamite, as they say, comes in small packages.'

'You're full of other people's sayings, aren't you?'

'Aren't we all? Have you ever used his cab?'

'No.' Rory raised an eyebrow to indicate she wouldn't be seen dead in a mini-cab.

'The night you came home and found your uncle, where had you been?'

'Thornton, I've already given the police all this information. It really isn't going to help you.'

'Maybe, maybe not. All right, let's move on. Mistresses.'

'No.'

'Gay?'

'No.'

'No sex life at all?'

'Whatever he did to relieve himself sexually I know nothing about it. He never married. There are no dirty magazines in the flat, straight or otherwise, no sex toys. The police went through it with a fine tooth comb. Certainly being shot in the chest by a crossbow bolt could hardly be in the nature of a masochistic sexual game gone wrong.'

There was an audible gasp from the Haw Haw's table and both Rory and Thornton turned to look. Thornton leaned back in his chair.

'If we had two more chairs placed at this table would you care to come over and join in the conversation?'

The male companion was absolutely horrified. His mouth started to quiver and it took a while for him to find his voice.

'I b... beg your p... pardon?'

'And so you should,' Thornton turned from him to her. 'Did your mother never tell you it is rude to listen in to other people's conversations?'

'I think we had better leave,' the companion said, rising. By now the whole restaurant had ears flapping fit to start a windstorm and all eyes were on Lady Haw Haw.

Blushing with embarrassment she got up, threw Thornton what she thought was a contemptuous glance, though it seemed in fact as though she was about to burst into tears, and they made for the door, there to wait by the desk for their bill. In their haste they had even forgotten to leave a tip and such was their state they would no doubt forget to leave one whilst paying. Out of sheer embarrassment they would not be returning to the Grise for a long time.

'The only reason I am pursuing this line of questioning,' Thornton said, turning back to Rory and wishing he didn't sound quite like Reg Venables, 'is because if he picked up a piece of rent or rough trade… '

'I told you, there was never anything like that.' She sounded rather annoyed but he went on regardless.

'Seeing as to how he would be considered a security risk he would more than likely keep it a secret from you and everyone else and rough trade can get very rough.'

'Forget it, Thornton. You're barking up the wrong tree. My God, we're full of the platitudes today, are we not?'

'All right then, what about foreign visitors, foreign correspondence? Could he have been blackmailed by a foreign power because of his work?'

'I suppose it's possible but he gave no signs of distress or being under any sort of pressure. Not to me he didn't. No, wait! The last week or so he did seem a little more preoccupied than usual but I just put it down to absentmindedness.'

'I'll check with one of my colleagues in the department.'

'Mike Aliff?'

'Certainly not Mike Aliff. No, I was thinking of my friend Holly, Holly Day.'

'Oh, yes, Mike mentioned her. If I recall he referred to her as that snooty stuck-up bitch.'

'He would,' Thornton chuckled. 'But snooty would have been enough. Stuck up is sheer tautology. Another question. How come there was a crossbow in the flat anyway?'

'Some time ago archery was my uncle's hobby, both longbow and crossbow. He wasn't into competition or anything like that, a bit too old for that sort of caper, but he took it up as a form of exercise. At one time he was quite serious about it and an excellent shot I am informed on good authority but I believe he hadn't pursued it for a while. That is except for a month or so ago when he said he had been invited to take part in a challenge match.'

'Neighbours.'

'What neighbours?'

'You live in a block of flats, you have neighbours.'

'Once upon a time people had neighbours but it was a long time ago, Thornton. During the war there were neighbours. Out in the country there used to be neighbours but even out in the country these days you're unlikely to have any because the cottage next to yours has been bought by city types as a second home and you never get to know them. They roll up on a Friday night in their Landrover or any other make of four wheel drive gas guzzler and their green wellies and before you can say hello across the hedge it's Sunday night and they're shooting back to their jobs in the city. They don't even use the local store but bring everything they need with them. Here now we have the sound of television sets. I wouldn't know any of our neighbours as you call them if I passed them in the street. That's the way it is today. Today neighbours are a scarcity. Today there is the sound of teevees, usually too loud and, in the summer, cheap music blaring out through open windows without a thought for other people. I suppose in a way we were partly to blame that we don't know anybody in the building. Sir Roger was hardly the gregarious type and I didn't exactly knock on doors. Isn't it sad?'

'Presumably the police questioned the people living in the building?'

'And got nothing. No one saw anything, no one heard anything, only their TV sets.'

'Then I had better start looking in other directions.'

'Yes, Thornton, you better had.'

CHAPTER TWO

Thornton was going through back copies of *The Times,* firstly the news reports of Sir Roger Pemberton's death. The reporting was very matter of fact as befits so august a newspaper, once known as "The Thunderer", and the articles ended with the coroner's verdict. Case closed.

As he went through it, Thornton couldn't help chuckling over the embarrassing mistake a nineteenth century compositor made when typesetting the story of Queen Victoria opening a bridge over the River Thames. "Having cut the ceremonial ribbon," the story ran, "Her Majesty proceeded to piss slowly across the bridge." Now where could he have read that and what must Her Maj have thought when she read it over breakfast in Buck House? We are not amused? Or was it discreetly kept from her? "I'm afraid the newspaper boy hasn't arrived today, ma'am." Had she been a monarch of an earlier age she would probably have ordered the man's head to appear on a pike. Never mind the fantasy, Thornton, keep to the job in hand.

He had previously gone through the tabloids which made much more of a gory meal of the scientist's death with photographs and illustrations of crossbows, crossbow bolts and the damage one could cause even through protective clothing, and an artist's impression of the scene. No one from the paper had actually gone into the Pemberton flat but another resident, screwing the paper for what it was worth, allowed the artist access to her kitchen that, she said, would be exactly the same layout-wise and the position of the body was anybody's guess. It was a little embarrassing when, after the inquest, they discovered it had been outlined in entirely the wrong place, but what the hell! Any journalist can make a mistake and these small mistakes are usually soon forgotten.

It wasn't guesswork for Thornton though. He knew exactly

where the body had lain as Aurora had shown him before leaving him to his own devices in the flat. He was seated at the kitchen table gazing at a door that led to a walk in pantry, on the floor in front of which the crossbow had been discovered, when Mrs McIvor arrived and nearly jumped out of her skin at discovering a strange man sitting in her kitchen. She did manage to control the urge to scream, a natural reaction after what had happened so recently in this very room.

'Good morning,' Thornton greeted her with a beaming smile. 'You must be Mrs McIvor.'

'Must I?' She snapped, once she had got her breath back. 'And just who might you be if I may ask?'

'My name's Thornton, Thornton King. I am a...' He was about to say a friend of Aurora's but she cut him off short with, 'And, if I might also ask, what are you doing in my kitchen? Giving a body a fright like that.'

Thornton couldn't help thinking she was modelling herself on Janet from *Doctor Finlay's Casebook* as, without waiting for a reply, she turned her back on him and went to hang up her hat and coat and collect her much worn faded floral pinny from a hook behind the inner door. She turned back and marched towards the sink, tying the pinafore strings as she went into a bow behind her back. She stood looking down into the sink for a long while as if mentally conjuring up a pile of dirty dishes to be dealt with but, as there was nothing there but a single coffee cup and saucer left by Aurora, she turned back to look at Thornton, eyes suspiciously narrowed.

'You haven't answered my question,' she said accusingly.

'I was about to when you...'

'Have you finished with that cup?' She nodded towards the cup on the table in front of him and started forward as if to collect it. Thornton wondered whether she ever let anyone finish a sentence. He picked up the cup.

'No I haven't as a matter of fact.' There was a slight edge to his voice. 'There's still some dregs to be sopped up.'

This brought her up short. She stood there looking very indecisive.

'Yes. Well I'd best be getting on then.' She brushed away a wisp of grey hair from her forehead and once again turned away.

'Not so fast please,' Thornton ordered. 'I have some questions I would like to ask you.'

She turned back. 'Oh! You're a policeman are you? I might have guessed.' She folded her arms and for a moment glowered at him and then returned to her coat, searched in a pocket and came out with a box of matches and a packet of fags. Returning to the sink she found the saucer used as an ashtray on the window ledge and, taking an already half-smoked cigarette from the packet, lit it, dropping the spent match in the saucer.

Thornton thought better than to disabuse her about his true vocation. Mrs McIvor blew out a cloud of smoke and followed it up with a cough and a sniff as she leaned back against the drainer.

'I take it Miss Aurora let you in before she left and you've been waiting for me, is that it? Well get on with it then because I've got work to do. Anyway I told your lot before, everything I know which is nothing. Poor Professor Pemberton, I always called him the Prof, poor man, what a way to go. I only hope it was dead quick so he didn't know anything about it.'

She moved back to the table, carrying her makeshift ashtray, pulled out a chair and sat down. She tapped her cigarette with a straight forefinger though there was as yet really no ash to knock off and wiped an eye with the back of her hand. Thornton wasn't sure whether the tears were caused by smoke or a genuine sentiment and almost expected her to produce a hankie from her pinafore pocket and snivel into it. He was quite disappointed when she didn't. Instead she indulged in something he really hated apart from people eating with their mouths open, chewing gum, or rattling coins in their pocket; she started to rap her fingers on the tabletop. Thornton watched for a moment. She glared at him. The fingers never stopped.

'Well, get on with it then,' she finally ordered and took another drag of her cigarette, 'what is it you want to know?'

'How's your Jimmy?' He asked. It was a shot in the dark but it seemed to hit the target. The fingers immediately stopped their rapping.

'My Jimmy? What kind of a question's that when it's at home? What's my Jimmy got to do with it?'

'He brings you to work doesn't he? Does he also pick you up when you've finished?'

'Yes. Sometimes I might have to wait a while if he's carrying a passenger somewhere.'

'I hear he's bought a new car.'

'So? His car is his living, innit? And the old one was on its last legs, or wheels I should say.' She smiled at her little jest.

'Quite an expensive model.'

'What?'

'The new car.'

'Good for business. Fares like to travel in a bit of comfort don't they? There's too many old rattle-bang jalopies about fit only for scrap. Accidents on wheels waiting to happen that's what they are. What else?'

'How did he pay for it?'

'Look, Mister Detective or whatever you are, what has all this got to do with the Prof? And who told you about the new car anyway?' Angrily she stubbed out her cigarette.

'Actually nobody told me. I happened to be looking out of a front window when he drove up and dropped you off.'

She stared at him for a long while, her clenched teeth a solid barrier, her mouth a thin line from which nothing was going to be allowed to escape if she could help it.

'Well?' Thornton prompted.

After a lengthy silence she obviously decided to reply.

'If you must know, he's paying for it on the never never. How else?'

'I see. Who do you bank with?'

'What?' It came out almost like a screech. 'What are you on about?'

'I asked about your bank. What...?'

Her chair scraped back on the stone floor making a sound like nails on a chalkboard as she levered herself up and moved from the table. 'Away with you,' she said, 'we're just ordinary working folk. We've no time for banks and the like.'

'Then from where did your Jimmy get the finance to buy his new car?'

This brought her up short once more but without turning around. 'You will have to ask him won't you? And I'm quite sure you'll get short shrift because it's got nothing whatsoever to do with you, or

Miss Pemberton if it comes to that.'

She opened the pantry door and went inside, obviously looking for something. She spotted what she wanted, a set of Tupperware containers on a high shelf and used a set of wooden steps to reach it. Thornton watched. Back on the floor again she upended the steps with one hand transforming them into a rather primitive and somewhat rickety kitchen chair. It would seem the screws in the hinges were rusting and coming slightly adrift.

It was the era of stripped pine and the gentrification of run-down neighbourhoods like Hackney. Dealers in salvaged building materials and second hand furniture had their acid baths in which layers of iron-hard Edwardian, Victorian, and even Georgian paint were removed from cupboards, settles, doors, pilasters, panelling, and sash windows. This chair cum small stepladder was possibly a Victorian invention, maybe even earlier and obviously quite useful, one moment a chair and the next a set of three steps. Thornton was quite intrigued but thought little more of it. Mrs McIvor returned to the sink to give the Tupperware a rinse before slapping the individual pieces upside down on the drainer. From the set of her shoulders Thornton realised he was going to get little if any more information from her so he got up and left the kitchen.

Though nobody outside his own milieu had ever heard of him, there were front-page headlines in the tabloids six inches high such as "World Famous Scientist Brutally Slain," and "The Crossbow Killing!" and "Horrific Death In Maida Vale!" The word murder was not used. The headlines needed to be that big as that was all readers glanced at before turning to either page three for titillating tits, "Phaw! Howzzat for a pair of knockers, mate!" or to the sports pages, starting with the racing because form needed to be studied before bets could be laid, and then the football, probably read with disgust because the home team had been trounced once more, or with delight if the trouncing were the opposite way, before perhaps idly turning back to possibly muse over the coverage of Sir Roger's death, one of so many news items quickly forgotten.

The body was discovered by his niece who returned home late at night or, to be more exact, in the early hours, to find him lying on the kitchen floor. He was face up so she could see immediately what had killed him. She called the police. He had been dead for some time. Where had she really been that evening? Thornton wondered. Her story didn't quite ring true. According to what she told the police, she had been to visit friends living near Hammersmith, dropping by on the off chance but finding them not at home. The police had checked and the friends were indeed out until late that evening. She then thought, as she was nearby, she might as well slip into the Kensington Odeon. She knew what was showing but then anyone passing by and reading the billboards would know what was showing. She said she didn't remember too much of the film because she was tired after a really heavy day and dozed off most of the time. What did she do after the movie? After all she did not get home until the early hours. She drove along The Embankment, stopped the car and sat looking at the river for a long while. When asked why she replied, 'Like the man once said, "sometimes I sits and thinks and sometimes I just sits."' Did anyone see her? No. What made her story difficult to believe was that no one at the cinema recalled her either and she wasn't a body to be easily missed. Could she be a suspect? The police would think so but Thornton was dubious. If she were responsible for her uncle's death why would she come to him asking for help in solving the case? Unless of course it was a red herring.

The man in charge of the investigation was Detective Inspector Reg Venables. Good grief! Thornton thought, didn't the police have any detectives other than poor old Reg? They were working the man to death and he was surely almost at retirement age. Remembering his own first encounter with Reg Venables he would lay odds of four to five on that he would have given Aurora a hard time in the station. Come to think of it though, being a feisty young lady she could very well have given Reg quite a hard time in return.

Still at *The Times* Thornton moved on to the obituary, which was a lengthy and laudatory one befitting a scientist, not quite in the Einstein class but of some repute nevertheless: a number of terminal degrees (Thornton always thought that sounded like the onset of a fatal illness) from prestigious universities, plus honorary ones from American, English, French and German seats of learning; nominated for the Nobel Prize, a spell with NASA and, of late, working in a British naval research establishment. Already an OBE it had been rumoured he was in line for a peerage at least.

Thornton discovered two things during his enquires that could possibly lead to something. Firstly it was confirmed the deceased was an extremely wealthy man, the sole beneficiary under his father's will, inheriting a chain of garages and service stations up north, and eccentric only in that he chose to devote himself to science rather than play around with his inherited wealth though, according to an earlier newspaper report, he had donated ten thousand pounds to an unspecified charity, the donation made through an organisation called FUNDRAISERS LIMITED. There was absolutely no reason why a man as wealthy as Sir Roger should not be a philanthropist but Thornton had never heard of this particular organisation and, if Rory was into charitable works, why did Sir Roger not keep it in the family and channel his largesse through her? Thornton decided a return visit to the flat was in order to go through Sir Roger's bank statements. Having in his time had more than one run in with bank managers he didn't think he would be allowed to get very far, if anywhere, with Sir Roger's bank.

'Sat there bold as brass he did.' Mrs McIvor, seated at the kitchen table, cigarette in one hand, coffee cup in the other, complained indignantly to Aurora who was somewhat of an indulgent employer, but then good domestic staff wasn't all that easy to get these days so there was little point in being all dictatorial with do's and do nots.

'Asking the most impertinent questions, he was. Yes, that's what they were. Oh, the cheek of it! Asking me about our private money affairs and things like that. I gave him short thrift I can tell you. Put him in his place I did and I've a good mind to register a severe complaint with his superiors.'

'He doesn't have any superiors,' Rory said, putting down her coffee cup and delicately touching the corner of her mouth with her serviette, pinkie poised, before throwing the napkin on the table and getting up.

'What? He must have if he's a policeman. What is he? Chief Constable then?'

'Did he say he was a policeman?' She was heading for the inner door.

'No.' Mrs McIvor stood up. 'But then he didn't say he wasn't neither and, if he's not a policeman, what is he then?'

'He's a private detective.' Aurora turned to look back. 'I hired him to investigate Sir Roger's death.'

With which she left the room and Mrs McIvor staring after her open-mouthed until the dog end burnt between her index and middle fingers and she hastily dropped it into her coffee cup where it sizzled out.

'Shit!' Mrs McIvor hissed, waggling her wounded fingers and making for the sink behind which, on the window ledge, stood an aloe vera already slightly sliced about because of various domestic mishaps. She cut off a small piece and rubbed the juice on her burns. 'Shit!' She said again, leaning on the sink and standing there for a long moment lost in thought, every now and again waggling her fingers and blowing on her injuries. 'What'd she want to go and do that for?'

'Do what for?'

This time she did let out a little shriek as she swung around.

'Good morning to you!' Thornton said jauntily.

'What's good about it?' Mrs McIvor snapped back. 'I suppose you make a habit of scaring a body half to death do you? Pussyfooting around like that? If you think you're going to ask me any more questions, mister whatever your name is, you got another think coming I can tell you for nothing, so don't waste your breath because I know what you are now and you're not legit.' She winced and gave her fingers another rub with the slice of aloe. 'Miss Pemberton let you in did she?'

'She noticed my shadow outside the door just as she was leaving and as I was about to put thumb to bell, she suggested I enter your domain and ask you if you would be so kind as to make me a cup of coffee. Would you be so kind as to make me a cup of coffee? Or is that request a waste of breath? Maybe your injury prohibits it. What have you done to your hand?'

'Burnt me fingers if it's any business of yours.'

'Ah. I presume that does mean then that you're too incapacitated to make me that cup of coffee?'

'Fancy talk! Fancy talk! That's all you are, full of hot air,' she said as she marched across to a Welsh dresser to collect another cup and saucer. Thornton noticed there was already coffee in the Cona percolator on the cooker. 'Milk and sugar?'

'No sugar thank you, I'm sweet enough.'

'Huh!' She collected a bottle of Express Dairy milk from the fridge and he watched as she poured out the coffee before advancing on the table, cup and saucer in one hand, milk bottle in the other. She slapped them down on the table with such force some of the coffee spilt over into the saucer and a few drops of milk onto the table which she immediately wiped away with a corner of her pinny before going back to the sink.

'Thank you,' Thornton said, added milk to his coffee and, taking up the cup, left the kitchen to make his way to Sir Roger's study, a small room that was obviously originally meant to be third bed or box room in the apartment. Here he seated himself at the large desk that took up almost the entire space and tried the first of the seven drawers, three on either side and a wide flattish one in the centre. Naturally the drawer was locked. He should have thought to ask Aurora for the keys. Not to worry, his handy Swiss knife would once more come into its own. He wondered if Reg had gone through these drawers looking for possible evidence of suicide. Probably not. If Sir Roger had left a note announcing his imminent death it would have been on the desktop not hidden away inside.

Having successfully unlocked it with apparently no damage done, the desk was pretty much scratched from long use anyway, Thornton pulled open the first drawer and a quick look told him what he wanted was not there. He wanted bank statements, returned cheques, cheque stubs but all he found was a plastic tray with compartments holding pens, pencils, a sharpener, stapler and spare staples, rubber bands, ink pads, gummed labels, paper fasteners, postage stamps. He wondered why on earth the drawer should have been locked in the first place when it contained absolutely nothing of importance or value but maybe that was just the way the professor was. Maybe Mrs McIvor was a stationery kleptomaniac and there is nothing more annoying than finding something has disappeared just when you needed it. Thornton closed the drawer and went to the top one on the other side and – Bingo! He closed the blade of his Swiss knife and slipped it back into his pocket before lifting out the contents of the drawer and laying the mass of papers on top of the desk.

Sir Roger banked with Messrs Coutts and Co., the queen's

own bankers in their magnificent building in the Strand. He most certainly would not have got very far with his enquiries there.

In the next half hour or so he discovered that the ten thousand pound gift to charity was not the first made through Fundraisers Limited but, in fact, was the last of a number starting off with a relatively modest one thousand and increasing with each donation and all within a matter of months. Why? And what charities benefited from this largesse? Nowhere among the papers were any named. Nowhere was there a letter of thanks for a generous donation but that could be explained if all the donations were made incognito. And why the ascending scale of payments? Was Sir Roger like a sponge being gradually squeezed dry? It certainly looked that way if the payments were in response to blackmail demands.

The second discovery Thornton made that morning was that the deceased had not, as Rory claimed, given up on his archery but had, until just two weeks before his death, been a paid up member of a club called THE BOWMEN OF ESSEX: by the membership fees charged, as Sir Roger's cheques bore witness, and by the quality of their embossed and elaborate stationery, it was a very exclusive archery club in the vicinity of Epping Forest.

Thornton folded a sheet of the club stationary, a reminder to Sir Roger that his subscription was overdue, and slipped it into his jacket pocket before he replaced the papers, pushed the drawer to and got up to leave. He turned around to find Mrs McIvor standing in the doorway. He had been so absorbed in what he was doing he had no idea how long she had been there.

'Come for my coffee cup then?' he enquired.

'No,' she replied, 'I've come to see what you're up to. No good I'll warrant.'

Warrant? Warrant? Where do people find these words they use so blithely?

'The cup's there on the desk,' he informed her, nodding towards it as he marched from the room forcing her to stand to one side to let him pass.

'Good morning!' He headed for the front door that could not be seen from the office. She kept her beady little eye on him until he had disappeared, shutting the door quite noisily behind him, then she turned back and went into the study.

The unlocked drawer had been pulled open and she was so busy inspecting the papers that when she sensed a presence and turned around she let out a shriek that would have done credit to a banshee, knocked over the still almost full coffee cup, threw her arms in the air and sent papers flying in all directions.

Thornton was standing at the study door.

*****

Holly had not had a good day. Not only was she overloaded at work but, carrying a heavy pile of files through one of the corridors of power, she had unfortunately bumped, literally, into Mike Aliff and the files were sent flying in all directions. She was quite sure Mike had done it deliberately and she stood there for a moment fuming.

'Sorry, old gal,' Mike grimaced in mock apology. 'Here, let me give you a hand.'

'Thank you, I can manage!' Holly snapped as she crouched down to retrieve the first file. She was quite sure the man would use his "giving a hand" in more ways than just picking up dropped files. He wasn't known in the department as "Master Groper" for nothing and he wasn't going to be fobbed off that easily. He too bent down to pick up a file and Holly felt his unseen hand gently brush a buttock. With no further ado, as he was picking the file off the floor, she slammed the heavy one she was holding edgeways onto the back of his hand. Mike let out a yell and withdrew the hand very fast.

'Sorry,' Holly said although sorry was not what her face was registering. 'Butter fingers. Dropped it. Wouldn't make the women's cricket team in a million years. Jolly heavy these files, aren't they?' Mike got to his feet and without a word affected a swagger as he moved off down the corridor for all the world as though nothing had happened. It wasn't until he turned the corner that he winced, swore under his breath, and rubbed the back of his hand to ease the hurt before continuing on his way.

Mike Aliff had been a pain in the arse ever since he had been transferred to her section a week or so previously. She wouldn't be surprised if he hadn't requested it. She wouldn't be surprised either that, if he kept crossing her path, she would shortly be indicted for murder. Fortunately she had a few days leave due her and fortunately now was the time she was taking it. She picked up the rest of the files and moved on, stopping only to exchange greetings with a colleague who informed her Mike, looking like the wrath of God, was storming down the corridor mumbling to himself. She had caught the words "bitch" and "who does she think she is?" Could it be that there was a slight contretemps and the bitch referred to actually be Holly Day?

Holly grinned and confirmed she was indeed the bitch referred to.

'He wasn't rubbing his hand by any chance was he?'

The colleague confirmed that yes indeed that was exactly what he was doing.

'Good,' Holly said, 'I hope it's his wanking hand and I hope he can't do a thing with it.'

'Have a good break,' her colleague said with a laugh as they both continued on their way.

Her journey home was hell. Moving about in London was becoming impossible. Ants and bees were better adapted to this sort of over-populated mayhem, they were programmed for it, but human beings suffered for it, and year by year it seemed to get worse.

Her shower did little to cool her temper but now, her feet up, she was watching *Coronation Street* and enjoying the Chinese takeaway she had stopped off for on the way home when the phone rang. Though she insisted on using them in order to be authentic, she was never all that adept at chopsticks and at this moment she lost control. They went a little skew-whiff, the ends crossing, and a lump of sweet and sour pork covered in sauce hit the ecru couch leaving a bright coloured ineradicable stain as far as domestic cleaning would be concerned. She exchanged her bowl of food for the telephone conveniently to hand on the coffee table and lifted the receiver.

'Yes?'

'Aw-aw!' He said, 'I've called at a bad time again.'

'You always do, Thornton, You simply have the knack, I can rely on it. What do you want this time?' She was desperately dabbing at the stain with a tissue but fighting a losing battle. It only seemed to be making matters worse. There was no sign of the piece of pork. Maybe it had rolled beneath the couch.

'Do you have any free time at the moment or coming up shortly?'

'Why? Have you got a sixth sense or something? It so happens the answer is yes, I have, but look, Thornton, there's been just a teensy-weensy accident here, if you can call the ruining of a brand new couch a teensy-weensy accident, so, are you at home?'

'I'm at home.'

'I'll call you back.'

She hung up and got to her feet, her bare foot treading the lump of pork into the carpet squelching the now cold sweet and sour sauce between her toes.

Holly, who was normally of a sanguine disposition, felt the urgent need to scream but there was also the urgent need to get something from the kitchen to clean up the mess, or at least attempt to, and that took precedence. Mind you, there was no reason why she couldn't scream on the way to the kitchen if she so felt like it and even on the way back if she still felt like it but she resisted the urge. She also decided, limping half way to the kitchen as she kept her saucy toes off the carpet that, urgent though it may be, she would leave the cleaning up for a while because Chinese food, delicious whilst hot, is not quite so tasty when cold and congealed and, after all, the damage had been done, so why not be philosophical about it? Wondering just what Thornton might want of her this time, she returned to the couch, her unfinished meal and *Coronation Street* just in time to hear that familiar music and see the end credits roll. Damn it! She had missed the tag.

*****

Reg Venables wasn't eating a Chinese takeaway; he was sitting in his office trying to nosh on a hot salt beef on rye with lashings of mustard, one of his all time favourites, when Police Constable Roper, back from his stint at Heathrow Airport, appeared at the office door and asked if the inspector was free and willing to see Mister Thornton King.

'What's he want?' Reg asked.

Roper lifted both shoulders and shook his head.

'Well you might have asked him. Oh, all right, send him in.' He sounded most disgruntled.

Reg for once wasn't particularly enjoying his sandwich because he had recently lost a filling and, although he desperately tried to avoid the offending tooth, the nerve was exposed every now and again to the piping hot silverside and reacted accordingly, the pain seemingly playing dodgems around his skull. He put down the remainder of half a sandwich, ran his tongue around his teeth to clear them of any remains and nodded. Roper left and a few moments later Thornton appeared with a cheery greeting.

'Afternoon, Reg. How's tricks? Banged up a few villains lately or are you hunting down the poor old motorist again? Whatever, looks good on the score card, hey?'

Reg grunted and probed the cavity in his tooth with the tip of his tongue. He was definitely going to have to see the dentist and was not looking forward to it. In fact he was virtually in fear and trembling. His own lovely Scots lassie from Edinburgh was away and this Rumanian butcher had taken her place. God alone knew where she had qualified but the first thing she said to him was, "I am never to give you an injection because I must be feeling for your reactions." She felt them all right because by the end of the treatment she was a trembling wreck and Reg was also, wondering if he could hold out until his own dear girl who was always so gentle with him came back from wherever she had gone to. If she was going to be permanently in Edinburgh he was prepared to take the train rather than face the Rumanian butcher again.

'You're in a bright and breezy mood, Thornton? Won the pools have you?'

'Chance would be a fine thing,' Thornton said. 'Anyway, how are you?' He advanced into the room and seated himself in front of the desk. The last time he was in that chair was as a murder suspect. There was an almost imperceptible raising of a Venables eyebrow.

'Well, if you must know, Thornton, old lad,' Reg had the look of a very sick bloodhound, 'I'm having a spot of bother with one of me molars. Care for half a salt beef sandwich?' He shoved the paper plate across the desk.

Thornton, who hadn't had lunch, accepted the offer. 'Don't mind if I do,' he said, 'ta,' and picked up the half sandwich. He wondered if he would ever get used to Reg's girlish voice. It just didn't seem right coming from that particular face.

'I'm a martyr to my teeth,' Reg moaned, 'and that's a fact, have been all my bloody life. Even as a kid before I got my second set. When a milk tooth became loose, my dad used to say, "Here, we'll tie a bit of cotton around it and tie the other end to the door handle, and then we'll slam the door and out will come the tooth, just like that. You won't feel a thing." Won't feel a thing? Who did he think he was kidding? I'd have probably ended up on the floor in a dead faint and that's a fact. Terrifying it was. Even the thought of tying that piece of cotton around the tooth was almost enough to give me the squitters never mind banging the bloody door. I never let him do it of course. Just used to sit there all miserable playing with it with my tongue or a finger and every time I tried to bite into anything tough I'd go through the roof and get blood all over my mashed potatoes. Don't know why God invented teeth in the first place, I really don't. There ought to have been a better way of arranging things.'

'Consider yourself lucky, Reg, that you live in the twentieth century and dentistry has advanced so much. When King Louis the Fourteenth of France had a top tooth extracted he lost half his upper jaw in the process.'

'Leave it out, Thornton.'

He picked up his pipe; the one Rita bought him in the south of France to replace the one he broke when in a bad temper with a French taxi driver he hit it too hard against the heel of his shoe and snapped off the stem, lit it with a Swan Vesta and drew in a satisfying lungful of Three Nuns. Thornton meanwhile didn't even stop to sympathise with Reg in his troubles but munched happily on what should have been the inspector's favourite lunch.

'Young Roper seems a bit on the melancholy side,' Thornton said. 'Never seen him with such a long face. Got toothache as well has he?'

'Nothing so simple,' Reg replied, 'and not half so painful. His face-ache's caused by a lover's tiff. He and his Welsh girlfriend, the one he met at Heathrow, have had a falling out.'

'Well the path of true love ne'er did run smooth, hey? Think of Romeo and Juliet.'

'Yes, yes, well never mind that, to what do I owe the honour of this visit?' Reg said. 'I take it it's not just a social call or to henquire after constable Roper's emotional state.'

'Half and half,' Thornton replied. 'How's the missus?'

'The missus is fine and dandy thank you very much and I don't believe you're here to henquire after the state of my Rita either.'

'And the kids?'

Reg burped loudly.

'Was that a comment?'

And grunted.

For a long while he puffed on his pipe regarding Thornton steadily all the while before finally saying, 'Are you going to get to the point, Thornton? It might not seem like it but I am a busy man you know. Your taxes go towards paying me to pursue criminals and reduce the crime rate, not that you'd really notice it diminishing but there you are. C'est la vie as the French say. Been burgled lately have you? We'll never catch the bastards you know, understaffed as we are; too many of them, too few of us, and should we by any chance nab one of the buggers all he'll get is a reprimand and a suspended sentence at the very worst so he can go out and do it again. Got the picture, have you? So just get your insurance to cough up and we will enter all the details in the incident book and think no more about it. Too much red tape, too many bloody forms to fill in, in triplicate. We've been chopped off at the knees, Thornton my old lad, castrated we are, knackerless, thanks to the lets be kind to the criminal because they're only human fraternity who seem to be having it all their own bloody way. It goes without saying that if one of them gets burgled or mugged he soon changes his bloody tune. Still, so long as the country's paying me to do my duty, I'll do my duty as I see it. Now, what can I do for you, lad?'

'The Pemberton case.'

'Oh yes? What about it?' Reg's eyes narrowed, not a good sign.

'I wondered if you could fill me in, not necessarily in triplicate,' Thornton smiled but his joke fell flat.

'Fill you in with what?'

'A few details.'

'Why?'

'I'm curious.'

'Why?'

'All right, if you must know, his niece has asked me to look into it.'

'Why?'

'Because she's not satisfied with the coroner's verdict.'

'If she's not satisfied with the coroner's verdict it means she believes I didn't do my job properly. Sorry, Thornton, can't be having that, old lad, case closed. Good day.'

'I haven't finished my sandwich.'

'Take it with you. It is, after all, a takeaway and it's all you will take away.' And Reg, momentarily forgetting his tooth, chortled merrily at his witticism and pretended to divert his attention to a stack of forms.

Wheeler Dealer Peter, elbow on the polished surface of his expansive desk, slowly with the top joints of index and middle fingers scratched beneath his chin where his goatee was itching and stonily regarded Mike Aliff seated opposite him.

'Believe me, everything's hunky-dory,' Mike was whining, sweating slightly. 'It's exactly as I expected. The man is running around in ever decreasing circles and soon he'll disappear up his own fundament.' He didn't think he should say "arsehole" in front of the big man. All very well being familiar and matey in a group but one to one was an entirely different matter. 'And that will be the end of that,' he concluded. 'Usually he gets his girl-friend, one Holly Day, to help him out but it appears this trip he hasn't approached her.'

'It's early days yet.'

'He's got absolutely nothing to go on,' Mike responded with apparently growing confidence, 'and I'm keeping a beady eye on Miss Day just in case.' This was a downright lie, as he hadn't a clue as to where she was, but he didn't think the lie would be found out.

'Well, I only hope you're right. There's a great deal hanging on the outcome of his investigations and should he stumble, however accidentally, on the truth, and accidental coincidences have been known to happen, like the discovery of penicillin or Madame Curie with her radium, well, I don't have to spell out the consequences do I?' Sir Peter didn't have a clue as to how penicillin or radium were discovered but then neither had Mike and it sounded good.

So Mike had no answer to this. Suddenly he wasn't quite so sure his plan had been such a good one.

'Leave it to me,' he said with a bravado he certainly didn't feel. 'If I think he's getting even within a mile of it, I'll sort it out.'

'I hope so,' Sir Peter said with a smile. 'Oh, I do hope so.'

Rory, having given him a spare key, Thornton let himself into the Pemberton flat. This visit was timed so as to avoid Mrs McIvor and he knew Rory would be out. He went firstly to the study to check on the desk. The drawer holding the bank papers had been re locked. Did Mrs McIvor do it or was it Aurora? He sat down and once again produced his trusty Swiss knife. It was as he had expected, all the paperwork relating to The Bowmen Of Essex had been removed. He was three quarters of the way to closing the drawer when she spoke.

'Well well well...'

At the sound of the first "well" it was Thornton's turn to take fright with one hand still in the drawer holding the papers flat. He jumped so hard he hit his knuckles on the underneath surface of the desktop, gritted his teeth as he sucked in a deep breath and waggled his damaged hand in the air. Then he sat massaging it as the pain gradually subsided. God! Whoever invented thumbscrews and slivers under the fingernails really knew what they were doing.

'Quits!' Mrs McIvor said gleefully. 'Serve you right, Mr Snooper, always nosing around. What is it you want this time, hey?' With which and not waiting for a reply she turned away and disappeared in the direction of the kitchen.

Thornton finished closing the drawer, got up, and followed her. She sat down at the kitchen table and stubbed out a cigarette she had left smouldering in the saucer that passed for an ashtray and immediately took another from the pack lying on the table and lit it. A cup of tea sat at her elbow and a large tin of assorted biscuits. She regarded Thornton with narrowed eyes as he walked in and joined her at the table.

'I thought I heard the front door when you came in. Suppose you'll be wanting a cup of tea, will you?'

'Not really,' Thornton said, 'thank you all the same.' He pulled the biscuit tin towards him and after a few moments deliberation, selected a cream puff and nibbled into it.

'I suppose you'll be wanting to ask me a lot of silly questions then.'

'Not really.'

'Well, what do you want? You're always snooping about aren't you?'

'It's what I'm paid to do.'

'Hmn... '

'Hmn... and I want to try and work out just how it was that Sir Roger got himself killed.'

'For goodness sake!' She sounded truly exasperated. 'You know how he got himself killed! He was killed with a crossbow bolt. You know that so what more is there to know?'

'A whole lot more I'm afraid.'

'Like what in particular, if I may be so bold as to enquire? You're up to no good or my name isn't Iris Delores McIvor.'

'Delores?'

'Are you married?'

'What on earth makes you ask that?' He was genuinely surprised.

'Well are you?'

'No, I'm not married.'

'I thought as much.' She gave out a snort followed by a sniff.

'What's that in aid of?' Thornton asked.

'I think...' She paused, nodding her head 'I think you're trying to take advantage of Miss Aurora. That's what I think.'

'Really.'

'Yes, really. You're after her millions aren't you?'

'Millions?'

'Well quite a lot anyway, however much there is.'

'I'm after some of it, that's quite true, but only through earning it by the sweat of my brow.'

'There you go, talking tripe again.' Iris Delores McIvor reclaimed her biscuit tin just as he was reaching for another cream puff, slammed down the lid and kept both hands firmly on it until she had to use one hand to remove the cigarette from her mouth because she was beginning to choke on the smoke going up her nostrils and her eyes were beginning to water again.

Thornton felt it would be a little infra dig to try a second time so sat regarding her for such a long time she began to feel most uncomfortable. She stubbed out the cigarette and got up to put the biscuit tin away in the pantry. He watched her go, open the door and turn the wooden chair back into a stepladder so that she could place the biscuit tin on a high shelf then, leaving the pantry door open, she returned to the kitchen to take off her pinafore and replace it with her coat. He noticed she had placed the biscuit tin in a position that, if he went for another biscuit and didn't put the tin back exactly as she had left it she would know he'd been thieving. Thornton smiled to himself.

'Why are you still here?' He asked. 'You should have left...' He looked at his watch... 'over an hour ago.'

'I was late getting in and my old man is very busy today so I'm making my own way home. I suppose I can safely leave you here? You're not going to burn the place down or anything like that?'

'What a peculiar idea. Why would I do that? Pyromania is not my bag.' He gave her his broadest smile.

'You do talk such a load of old codswallop, you really do.' With which, leaving Thornton still seated at the table, she slapped on her hat and left, shaking her head as she went.

For a long while after he heard the front door bang too he sat quite still staring into the pantry and looking firstly at the carefully positioned biscuit tin and then at the chair-cum-steps. Somehow he felt the secret of the scientist's death lay in that very ordinary piece of domestic furniture. It was the "what a peculiar idea" that had set him thinking. It was actually a quite peculiar piece of furniture obviously, by its rough appearance, homemade. No craftsman would ever own up to making it. He got up and walked to it, stood for a moment looking at the stepladder-chair, chair-stepladder, opened and closed the pantry door a few times, went back to the table and sat there thinking, returned to the pantry and converted the stepladder back into the chair, the seat facing the door, squatted behind and angled it so it was square on to the position where the body was found. Next he closed the pantry door and placed the chair almost immediately behind it and pushed the door open again. He went back into the kitchen and looked around for something long, thin, and sturdy and found what he wanted in a mop handle, retrieving the mop from its bucket on the fire escape. Returning to stand outside and to one side of the pantry door he held the handle over the chair as though he were holding a fairly large object upright and started to close the door. At the last inch, before it finally closed, he swiftly removed the handle.

'Ingenious,' he said to himself, 'bloody ingenious! I wonder who it was thought of that.'

*****

'How are you getting on?' Rory asked as she poured the tea. Afternoon tea at The Savoy was one of her favourite occasional treats - occasional because one didn't want to overdo a good thing that in time would lose its allure and become commonplace - overlooking The Embankment and the river, the piano providing soft music, the pianist providing a sugary sweet smile, the uniformed waiters providing just the right kind of service, the delicious cucumber sandwiches, the dainty fairy cakes, the murmur of conversation spiced with merry laughter, and the ambience, who could ask for anything more?

'Tell me, Rory, did you and your uncle never talk to each other?'

'What an odd question but, come to think of it, not all that often. Sir Roger wasn't what everyone imagines an absent-minded professor to be but I suppose he did live in a world of his own rather, always brooding over some problem or other to do with his work. There was no point his discussing it with me; I have never been of a scientific bent, no not at all. Also I am away quite a lot but when our paths did cross it was usually small talk like how've you been, how's the work going? Things like that. Why do you ask?'

'Because you told me he had given up on his archery whereas as a matter of fact he was a member of his club until almost the day he died.'

'Oh!' She thought about this for a while and then gave a little shrug. 'I don't see that that's so important.'

Thornton shook his head. 'It could be very important but we will see. What made you take up charity work?'

'Really, Thornton, you are asking some strange questions today. If you must know, and I don't see that it has anything to do with you or my uncle, it was because I was over-qualified for everything I applied for. I have had a first class education, thanks to my late guardian. I believe I am intelligent, talented even and I think, when prospective employers perused my curriculum vitae they freaked out, decided I was too clever by half, would probably show up their own inadequacies, make them look ridiculous or put their jobs in jeopardy, and wrote me off before I could even get an interview, most of them having got their own positions simply by chutzpah or gift of the gab. There, does that tell you everything?'

'In a nutshell.'

'So can we get back to what you have discovered so far?'

'It was an accident,' Thornton said.

For a moment the teapot remained suspended in mid-air as in a stop-frame. This was not what Rory was expecting to hear so convinced was she in her own mind that her guardian had been deliberately done away with.

'Accident? I don't believe it. I'm sorry, Thornton,' she continued to pour the tea, 'I simply will not believe it.'

'It was an accident, Rory, I promise you. That is, I'm almost certain of it, an accident that went wrong and resulted in his murder.'

'Aaaah!' That was better. She lowered the teapot and passed Thornton his cup. 'The cucumber sandwiches are a real treat, Thornton, nobody makes them better so don't hold back. We can always order more. Now tell me what you mean by an accident resulting in murder.'

'Well...' He took a bite of his first cucumber sandwich, a small bite so that he could talk and carry on eating without actually having his mouth full as it were. 'As I see it, the plan was actually for your uncle to be given a scare. He was stepping out of line... '

'I don't understand.'

'For some reason he was being blackmailed, I don't know why, and I believe he finally decided enough was enough so whoever was doing the blackmailing decided to put the frighteners on him and, I am afraid, Rory, your Mrs McIvor and her Jimmy were in on the whole thing.'

'Never!' She put down her teacup with such force she almost broke it. 'Oh, no, don't say that, Thornton. What proof do you have?'

'I don't have proof, Rory, but I believe this is how it was worked. That day there was no one around in the early evening, when your uncle was killed, if the medical report is correct, which is why no one saw anything suspicious at that time. Sir Roger was alone in the flat having come in from work. You were gone for the day and wouldn't be back till late. You more than likely let on to that fact to Mrs McIvor before you left the flat. Sometime during that morning after you had gone Jimmy McIvor was in the flat setting a trap, the trap being the crossbow. It was set up almost vertically, but not quite, on that wooden chair in the pantry, placed so that it was leaning on the closed door and when someone, in this case your uncle, opened the door, the bow dropped with a jolt and was triggered. You know, there's been many a genuine accident with guns being dropped or bumped and going off. Now the reason I say it was an accident is because the seat of the chair of course isn't very high and, had the bow dropped to the horizontal position which was intended the bolt, if it had hit your uncle at all, would have done so round about knee height. Kneecapping may have been the object of the exercise. For some reason the bow was triggered too soon, I don't know the reason for it but that is why the bolt went in at an upward angle under the ribs. The reason why I say his death was accidental is because you don't slay the golden goose if you can help it. There was still plenty of money to be squeezed out of this one I'm sure. Are you following me?'

'Yes.' It was almost a whisper.

'This is mere conjecture but I imagine Sir Roger might have received a phone call that piqued his curiosity so that he opened the pantry door, and curiosity as you are now aware, led to the death of this particular cat. It would have been too bad if you had a change of plans and returned early, before your uncle that is. You could have copped it instead of him, though I'm sure Jimmy or Iris Delores' – Thornton seemed to like the sound of those names together, they sounded like the title of a popular song - 'or both were lurking about somewhere to ensure that didn't happen. Had you approached the building, one of them could have delayed you under some pretext or other while the other scurried off upstairs to disarm the booby trap as it were. I assume the crossbow in question was your uncle's personal property so no one would question it being there.'

Rory nodded and they sat for a moment in silence. Thornton helped himself to another cucumber sandwich and this time took a healthier bite. He had made his pitch.

'Are you positive the McIvors had something to do with it?'

'What makes me believe so is the sudden acquisition of a brand new pretty pricey motor which was bought for cash.'

'How do you know that?'

'Because I went to the dealer who sold it to our Jimmy and he confirmed it was a cash deal.'

'He told you all about another man's business? Not very ethical I must say.'

'There are ways of asking questions that don't seem like questions or at least questions that seem pretty innocuous. I merely happened to mention a very good friend of mine had recently bought the model I was interested in and got a good deal for cash. "That would be Mr McIvor would it?" He asked. "Yes, indeed," I replied and, "being a Scot, Jimmy would know how to clinch a bargain." That last was said to make the fellow believe Jimmy really was a close friend.'

'How did you know where he bought it?'

'The dealer's name is on the rear window and on the number plate. Mrs M. insisted it was bought on the never never but the McIvors are not exactly the kind of people who would be granted hire purchase facilities from a mainstream house. Pawnbrokers and loan sharks for small amounts at exorbitant rates of interest, that's more in their line. Sir Roger could have lent them the money but I don't believe he did. I found no evidence pointing towards it. You could have lent it but you didn't. So where did they get it?'

'Well, if what you say is true, then the question to be answered is, who was responsible?'

'That,' Thornton said with his mouth full, and he hadn't even started on the fairy cakes, 'is what I have to find out.'

CHAPTER THREE

Thornton felt as he was obviously to blame, or so Holly led him to believe in no uncertain terms, she could call in a firm of professional cleaners to set the couch to rights and charge it as expenses to Aurora Pemberton. After all, he was seeking Holly's help when he telephoned so it was all in the line of duty as it were. He finished inspecting the unfortunate brown stain and sat down to one side of it.

'I must confess it does look rather obscene,' he remarked.

'Never mind the obscene bit, Thornton, what is all this air of mystery in aid of?' she asked.

'Murder.'

'That is always obscene,' she said, opening her eyes very wide. 'Who have you murdered?'

'No joking, Holly, I'm deadly serious.'

'Murder is for the police to look into, Thornton, not you.'

'They've already looked into it with no success. As far as they're concerned the coroner's report means it's over and done with, the case is closed.'

'Of course, but you don't agree, so all right then, go ahead, tell me all.'

'Well, you know about Sir Roger Pemberton... '

'Of course. As a possible security risk he was on file at the department for some time. I must admit the whole business did seem, how shall I put this? A bit bizarre? There was great debate in the department as to whether or not we should poke our noses in just in case it had all the makings of an international incident. That's putting it nicely.'

'Bizarre is the word for it, Holly and that is what his niece thinks and why she's hired me to investigate.'

Holly nodded and hugged her knees. 'And you want a little assistance from me. Information?'

'More than that.'

Holly raised an eyebrow.

'Active participation.'

'Meaning what exactly? Want me to watch your back again?'

'No. How good are you with a bow and arrow?'

Holly couldn't help it. She burst into laughter. Thornton waited for her to calm down. Her fit having subsided she looked hard at his solemn face.

'You are serious I take it.'

'Never more so.'

'Well then, to answer your question quite bluntly I've never in my life held a bow or fired an arrow.'

'Never mind, a couple of lessons and you'll be up to Robin Hood or William Tell standard. We might even have you entered for the Olympic Games and whoever's playing the latter day equivalent of the Sheriff of Nottingham will be completely fooled by your brilliant disguise as you walk away with the golden arrow.'

'Thornton, are you fantasising again or are you quite sure this is necessary?'

'Oh, absolutely.'

'Because Sir Roger met his death by means of a crossbow bolt?'

'Exactly.'

She sat regarding him for a long moment while she ruminated on this then, 'What is the connection?' she asked.

'The Bowmen of Essex', he replied. He took the filched letter from his pocket and passed it to her.

*****

The small highly polished brass plaque beside the door was most discreet. It gave no information other than the number of the building and the name of the company, Fundraisers Ltd.

Holly, acting as secretary to a Mister Kenton, he being trustee of a brand new charity being set up to assist in the protection of the endangered species of turtle, caritta caritta, (something actually close to Thornton's heart), telephoned to make an appointment and the said Mister Kenton duly presented himself at the designated time for his appointment at the offices of Fundraisers Ltd. It was actually a toss-up between the magnificent but fast disappearing gorillas of West Africa being hunted to extinction for bush meat and the turtle. It was Thornton's firm belief that human beings are predators of the worst kind on this planet, killing for so-called sport, killing just for the hell of it, killing unnecessarily for the thrill of exotic food to satisfy jaded appetites. He was served turtle soup once at a posh dinner. It had the viscosity of slightly watered down horse hoof glue and most probably tasted like it as well. It clung with all the tenacity of a barnacle to lips, teeth, and every other part of the mouth until more or less washed away by copious drafts of wine and the following courses. Even so he couldn't wait to get home to brush his teeth and use a mouthwash.

His briefcase was stuffed, thanks to Rory's expense account, with relative material: pamphlets, letterheads, information; aims and objects of the new charity. He had taken the liberty of using Harold Norris's address as its headquarters. A used car lot with a prefabricated office was as good as any unless it was going to be checked out in person. The telephone number though was his.

Rory had also briefed him quite thoroughly in the way he should conduct himself at an interview. No, she said, she had never heard of a company called Fundraisers Ltd., and would be more than interested to know all about it. She somehow doubted if they really were into raising money for charity. As far as she was concerned the whole thing sounded very dodgy. It also sounded extremely dodgy as far as Thornton was concerned which was why he was now seated in the small reception area of the company's offices, a room that was positively Dickensian. A twentieth century Uriah Heep character had obsequiously greeted him, introducing himself as Seymour Goodwin. Thornton wasn't too sure whether this was a pseudonym or not, and was surprised the character wasn't either rubbing his hands together or holding in ink-stained bony fingers a quill pen and sitting on a high stool pouring over a heavy ledger by the light of a guttering candle. If Thornton continued to fail as a private detective he thought he might turn his hand to a spot of writing, not high literature necessarily but books purely to amuse.

Politely requested by Mister Goodwin to wait just a few moments whilst Mr Fund Raiser himself, that is Mister Nikos Filodopoulis, finished making a rather important telephone call, Thornton seated himself in an extremely comfortable leather armchair and, resigned to a possibly long enforced wait he was about to pick up a copy of *The Financial Times* from the table in front of him to keep himself occupied, when the inner door opened and Mr Filodopoulis entered. Thornton had him summed up in three words: money, money, money.

As a young man, not that he was that much older now, Nikos Filodopoulis must have been extremely good looking. Eyelashes many women can only dream about framed his enormous brown eyes. The mouth was perhaps a little too sensual but on the whole the remains of his looks were still evident. Unfortunately, as with so many Mediterranean men, as they reach the middle twenties when the love handles and the belly have developed and the breasts are beginning to show a distinct wobbly prominence, he was well passed his sell-by date. Even his wife who married him for his looks no longer found him attractive but sighed over the memory of her young Adonis, which didn't matter all that much as there were girls aplenty who found his money so alluring they were prepared to put up with anything, even the garlic which he was in the habit of chewing raw.

'Mr Kenton,' Filodopoulis extended a set of podgy ringed fingers that Thornton briefly took, 'so sorry to have kept you waiting. Won't you please step inside?' There was no trace of an accent and he waved an arm towards his office door, stood aside so that Mr Kenton, alias Thornton King, could enter and followed, closing the door behind him, behind Thornton's back giving a smirking Uriah a big wink as he did so.

'Please sit down.' Nikos held out a hand indicating the chair in front of his desk as he walked around and ensconced himself in the high back, black leather, swivel executive chair on the other side.

'Now then, Mr Kenton, where shall we begin? Why have you come to see us?'

'As I believe my secretary informed you on the telephone, we are setting up a new charity.'

'Ah yes...' He glanced down at a slip of paper on which he had obviously scribbled some notes. 'To save the turtle, caritta caritta, an endangered species. Even the spelling of its name is endangered. Some spell it with one T, others with two but however it is spelt, I am wholeheartedly with you on this one. Yes, indeed. But still, why have you come to us? There is an organisation that could help you, the Charities Information Trust. Why did you not go straight to them?'

'You were recommended to me.'

'Oh, yes? That is most interesting. I would be most interested to know by whom, that is, if I may ask?'

'Who?'

'Indeed, yes. Who was it recommended us to you?'

'Do you know...' Thornton laughed with genuine embarrassment and tapped his temple to indicate what a klutz he was, but he needed to think fast. 'I don't actually recall his name? I did hear it of course because naturally he introduced himself. This was on the plane you see. He mentioned his name of course, sort of introducing himself, but at that precise moment our hostess was offering us drinks, which diverted my attention and that was why I didn't catch it. I should have got him to repeat it of course, or write it down, or offer me his card, but I didn't think of it at the time. Anyway we got into conversation and...'

'And he told you all about Fundraisers Ltd.'

Thornton was beginning to feel a trifle nervous. Nikos, gently tapping a gold fountain pen on his desktop, seemed to be giving him the hard stare.

'This plane you were on, where were you flying from?'

'From Greece. Athens airport. Isn't it the pits? Like Luton and Naples. One day they'll really have to build a new one.'

'I'm sure they will. Luton and Naples as well I shouldn't wonder. But tell me, how did we happen to enter the conversation?'

'Because I was returning from a field trip. As you know only too well, more than likely, being Greek... you are Greek I take it? Maybe Cypriot?'

'I am Greek. From a little village in the Peloponnese.' He pronounced it the Greek way – Pelopónnisos.

'Well then, you are aware there are beaches where the turtle lays her eggs and these beaches are in grave danger, at the moment from hordes of hippies from all over Europe, camping overnight, lighting fires, disturbing the turtles in their laying. But it is the future we are even more worried about.'

'How so?'

'Well, British holidaymakers seeking the sun at the moment take their two weeks or so on the Costas, right? I'm talking about the ordinary man in the street as it were seeking sun, sex, and sangria as the saying goes but, as package holidays get cheaper and flights more available, they will want to travel further afield and the next destination will be Greece. Greece of course will welcome these tourists bringing in much needed income but I can foresee the day when the nesting beaches will fast disappear under an encroaching avalanche of sun beds and beach umbrellas and hordes of sun worshipers. Sun, sex, and Retsina, yes?'

Filodopoulis kept a perfectly straight face and Thornton's smile gradually disappeared.

Finally, 'You make it sound very dramatic,' he said, 'An avalanche?'

'Believe me Mister Filodopoulis, the matter is very serious. These nesting places are sacrosanct, out of bounds and meant to be undisturbed but...'

'But human beings being what they are they couldn't give a tinker's farting fuck, am I right?'

'Unfortunately you are right,' a slightly startled Thornton replied wondering where on earth Filodopoulis could have picked up that expression and did he use it frequently in business dealings? But wait a moment. Hadn't he heard someone use that expression before? Where? And who? He tried hard to recall who it could have been.

'And you hope to pre-empt this?'

Thornton came back to earth. 'I beg your pardon?'

'I said, and you hope to pre-empt this.'

'We can at least try to educate...'

Nikos laughed. It wasn't a pleasant sound. 'Mr Kenton, what's the expression I need here? You are flogging a dead horse. By the way do you know the joke about the guy wanting to know if he was flogging a dead horse?'

It was Thornton's turn to stare stonily at Mr Filodopoulis. He was there to discuss the plight of the caritta caritta not listen to jokes that came out of the ark. No, that wasn't actually true. He was ostensibly there to discuss the plight of the caritta caritta. What he was actually there for was to discover a possible link between Sir Roger Pemberton's death and Fundraisers Ltd. Nikos stopped laughing and shook his head. Rather than tapping with it, he was now rolling his gold pen around the desk with the flat of his chubby hand.

'Mr Kenton, people have to earn a living and people wish to enjoy themselves, especially in Greece where the law is there for other people to observe and really never has anything to do with you personally unless you are the complainant. The ones enjoying themselves are helping the first lot to earn a living, these will be the owners of the beach umbrellas and the sun beds and the ones that run the tavernas. As a matter of fact I have a couple of cousins who are exactly in that position. I also have a couple of cousins who are policemen and who will no doubt, for their cousins' sake, turn a blind eye to any infringement of the law they don't consider exactly criminal, merely a minor bit of naughtiness, if you know what I mean, something those rascally politicians with nothing better to do dreamed up to harass the ordinary man going about his business. Do you really believe for one moment you are going to make any kind of impression on these people? I am sorry but I very much doubt it. So, Mr Kenton, so please come off the bush and give me your real reason for being here.'

Thornton was by now really worried. Something was going drastically wrong. It was he who was supposed to be asking the questions, not the other way around. He had got nowhere with Reg Venables, he was getting nowhere with Filodopoulis. His brain seemed suddenly scrambled as he sought desperately for something to say. Filodopoulis was smiling a Gioconda smile that was most unpleasant. There was silence for a while before he spoke again. His voice was very quiet, only just audible.

'Nothing to say, Mr King?'

The silence this time was even longer. Thornton didn't actually feel any of those symptoms writers are always writing about in just such a situation. He didn't feel his blood run cold or a tingling in his groin or his heart beating any faster or his toes curling or the sweat standing out on his brow or trickling down his back. He didn't even drop his jaw. He merely sat like a ventriloquist's dummy minus the hand of the ventriloquist as Nikos Filodopoulis continued.

'You were not on your way back from Greece, Mr King, that is, unless France or Sicily have suddenly become part of my patritha. Let me offer you a word of advice, if you want to play at being a private detective…' and here Nikos produced from behind his desk a daily paper opened at the relevant page with a photograph of Thornton and a column on the great diamond heist… 'I would advise you to shun all publicity. Anonymity is a great advantage in your line of business. You came here to get information but you leave with nothing, nix, nil, niente, tipota. Seymour will see you out.'

The shakes only started for Thornton as the front door of Fundraisers Ltd. closed behind him finally obscuring the grinning countenance of one Seymour Goodwin. He stood for a moment on the pavement, oblivious to everything but his own sense of failure. It was true. The visit had got him absolutely nowhere: had more than likely alerted any guilty party that he could be on their trail. He badly needed a stiff one to calm himself down. There were secrets in that building, secrets he would never be privy to unless he were to break in and that would just be stupid. Of course Fundraisers was on the surface a legitimate business: registered at Companies House as all businesses are meant to be; into banking, insurance, investment; publishing their yearly audited accounts, no doubt paying their taxes and their VAT all up to date, with the charitable aspect only a sideline and, Thornton was convinced, something like blackmail and money-laundering, but there was no way he was going to prove anything now, his cover having been well and truly blown.

He had been walking some distance, trying to fathom out his next step when he found himself outside *The Wig And Gown* and his next step took him through its swing doors and into the smoke filled bar.

'You should have seen her costume! A tassel for each tit and a ruby in her navel! Haw haw haw haw! Mind you, she could have been wearing a merkin but I couldn't get close enough to have a good look-see. Thornton, old lad! What're you doing in this neck of the woods?'

Mike Aliff was the last person in the world Thornton wanted to bump into after what he had just been through but fate had directed his footsteps and he guessed he was stuck with him. 'What's your poison?' Mike asked. This was unusual. Mike Aliff was not noted for generosity at the bar but he was probably out to impress.

'You're not going to like this,' Thornton said, 'but seeing as to how you're offering, I'll have a large scotch.'

There was sudden intake of breath from Mike but, for once as good as his word, he clicked his fingers at the barman and ordered Thornton's drink, at the same time eyeing him with some distaste. 'Why the sudden need for the comfort of alcohol, old chum, if one may ask?'

'Just gone through a terrible interview,' Thornton said.

'Oh yes?'

'At a firm called Fundraisers Ltd.

'With the Gree...' Mike could have bitten off his tongue.

'You know him?'

'Who?'

'Nikos the Greek.'

'Well, to be honest, Thornton...' Mike was winging it. 'Not personally you understand, only through the department. We had reason to believe at one time he might be a security risk. We didn't find anything though.' He could only hope Thornton had swallowed it.

'I don't remember that but maybe his file never came my way. In what way would he have been a security risk?'

'You know what these Middle Eastern types are like. Can't trust any of them an inch, least of all a Cypriot. They hate our guts you know.'

'Strange, he distinctly told me he's Greek. A small village in the Peloponnese he said.'

'Did he now? Here's your drink. Cheers!' as he slid the glass in Thornton's direction and paid the barman.

'Cheers!' Thornton said and took a swig at his whisky. 'Good,' he said. 'Now tell me, Mike, I hear you recommended me to Aurora Pemberton, would that be right?'

'Of course.'

'Why?'

'Why?'

'Yes, why?'

'Why not?'

'Why not is not the question. The question is why?'

'Simple, old chum. She wanted to hire a private detective and you are a private detective, are you not?'

'There are no others?'

'Not ones I personally know. Anyway, how are you getting on with the task at hand? Any conclusions as yet?'

'Early days, Mike, early days, but I do have my suspicions.' With which Thornton with a gulp swallowed the remains of his whisky and placed the glass on the counter. 'Thanks for the drink. It's on me next time. Be seeing you.' He turned to leave but turned back.

'By the way, what do you know about this company, Fundraisers?'

'Don't know a thing, nothing at all.'

It was a little too emphatic Thornton thought and once more turned away, leaving Mike Aliff, a trifle bemused, staring after him.

At the door Thornton suddenly came to a grinding halt and turned to look back at Mike who was now deep in conversation or giving out with more of his globe-trotting sexual adventures and triumphs with those around him. That was where Thornton had heard the bizarre expression used by Nikos Filodopoulis.

*****

Holly's Bermuda based heiress friend Carmen Inez Hernandez was at the Dorchester for a few days and Holly, having received her phone call, wasted no time in visiting her in her suite. No argument, this definitely was fate. It couldn't have been more convenient. She had been racking her brains for a way of proceeding in the investigation of the *Bowmen Of Essex* and had come up with absolutely nothing, but Carmen's presence in town could solve the problem.

They had not seen each other for some time and there were hugs and air kisses galore and delighted shrieks from Carmen. Holly was not the shrieking type. Carmen took her by the hand and led her to the sofa where they sat facing each other, Holly a little on the demure side, Carmen, laughing happily, landing with an abandoned plump.

'Holly! How wonderful to see you! Let me get you a drink.' She was immediately on her feet again and crossing over to the bar where she turned to look back with a smile. 'What will it be? There's everything here and, if there's not, I can have it sent up. Oh, it is so good to see you! It's been far too long. What did you say you wanted?'

'A gin and It if I may.'

'Of course you may. Two gin and Its coming up,' and she set about pouring them.

'How are the bananas?' Holly asked.

'The bananas are just dandy. So is the coffee, so are the pineapples, so is the sugar and so is the beef and I believe daddy, like little Jack Horner, is poking his finger into a couple of new pies, not illegal ones I hasten to add, but what a clever old boy he is, thank the Lord!' She crossed back to the sofa with the two glasses filled almost to the brim, and handed one to Holly. 'Cheers' she said.

'Bottoms up!'

Carmen sat and they clinked glasses, a little too enthusiastically as Carmen was splashed with a not inconsiderable amount of gin and Italian.

'Oh, me! Oh, my! Silly mois.' She brushed herself down with slender fingers and flicked her fingers towards the carpet.

'Mummy of course is as big an embarrassment as ever, maybe even bigger. She insists upon thinking of herself as being at least twenty-five years younger than she is, acting like she's my sister, wearing the most outrageous outfits. She has absolutely no taste in clothes. She goes to bars and flirts outrageously with men young enough to be her own sons and she simply refuses to grow old gracefully. But there you are, what can one do but stay as far away from her as is possible? Not a nice thing to have to say about a parent but, if parents can't behave like normal human beings, what can one do? Now, fill me in with absolutely everything that's been happening to you,' Carmen gushed, kicking off her shoes and folding her long legs beneath her.

'It would take too long,' Holly replied, laughing. 'And not really all that interesting.'

'Don't be so modest. Are you still with the hush hush department?'

'Afraid so. Are you still with the same fella?'

'That depends.'

'Depends on what?'

'Which fella I was with when we last saw each other.'

'Oh. I seem to remember it was a Warren something or other.'

Carmen gave another shriek and spilled some more gin down her front. 'Warren something or other is ancient history, my dear! I can't for the life of me even remember what he looks like. Oh yes I can! Whatever did I see in him? He seemed every girl's dream boat at the time but you wake up one day and the dream boat has sunk to the bottom of the ocean or, in Warren's case, the bottom of a murky river. He was a slime ball if ever there was one. Here, hold this.' She handed Holly her glass and got to her feet to head for the bathroom ostensibly to do something about the spilled gin but half way there changed her mind and headed back for the sofa.

'Silly me,' she said, 'clumsy as ever. Do you remember at school I practically trashed any and everything that came my way? Madame said if I stepped on board a battleship it would sink immediately. I'll change in a minute and this can go to the cleaners.'

'Just like my brand new couch,' Holly said.

'What happened to your couch?'

'Sweet and Sour Pork happened to it.'

'Ouch!'

'Tell me, Carmen, I couldn't believe it was really you when you called. How long are you in London for?'

'Just long enough to see a few old friends. I don't mean old old friends, just old friends. You were the first on the list, and, when I've been through the list, it's off to Monte. There's a dear sweet li'l old yacht waiting for me there with a dear sweet li'l old captain who doesn't look a day over thirty, and a dear sweet li'l old crew to steer me around Mediterranean hotspots, what more could any girl want?'

'Are you, as a world-famous newsworthy heiress and jetsetter, still being photographed by the paparazzi wherever you go?'

'Absolutely no one, darling, knows I'm here or has the slightest clue as to what I look like. It's a dead secret. When I go out I am but totally in disguise, dark glasses, heavy wig, you name it. And I'll tell you something else,' she dropped her voice to a whisper, 'I'm registered here under a false name.'

'How did you manage that?'

'Aha!' Carmen tapped the side of her nose. 'Little Miss Muck here has ways and means. Everything's actually legit and aboveboard. It's just that I didn't want any of the staff to know who I am and give the game away. That way no paparazzi, no need for bodyguards, free as a bird.'

'I'm sure daddy would not approve if he knew. Have you any idea the size of the ransom somebody could ask for you? But this is very interesting because coincidentally I was going to ask a simply enormous favour of you.'

'Oh yes?' There was nothing guarded or reluctant about this "Oh, yes." It was simply an interjection. Carmen was always most forthcoming with her close friends and unwilling to deny them anything if it were in her power to oblige.

'While you are in London travelling incognito I would like to steal your identity.'

There was a long silence as Carmen stared at her friend, trying to digest what she had just heard.

'You want to be me for a few days?'

'Hmn-Hmn.' Holly smiled and took a sip of her drink.

'What an extraordinary request! Her eyes were opened so wide it was a miracle they didn't pop out of her head. 'I hope it's is not for any illegal purpose.'

'Well in a way, impersonating someone else to all and sundry I suppose could be considered illegal under certain circumstances but in actual fact, unorthodox as it may seem, it's to set a trap, a trap to catch a killer… '

'A killer!' There was yet another, even wilder shriek from Miss Hernandez.

Or perhaps more than one and, in order to do it, I need to be mega mega rich. You are mega rich, I am not, so I need to pretend to be you. Are you game?'

Carmen raised a thumb. 'Count me in,' she said. 'How exciting! Now I'll go change my dress.'

*****

Harold Norris, overcoat collar turned up to his cheeks in a vain effort to keep out the cold, was doing what for him came naturally, polishing one of his cars with a soft yellow duster only recently out of its cellophane. Trade had been slack of late and he was feeling the pinch. His nose was running and he was rummaging in a pocket for a handkerchief to stem the flow when a familiar voice greeted him with a cheery "Hello." He didn't even bother to turn around.

'Hello, Thornton,' he said, 'and what can I do you for on this bitterly cold morning?'

'I need to hire a car,' Thornton said.

Now Harold did turn around to cast a rheumy eye in Thornton's direction.

'I hear you've now gone in for the hiring racket… '

'Racket?'

'… as well as the buying and selling.'

'You hear correct. What kind of car do you wish to hire and, more important, how do you intend to pay for it?'

'Aha, Harold, something you haven't heard. At the moment I am gainfully employed and this hiring lark is to be paid for by my employer as a legitimate expense.'

'And just who might this employer be?'

'Can't tell you that. Ethics and all that don't you know.'

Harold snorted which was a mistake and required a quick rub down of his coat front with the handkerchief.

'I can only tell you she's as rich as Croesus.'

'Oh, it's for Holly is it?'

'On the nail, old chum. The car is for Holly's use but Holly is not as rich as Croesus. Her daddy is. But daddy is not paying for the car. My employer is.'

'God, you do go around in circles, Thornton. One day you're going to disappear up your own… Okay, what kind of car do you want? Let's get out of this bleeding cold. It's enough to freeze the balls off a brass monkey as the old saying has it. Come to the office.' They set off across the yard, Harold a step ahead. 'How about this one? Beautiful bit of engineering we have here. Real class, a work of art, British craftsmanship at its best. No Johnny Foreigner could beat that, not even the Japanese whose cars it seems are becoming quite popular.' He was pointing to a silvery-grey Bentley.

'I don't think so, Harold. Would suit her daddy but not the kind of car a feisty young gal would drive. A wee bit on the stately side don't you think? I know women join the army to enjoy the thrill of driving tanks these days but it's not Holly's style. Holly would be more Formula One. This, I would say, is more in her line.'

'The Jensen! The Jensen?' Harold looked at his prospective client as if he had gone right off his rocker. 'Thornton, do you know what that will cost? On my life, boy, the insurance premiums on that car would pay your office expenses for a year.'

'Definitely that's the one,' Thornton said, giving it a friendly pat that left finger marks on the paintwork and almost caused the fibrillation of Harold's heart.

'Give us a discount for cash.'

CHAPTER FOUR

Holly loved it. The car purred like a contented pussycat. She only wished she could put her foot down and experience its speed but English roads and the amount of traffic on them make it impossible for the most part to floor the accelerator and she knew perfectly well that even if she tried, within seconds there would be a cop car on her tail, siren wailing, before she could say Heath Robinson.

She enjoyed the good-hearted banter, the wolf whistles, the "Hello darlings," she received from builders, tradesmen, other drivers. The time would come when such natural reactions would be outlawed, would be considered sexual harassment, could be cause for massive compensation claims for psychological distress and all the rest of that bullshit, but at the beginning of the seventies this kind of politically correct nonsense, although beginning to take root, had fortunately not gone that far and Holly enjoyed being the centre of masculine admiration. Of course there had to be the one or two who accompanied their banter with an obscene gesture but there would always be those who would never know any better.

She half circled the Clapton roundabout and headed down the Leigh Bridge Road for Walthamstow and on toward Epping.

There is nothing in the legend that says Maid Marian ever pulled a bowstring but, as befitted her incipient role, Holly was a vision in Lincoln green. For a good while her costume appeared to be about the only indication of her mission, and as far as she was going to get, as there was absolutely no clue as to where the *Bowmen Of Essex* hung out. The club was obviously so exclusive it had no need to publicly advertise, not even by so much as a sign. Membership was obviously by proposal.

She must have done an extra fifteen miles or more when she passed for the third time a dirt track to her left, and took notice for the first time that a short way down, tall trees and glorious purple rhododendrons flanking them, there was a pair of quite handsome, white painted wooden gates. She stopped, put the car into reverse and backed up, sat for a while contemplating the gates, then turned the Jensen onto the track, steering the car at a slight angle so that she completely blocked the way.

She took something from her purse, slipped out of the car and walked around to the front. Looking around to make sure she was unobserved she bent down and placed an inch and a half nail against the tyre and then pushed it right in with her boot. Then she crouched down beside the wheel, unscrewed the cap from the valve, let out all the air and replaced the cap. Now it was just a question of waiting, hopefully not for too long and hopefully also that her sixth sense hadn't let her down and she was in the right place.

A good half hour passed. Cars drove by on the main road but no one took any interest in Holly or her car. There was an ominous distant roll of thunder and she glanced nervously upwards. Solid black clouds seemed to be scudding in her direction at the rate of knots and the few advance messengers heralding a heavy shower, if not a tropical downpour, spattered on the bonnet of the car and on her Lincoln green. Holly looked down at the tyre she had only just flattened.

'Shit!' She said. 'This is all I need.'

Making his way towards Finsbury Pavement, Thornton also felt the first spatter of rain. Turning up his coat collar and hunching into it he quickened his step before the storm could hit, silently cursing that he had travelled by underground instead of taking a taxi - he was after all on expenses – and also that he had come out without his trusty umbrella.

In the nick of time he barged through the tax office doors just as there was a crash of thunder virtually overhead and the heavens opened. For a few moments he stood inside the door looking out at the deluge that would have soaked him to the skin within seconds and was in fact doing just that to those scurrying by who hadn't managed to find shelter. Then he turned back to make his way to the second floor and a meeting with his second best bete noir, his first bete noir of course being his smarmy bank manager who he hoped one day to see standing outside his very own bank, cap in hand, doggy on a tatty blanket at his feet, begging alms from passers by; a fantasy that had no chance of ever coming true but a pleasant daydream nevertheless, nice to conjure up and comfort oneself with every now and again.

Mister Jason Alexander Augustus Pinner, one of Her Majesty's Inspector of Taxes, a monumental set of first names for one who could only be described as a weed, being no more than five foot three or four inches tall and as skinny as the proverbial rake as Thornton's mother was wont to say. This was usually dredged up at mealtimes when, as a child, he baulked at eating his vegetables, Brussels sprouts or spinach in particular. "Thornton, you will grow up looking like a matchstick man." Mister Pinner quite obviously did not relish his vegetables as a child and still didn't if the pallor of his complexion was anything to go by, appearing even more jaundiced under the harsh glare of the strip lighting and in contrast to his watery blue eyes, the bright red of his hair and rather droopy nicotine stained moustache.

With his back to the door he was busy thumbing through a number of files in the drawer of a tall and somewhat battered metal filing cabinet when Thornton entered the office and stood silently waiting. Having found the file he wanted, Pinner slammed closed the cabinet drawer and turned around to see Thornton stranding there. As though startled, he took a dramatic step back, tucking his chin into his scrawny neck and then, 'Well bless my soul,' he said with a smile. 'Would you credit it? Look who's here? Mister King isn't it?'

He knew perfectly well it was Mister King. He never forgot a face and had experienced great pleasure on a couple of previous occasions in giving Thornton the third degree in this very office, casting aspersions on his tax returns, demanding to know how Thornton could live off the smell of an oil rag and was he by any chance part of the black economy that was leading the United Kingdom into a steady decline and having a deleterious effect on the country's balance of payments? At the time Thornton decided Pinner was as mad as a hatter and probably believed England was still paying back lend-lease. Come to think of it, maybe it was.

'And to what do we owe the pleasure of your company this fine day? Oops! I do beg your pardon. It was a fine day just a few moments ago, was it not? Perchance you brought this inclement weather with you.' By this time, after a quick glance out the rain-spattered window, he had seated himself behind his desk and extended a crabby milk-white, blue-veined hand to indicate Thornton was permitted to sit opposite him. Thornton was glad he wasn't expected to shake the hand. He would have been unable to repress a shudder.

'I have no recollection of us having an appointment, Mister King?' Pinner laid his elbows on the desk and steepled his fingers, the tips of his index fingers just touching his nostrils as though to push back the hair that protruded there.

'We don't. Not officially that is. I popped in on the off chance we could have a little chat.'

'A little chat? A little chat indeed. Well I never. There's a novelty. I'm certainly not used to members of the public just popping in for a little chat. Bearding the lion in its den are you?' He permitted himself a wry little smile. 'Well then, a little chat about what does one suppose? Your complicated tax affairs I take it.'

'Actually, no. My tax affairs are smack up to date I'm glad to say.' Was it his imagination or did Pinner's face fall slightly? 'A little chat about somebody else's complicated tax affairs, the affairs of a company in fact.'

'You have some connection with this aforementioned company?'

'In a roundabout way.'

'Which means no.'

'Which roughly means in a roundabout way. I have been asked by a client to investigate the company's affairs and I thought...'

'You thought wrong, Mr King.' He unsteepled his fingers and used the index finger and spatulate thumb of one hand to stroke the base of his nose as he spoke. 'I cannot possibly divulge information confidential to this department just because you have a client... what does your client wish to know and, just as importantly, why?'

'I am trying to solve a murder.'

'Goodness gracious me! A murder indeed! Well I never.' There was a long pause as he sat back in his chair and stared at Thornton and then, 'But surely, Mister King, solving a murder is the province of the metropolitan police or Scotland Yard, the CID? Why should it be left up to you to attempt a solution? Who, if I may so enquire, has been murdered?'

'Well, as yet there is no actual proof... '

'Aaaah!'

'That is what I am looking for.'

'I see.'

Jason Pinner was beginning to wonder if there was to be a little excitement in his life other than facts and figures and harassing quailing miscreants sweating on the other side of his desk who had mistakenly, so they always maintained, under-estimated their income or over estimated their expenses and consequently reduced their tax liabilities. It's called evasion he would say to himself, steeling his heart against every sob story and, in the course of his long career with Her Majesty's Inland Revenue Service he believed he had heard just about every sob story going.

'You no doubt heard about the strange death of Sir Roger Pemberton.' It wasn't a question from Thornton, just a statement of fact.

'His tax affairs weren't handled by this department,' Jason said, 'But ye-es, I read all about it in the papers and, of course, saw it on the telly but at no time was the word murder expressed. I remember my lady wife over supper one evening asking me if he was one of mine, tax wise I mean, but unfortunately I had to answer in the negative. His estate must be worth a pretty penny in death duties wouldn't you say? Who is to benefit from the residue?'

'His niece and ward, Aurora Pemberton. It is she who has hired me.'

'I see. But, if I may enquire, this company you are asking about, what does it have to do with Sir Roger, alive or dead?'

'Sir Roger made some quite substantial payments to it that I feel need investigating.'

'Oh, yes?' Even if he hadn't been before, Jason was now definitely interested. 'From what point of view?'

'The reasons as to why he made those payments. Ostensibly it was for charity.'

'I see. You think maybe it was a tax dodge?'

'No. I think it has more sinister connotations than that.'

'Like what?'

'Like blackmail?'

'And what may the name of this company be?'

'Fundraisers Limited.'

There was quite a long silence as Pinner pursed his lips and thought about this.

'Hmn... A most interesting establishment that. They use a firm of accountants I am fully acquainted with and with whom I am, between you, me, and the gatepost, constantly at daggers drawn. They can turn profit into loss at the drop of a decimal point. Maybe it's their accountants you should be investigating, Mister King. You know of course, or maybe you don't, that Fundraisers Limited is a subsidiary company of Wheeler & Co, another very interesting set-up if I may say so. On the surface, I really shouldn't be telling you this, Mister King, this is strictly entree nous... '

Thornton nodded.

'It all seems to be so respectable but I have deep dark suspicions that we see only the tip of the iceberg as it were and beneath the surface all is not as it should be.'

'In what way, if I may ask?'

'In the way of dividends, Mister King, which always strike me as being inordinately high. I am forever suspicious of companies that pay shareholders dividends way above what one would expect. Perhaps you would like to see a list of shareholders. This is all strictly between us you understand, or have I already said that?'

Jason was obviously fairly nervous at this point. If any of this conversation became public knowledge it could mean the end of his employment and a consequent reduction in pension.

'You have and my lips are sealed.' For emphasis Thornton made a zip movement across his mouth.

'I just had to make that point absolutely clear. I'm glad you came to me, Mister King, because I have been wanting to nail these...'

Pinner realised where he was going and stopped to clear his throat rather loudly before lowering his voice. 'I feel sure you will respect my confiding in you when I say I have had my suspicions for some considerable time and have been doing a little ferreting out of my own but this is strictly off the record you understand.'

'Perfectly.' Thornton wished he would get on with it. He'd already given his word he would remain as silent as the grave.

Pinner sat very still for a minute obviously contemplating as to whether Thornton was as trustworthy as he maintained or whether he was still about to put his pension on the line here, and then he got up and went back to the filing cabinet for another folder, returning with it to the desk. He opened it and slipped a sheet of yellow legal pad paper across to Thornton.

'These are members of the board of Wheeler & Co. Is there anything there that helps?'

There was. One name that almost flew off the page – MIKE ALIFF!

*****

Holly was wondering what gods she may have offended, as she stood chilled to the bone, drenched, and looking, she imagined, like a bedraggled hen. She gave the flat tyre a hearty kick that did nothing to ease either the situation or her feelings, if anything it made them worse. It was at this moment when she was wondering whether she dared abandon the Jensen and hit the main road to try and hitch a lift somewhere, anywhere, when a vintage Rolls with a uniformed chauffeur at the wheel pulled into the track and came to a stop. There were a couple of seconds before a tattoo was played on the horn to which Holly lifted both arms wide as much as to say would I be standing here in the pouring bloody rain if I could be anywhere else? A few more seconds elapsed before simultaneously both the driver's door and a passenger's door opened: the chauffeur, holding a large umbrella stepped out from the front and, opening the umbrella, held it over a rather florid gentleman as he eased himself with some difficulty from the back. Both the car's doors were slammed shut and the pair advanced a couple of paces towards Holly.

'Young lady,' the florid gentleman said, 'just what do you think you're doing?'

'What do I think I'm doing?' Holly looked around as though expecting to be backed up by invisible companions before turning back to glare at the men in front of her. 'I am not singing in the rain if that's what you think. As a matter of fact...' A tickling rivulet of rain ran down her nose causing her to sneeze before she wiped it away with the back of a wet hand. 'I think I'm getting the mother and father of all colds, that's what I think. In fact I think I might

72

just stand here until I develop pneumonia. Does that answer your question?'

'No it doesn't. You do realise you are totally blocking the roadway.'

Holly looked around again, both to indicate to her invisible companions that this man had to be the biggest klutz of all time and to ascertain whether she was in truth blocking the road.

'Oh!' she exclaimed. 'Am I?' She could have been addressing a three year old. 'I didn't realise. Did you want to get by in your nice big shiny motor car?'

'There is no need for sarcasm young lady.'

Holly blew.

'You great steaming turd!' she yelled.

'I beg your…'

Holly had never been to the Royal Academy of Dramatic Art or taken voice lessons in any other esteemed institution for the training of budding thespians but her voice was stentorian when she chose to use it and right at this moment she chose to use it.

'You prick of the first water!'

'I beg your…'

'Standing there bone dry under your filthy great umbrella uttering inanities instead of coming to the rescue of a lady in distress! Arsehole! Craphound! What kind of a gentleman are you?'

'I… I… I…'

The chauffeur, who bore a distinct resemblance to the deceased film star, Cord Wainer so that Holly had already clocked him as being extremely dishy, had turned his head away in order to hide his smile. His employer was staring goggle-eyed at Holly and had now apparently been rendered speechless. The man had turned puce, so much so that the thread veins on his cheeks, previously so obvious, totally disappeared.

'I can't move my fucking car, you blithering idiot, because my fucking car has a fucking great puncture in one of the front fucking wheels! Do I make myself absolutely fucking clear or am I talking fucking Chinese here?'

Holly had once had a very brief fling with a young merchant navy steward who couldn't string two words together without that particular expletive in between, and he wasn't even upset.

'Young lady, young lady, please!' the owner of the Rolls bleated. 'There is absolutely no need for such language, no need whatsoever.'

Holly tut tutted, raised her eyebrows and turned her head away.

'There is also no point us standing here in the rain fighting like alley cats...'

'Alley cats? Who are you calling an alley cat?'

'No no, I didn't mean...' He turned towards the chauffeur. 'Albert, see what you can do to help the young lady.'

'Thank you.' Holly was suddenly all sweetness and light. 'I apologise for losing my temper.'

'Understandable, my dear, quite understandable er... under the circumstances.'

Holly's Lincoln green having been thoroughly drenched and clinging to her to now show every curve had both Albert's and the gentleman's eyes virtually popping out of their heads. She would have won a wet T-shirt contest hands down.

'Albert! What are you waiting for?' the man barked.

'Here,' Holly said, 'give me the umbrella and I'll hold it over Albert and keep the rain off him while he changes the wheel. You get back in the car where you'll remain dry.'

'Why don't we both hold the umbrella over Albert?'

'I don't think that will be necessary,' Holly objected, detecting what looked suspiciously like the sudden lecherous gleam in the man's eye and the thought of close proximity under the brolly with possibly a sneaky arm around her waist filled her with horror. 'As I am already wet and, I could add, chilled to the marrow, it might as well be me keeping the rain off our friend here. He'll get muddy knees of course but then I don't think that will worry him much. Will it worry you, Albert? I should think Albert is quite used to being on his knees, aren't you, Albert?' She favoured young Albert with one of her most ravishing smiles and Albert, trying to keep his own smile to himself, turned and walked towards the Jensen. Holly quickly followed and the man made a bolt for the warmth and comfort of the Rolls. Once safely inside he rolled down the window to say, 'My name's Maurice by the way, Maurice Chinnery.'

'How do you do?' Holly said, momentarily turning her head to look at him and then back to Albert, 'Come on. Let's get on with it, shall we?'

Albert wondered whether or not he sensed a double meaning in that remark and hoped he had. He imagined, after changing the wheel, they would definitely be seeing more of each other in every sense of the word.

'When Albert's changed your wheel,' Maurice shouted, 'you'd better drive on down to the club and we'll find some dry clothes for you. Fortunately our caretaker chappie has a wife. Not as slim and presentable as you of course' – Holly and Albert, their backs to the Rolls, both raised eyebrows - 'but dry clothes are dry clothes after all. By the way you haven't told me your name.'

'If I were you,' Holly said, 'I'd close that window. The upholstery's getting wet.'

*****

'It would seem,' Sir Peter said, his voice a dark brown full of foreboding, 'that this man King is not the nincompoop Mike here led us to believe.' He raised his hand. 'No, don't interrupt Mike, please. The fact is he has been making enquiries in a number of places that, even if they haven't paid any dividends as yet, could still lead us into a great deal of trouble, all in line for a date with a cheap and chippy chopper on a big black block.' Sir Peter was yet another elderly avid fan of Messrs Gilbert and Sullivan and, as well as being a stalwart member of his local amateur operatic and dramatic society where he had been having a clandestine affair - that everyone knew about - with the secretary, Beatrice Peabody, for a number of years. The society had just produced with great success and a small profit due to the sale of raffle tickets, *The Mikado*, fondly known in theatrical circles as *The Mickadoo*, and Sir Peter could never resist either humming a snatch or coming out with a quotation now and again. The fact that cheap and chippy choppers had been out of fashion for three hundred years or more didn't as far as Sir Peter was concerned in the least reduce the effectiveness of his quote. The only thing the board members were grateful for was he didn't try at this point in the meeting to sing even that short phrase in his slightly off-key baritone. Next year it was to be *Ruddigore*, not very often performed but one of his favourites. 'Now, Mike, you may speak. What do you say to this?'

Mike cleared his throat. 'I still maintain he's flogging a dead horse. By the way does anybody know that joke about the guy who wanted to know if he was flogging a dead...'

'Do you mind?' Sir Peter almost bellowed. He seldom raised his voice, there was seldom any need for it, but right at this minute, despite his own inconsequential quotation of a G and S number from a spoof Japanese operetta, he had no time for someone like Mike Aliff who, finding himself between a rock and a hard place, endeavoured to lighten proceedings or escape censure by telling a joke that had whiskers on it as long as Methuselah's, even if the old jokes are reputedly the best; but Mike was never one noted for his tact.

'Forgive me,' he grovelled. 'It's just that I cannot seriously believe Thornton capable of anything but making the biggest hash up of any undertaking. Why else was he made redundant from the department? Why wasn't I made redundant?' There was a heavy accent on the "I". The unspoken answer to this was of course because he, Mike Aliff, was absolutely tip-top at his job and much too important, indispensable in fact. He carried the whole safety of the realm on his shoulders. 'I wouldn't have recommended King to Miss Pemberton if I thought any different and I remain convinced I was right, am right,' he corrected himself. 'However...' and here there was a dramatic pause as Mike looked around the table, all accusing faces, stern of expression, turned in his direction... 'should it come to the point of no return as it were,' Mike also had an unfortunate turn of phrase that didn't really mean much though it might sound like it, 'I will make sure Mr King is terminated, if you understand me.'

'I must assume that has an ex in front of it,' Sir Peter said, 'and just how will you accomplish it?' he went on to ask. He had been parachuted into France during the war to work with the underground and having dispatched a number of the enemy in various ways, painful if possible, was interested in all forms of assassination. In fact, in between rehearsing Gilbert and Sullivan, his affair with Beatrice Peabody, and seeing to the smooth running of his companies, he was writing a book on his experiences, though he found the act of writing pretty hard going which was why it was taking such an interminable time. It did though give him immense satisfaction sometimes to read over an episode and relive, in all its bloodlust, the excitement of that distant moment.

*****

Holly, wrapped in a one piece brown nylon cat suit six sizes too large for her and in which she would normally not be seen dead even if it were her size, was ensconced in the quite luxurious club bar, nursing a brandy and ginger ale, her favourite drink on a cold day, and seated opposite Maurice Chinnery who was nursing a double brandy, also his favourite drink but on any kind of day and without the ginger ale. Though invited to sit cosily beside him on the banquette she had managed to keep her distance by dropping into a chair whilst he was engaged in attracting the attention of the club steward. She had a quick vision of the last time she sat in a club bar such as this and ended up in a police station being quizzed on the death of poor old Colonel Montcliff blown to pieces by hitting a booby-trapped golf ball with his driver. Holly quickly dismissed the memory and after the original "cheers – cheers!" rigmarole, decided to jump straight in with a spot of seemingly innocent questioning, but Maurice beat her to it.

'So, mystery lady,' he said, 'you still haven't told me your name.'

'Carmen.' She smiled over the rim of her glass.

'Carmen? Carmen are you beezay tonight? Haw haw haw!'

Oh, my God! Holly thought. Where on earth is this guy coming from? Am I really going to have to put up with this?

'Carmen Inez Hernandez.' The "Her" was pure Castilian coming from the soft palate, the "z's" sounded as though a viper had been let loose.

'Spanish?'

'Argentinean father, English mother.'

'Oh yes? And what does your Argentinean father do? He's into cattle I take it. Magnificent hacienda, a positive army of gauchos, enormous herds of prime steak on the hoof spreading out across the pampas? Canning factory to corn his beef?'

'My father is into any commodity that makes oodles and oodles of dough which is why for the most part, when I'm not globe-trotting that is, I can afford to live in Bermuda in luxurious style.' Holly had

77

vacationed in Bermuda more than once so any questions there could be answered fairly convincingly she thought, and she had taken the trouble to do a spot of homework as well.

'Really? Yes, I should have known by the car you drive.'

'Oh, don't be taken in by that. That's borrowed.'

'I'm impressed!' And he really was. 'Friends don't usually lend that sort of vehicle to friends unless they really are very good friends.' The innuendo was made too painfully obvious. 'I mean, there is absolutely no way I would dream of lending the Rolls, my baby, even to my nearest and dearest. Hernandez... Hernandez... Yes, I seem to know the name.'

'It's quite a common one really, like Jones, or Smith, or Brown. Can I get you another drink? I don't have any cash on me... '

'Like the queen.'

'What?'

'I am led to believe the queen never carries any money.'

'No reason why she should really. I would think for the prestige of her patronage everybody would be falling over themselves to give her whatever she was after. I should think Eva Peron was exactly the same. Unfortunately we seem to be entering an age when every Tom, Dick, or Harriet seems to want something for nothing, or is that the way it's always been and it's now just that bit more obvious? But as I was saying, I don't have any cash but would they take a platinum card at your bar? I have a selection.'

Maurice ran his tongue over his upper lip. 'Oh, no! Please! Only too happy to do the honours.' As good as his word he raised a hand and indicated to the barman their need for two more brandies.

'So, Carmen, where are you staying whilst in our great metropolis?'

Holly was prepared for this one as well and had made prior arrangements with yet another friend who owned and ran a boutique hotel that, should anyone make enquiries about a Carmen Inez Hernandez, yes indeed she was staying at that particular hotel.

'The Hotel Diana, Bayswater. Very small, very chic.'

'Don't know it. Very expensive no doubt.'

'Very private. You get what you pay for.' Holly looked around her as the barman approached their table with the fresh drinks.

'Well,' she said, 'this is very nice. What exactly is this club?'

The drinks were placed on the table.'

'On my tab,' Maurice said as the man, without a word but with an appreciative glance in Holly's direction, retreated. 'This bar is called The Robin Hood,' Maurice said, 'and the members of the club are known as The Bowmen Of Essex. On the door to the men's toilets and changing rooms there is a ceramic plaque showing Robin himself aiming his arrow skywards, and on the door of the ladies' there is Maid Marion holding the accepted female symbol in both hands: you know, the circle with the little cross at the bottom. Does that tell you what you want to know?'

'Couldn't be more plain. An archery club, how fascinating. I've always thought I'd like to take up archery.'

'Really?'

'Do you think it was fate, or coincidence, that led me here? And did you know in fifteen forty five a man by the name of Roger Ascham wrote a treatise on archery entitled "Toxophiles?"'

'No, I didn't know that. I'm afraid I'm not much of a literary chap myself. Not a Shakespeare wallah at all if you know what I mean.'

'I know what you mean. A real action man, hey?' A proper rugger bugger.' Had she been within range she might have been tempted to give him four knuckles on his upper arm but contented herself by executing a small punching motion with her fist for emphasis.

'Well I wouldn't put it like that exactly.'

'Toxophiles... I suppose a rough translation would be "love of the bow."'

'Really? What a clever little minx you are.'

Holly's nerve ends went into overdrive. Did she sense a dangerous snide quality to his voice, a hint of suspicion as to her true reason for being there, or was the man merely being his normal stupid, male chauvinist self? Whatever, she inwardly squirmed, screamed, and wondered for a moment whether a karate chop across the Adam's apple might not put paid to his ever uttering such inanities again. Fortunately she was a girl with a great deal of self-control and all she appeared to do was smile as she pushed away the glass in front of her.

'On second thoughts I don't think I'd better have that,' she said. 'Have to drive back to town you know.'

'Oh, you won't be going anywhere for ages yet,' Maurice said and again Holly found herself tensing just a fraction.

'Will I not?'

'Well, first of all your clothes are still drying…'

'In front of an Aga that should take no time at all. Nice kitchen you have. I take it all the exercise of pulling strings, makes for quite an appetite. Do you pull strings, Maurice?'

'Maurice was beginning to seriously wonder if this little kitten was being coquettish and what his chances were.

'And secondly, Albert is busy valeting your car… your friend's car rather. You wouldn't want to return it in a state, now would you?'

'That's very kind of you.'

'Not at all. Anything to help a lady in distress.' He would have liked to have patted her hand but realised it was out of reach and, if she weren't in fact giving him the come-on, he would look a bit foolish groping for it, especially if she hurriedly removed it, which he fully expected she would do. Instead he said, while Holly was picturing Albert valeting the Jensen, 'So, Miss Hernandez, what brings you to this neck of the woods anyway?'

There it was, the true reason for her being there and this was one Holly, who usually thought of everything, hadn't prepared for. She had to mentally double-declutch before roaring away at speed. 'Saffron Walden!' she squeaked.

'Saffron Walden?'

'Yes, I was on my way there when I had the flat.'

'Looking at the way your car was facing you were going in the wrong direction.'

'I have to admit I was a wee bit off course.' She was doing the aren't I a silly little girl bit and waited for him to say something derogatory about women drivers but he merely sat there regarding her with those pink rimmed eyes. 'There's this delightful little antique shop there. I visited it once before and I wanted to see it again.'

'Why?

'Why?'

'Yes, why? Chelsea, South Kensington, the Fulham Road, The Angel, Islington, choc-a-block with antique shops. More upmarket ones in the West End, or there's the street markets, Portobello Road for example. London is bursting at the seams with bloody antique rip-off merchants. They go traipsing all over the countryside ripping off little old grannies who are unknowingly sitting on an heirloom or two worth a small fortune and then return to London to flog off at exorbitant prices what they have acquired. What's so special about Saffron Walden? And, apart from ringing at auction sales and cannibalising bits and pieces, they sell to each other, raising the price each time depending upon their geographical location.' Maurice was obviously not too fond of antique dealers. Perhaps he had been ripped off once too often.

'Visiting antique shops in Chelsea or the West End you don't get to enjoy a lovely drive into the countryside.'

'A lovely drive, hey? In winter? When it's more'n likely to piss down, if you'll pardon the expression, at any moment, as has been proved by today's downpour.' He waved towards a window through which it could be seen to be still pissing down.

There really was no answer to this so Holly merely shrugged and pouted.

'And the last time you were in this delightful little antique shop in Saffron Walden,' he continued, 'what exactly did you purchase that made the event so memorable?'

All this questioning was getting a bit hairy and Holly was wondering how long it would be before she could take the initiative.

'A pair of lovely ginger Staffordshire cats,' she said. 'Huge ones with curly fur, smiley mouths and emerald green glass eyes. Most unusual.'

'Really? You don't strike me as the kind of girl who would go in for Staffordshire cats, usual or unusual.'

'I'm not. They were a present for my mother. She's crazy for Staffordshire. She's got oodles and oodles of Poodles and Pugs so I thought cats would be something different for her. I'm into Limoges myself, Limoges and Dresden, particularly shepherds and shepherdesses, very romantic.'

Maurice slowly nodded and never took his eyes off her as he lifted up his brandy. Holly smiled as if butter wouldn't melt in her mouth.

Thornton was seated on a banquette in The Wig And Gown.

Instead of carefully nursing a half pint and making it go an awful long way, his usual public house modus operandi, he was enjoying a scotch on the rocks. He really could get used to this living on expenses caper. He was hoping Mike Aliff would soon put in an appearance. Although he might be tempted to enjoy a second, more than one scotch would not be conducive to intelligent and subtle questioning, especially with a smarmy operative like Mike. Even though he didn't hold too high an opinion of his one-time colleague, the man did after all have some experience in espionage and in the words of Mister George Bernard Shaw, "you never can tell" or in those of that old comedian Rob Wilton, "You can't always sometimes tell what's least expected most."

Thornton had already ascertained from the barman that Mike had of late considered The Wig And Gown his local and turned up round about this time most evenings. Why he should do so as it was patronised almost exclusively by legal eagles, most of them as dry as dust from too much court work and poking their noses into ancient statutes and precedents, was a mystery to Thornton until the swing doors opened and Mike appeared accompanied by an extremely attractive woman whose appearance almost caused Thornton to whistle his appreciation. Of course, not all legal eagles were male, over the hill and dry as dust with port decanter noses from too many Corporation and Guild dinners. There were some young lions, gowns flapping like black wings, roaring in and around the Inns of Court, their eyes fixed firmly on silk and the inflated fees they would one day earn once they became barristers; Queen's Councils. And, of course, there were also some extremely talented female legal eagles. Maybe they should be called eaglettes but no, this was after all the age of female emancipation and equality, and to harp in any way on their femininity, no matter how attractive, was likely to get one into a great deal of hot water. If this was one of those female barristers and, looking at the briefcase she carried, Thornton felt sure she was, he wondered how an obviously extremely intelligent and beautiful woman could put up with Mike Aliff for more than a few minutes but then remembered the wise words of Rob Wilton.

Mike, wondering who might be in the bar to take envious note of his prize, took a quick shufty around the already quite crowded room and scowled noticeably when he saw Thornton, the last person he expected to be there, who gave him the friendliest smile back, a waggle of fingers, and indicated the empty spaces on his banquette. In response Mike, with a querying look, raised a hand and twisted it vertically a couple of time in front of his mouth to indicate a glass, meaning did Thornton want a refill. This was more than likely merely a gesture in every sense, showing off in front of his companion; what a devil may care, easy-going, live for today for tomorrow we die, generous sort of chappie he was. Having already stood Thornton one drink in a lifetime, he hoped the response would be negative which, to his relief, it was, so he turned to the waiting barman to order for himself and his lady friend who, with just the hint of a smile, had been watching this little pantomime with some interest. Now she leaned towards him to whisper something. He turned his head to glance briefly in Thornton's direction, then looked back and nodded. Their drinks having arrived he brought both glasses and the lady to Thornton's table. Thornton, being the gentleman he was, immediately rose to his feet to be introduced.

'Thornton, old man,' was Mike's breezy greeting, 'you here again? To what does this prestigious establishment owe the pleasure of your company this time? It isn't your usual watering hole. Allow me to introduce Miss Annette Friedman Q.C.' He never mentioned Thornton's surname having obviously filled in Annette with the necessary information at the bar.

Thornton extended his hand, which she took and held, he believed, just a fraction longer than was necessary before, smoothing her skirt beneath her and placing her briefcase on the banquette beside her, she sat down. The men followed suit without the necessity of smoothing or rearranging anything.

'Well, Thornton?'

'Well what, Mike?'

'Why are you imbibing in The Wig And Gown, old man?'

'I've been doing some research, going over old newspapers which can be quite a draining occupation, so I thought I'd pop in for a quickie before making my way home. My bus happens to pass this way.'

'You should take a cab,' she said, 'I always do. London cabs are the best thing since sliced bread.'

'Unfortunately, Miss Friedman...'

'Annette.'

'Annette. My bread doesn't always rise to the occasion.' That was a rather stupid way of putting it, he thought, pun or no pun but she smiled showing absolutely perfect teeth behind those rather sensuous lips.

'You have a nice way of putting things,' she said.

Thornton was tempted to inform her he had an even nicer way of putting things but realised this would more than likely queer his pitch with Mike, if not her on first acquaintance, so let the moment pass. The look on his face though told her everything.

Mike was getting a bit edgy over what seemed like a mite too much chumminess developing far too quickly here.

'Thornton,' he said to her, 'used, until fairly recently, to be with the department and is now establishing himself as a private eye.' Did Thornton catch the hint of a snigger on private eye? 'At the moment he's snooping...'

'Snooping!'

'... into the death of Sir Roger Pemberton.'

'Oh, yes,' she answered, 'I was quite fascinated with the case as it so happens. So, tell me, Mr King...'

'Thornton.'

'Thornton. How are your enquiries going? Are you close to reaching any conclusion?'

'Well, yes...' He took a sip of his drink in order to artificially engineer a dramatic pause. '... as a matter of fact I am.' He was watching Mike as he said it and noticed the change of direction of Mike's glance from Annette to somewhere in the far corner of the room. Otherwise there was no reaction.

'Tell me,' she said, her voice growing husky.

Mike turned his look from across a crowded room back to her and lifted his glass. 'Cheers!' he said as though this would change the direction in which the conversation was going. She ignored him, which he was definitely not pleased about.

'Sir Roger was murdered.'

Mike choked on his drink.

CHAPTER FIVE

Harold Norris, starting with Dinky Toys, had been fanatical about cars from an early age. A skinny nondescript kid who found it difficult to make friends he was, like so many small boys, almost besotted with them and, like so many small boys, just couldn't wait to get behind a steering wheel. So it was natural that as a grown man cars would be his business. He never had the capital to go in for it in a big swanky way. No Berkeley Square dealings for him, but in his own small way his needs were few and he was happy with his lot. Well, for the most part he was happy with his lot. He would have liked to have had children, but either his long-suffering stay at home wife, Clarice – named after the famous art nouveaux designer of chinaware – was barren, or his sperm count wasn't up to scratch and neither of them had ever had the courage to see a doctor and sort it out. It would have been too embarrassing and was a subject they never discussed. Anyway, all things considered, it was a matter for regret but too late to think of it being any different.

It was true not all his dealings in the second-hand car trade carried the seal of legitimacy and it was true he had a cash box under the floorboards nobody was supposed to know about, least of all the department of internal revenue, and it was true he had a few dodgy acquaintances and it was true his cars sometimes would not be approved by an inspector from the Automobile Association or the Royal Automobile Club, not without a great deal of expensive work needing to be done first, and it was true the boys in blue paid him an occasional visit but he always greeted them with the greatest respect and they had never been able to pin the slightest misdemeanour on him. Apart from all that and an expression like a ferret caught eating eggs, Harold Norris wasn't a bad guy to know.

He was not one to fret unduly about the fate of most of his cars.

They were, after all, well insured, but a Jensen was something else. It was most certainly not your everyday jalopy by a long stretch but he was wondering just what Thornton might be up to. The man had come into the office and requested the hire of a second car, this time a Ford station wagon with mock wooden panels. Two cars before even a week was out? Who would be driving this one? Thornton would to begin with, he said, just for a day to visit his folks in the country, and then Holly when she returned the Jensen.

Harold trusted Holly implicitly. He knew she had taken her advanced driving test and, if anyone was one hundred percent safe behind the wheel, it was she, but the roads were full of idiots, some of whom imagined the streets of London were the same as the circuit at Monte Carlo, Le Mans, or Silverstone. He had been one of those himself in earlier years before he learned his lesson the hard way as an almost imperceptible limp could testify. Fortunately no other person was involved so he never had that on his conscience. There are others who, with no thought of the consequences, no will power and despite all warnings, think nothing of tanking up on ten pints of lager and imagining they are still fit to drive. When the Jensen came back he was going to sell it. This was one he did fret about and he couldn't stand the strain. To ease the immediate tension and with nothing better to do he set about simonising the bodywork nearest to hand; it was good exercise and excellent therapy and for a contented while he no longer had that furtive ferrety look.

Thornton finished his careful survey of the couch on which not a mark could be seen. He had walked around it three or four times and examined it from afar and in big close-up from all angles and, well satisfied, now sat himself down. It had cost a pretty penny of Rory's money for the specialists to get rid of the sweet and sour stain as, naturally, they had to clean the whole couch to keep the colour all of a kind; otherwise there would have been two shades of ecru, a dark and a light, but the money he reckoned had been well spent.

'How did you manage to get it done so quickly?' he asked. 'Normally it takes weeks for these people to even come around to take a look and give a quote, let alone actually getting the job done.'

'Speedyclean by name, Speedy clean by nature. They claim to be the fastest in the business, besides which the boss owed me a favour.'

'I bet he didn't knock anything off the price though.'

She handed him the bill.

'So,' Thornton said, giving the back of the couch a final flick with the back of his hand and putting the account in his pocket without so much as a glance. Amazing how blasé you can get when someone else is footing the bill. 'How did it go with the Bowmen of Essex? Where you a big hit? Quite unnecessary question.'

'I was entertained, if that is the correct word to use, by one over-inflated in every sense of the word ponce... '

'Ponce?'

'By the name of Maurice Chinnery.'

'Ah yes, a member of the board of Wheeler & Co. A very wealthy man in his own right I believe but always out for more no doubt. Some people just can't get enough, money I mean, and their greed becomes obscene. It's all very well accumulating the stuff but, if it gets to the point when money is making more money faster than you can unload it, what is the point? Have we had this conversation before, Holly?'

'More than likely, Thornton, more than likely. You're not just a wee bit jealous by any chance?'

He thought about this for a moment. 'I don't think so,' he said. 'Of course I hope the time will come, preferably not too far distant, when I don't have to penny-pinch or worry about where the next meal is coming from or be invited in for a friendly chat with my bank manager because I simply don't have the means of reducing my overdraft. I have dreams about that you know, nightmares I mean. Actor friends tell me there is such a thing as actor's nightmare where they are on stage or the curtain's about to go up and they don't know their lines or sometimes even what play they're in. I dream I am in hock way over my head in at least three different banks and, in reality I don't have an account in three different banks, I mean I should be so lucky, and I am called in to discuss the matter because the overdraft's getting bigger and bigger and I am now paying interest on the interest. My bank manager, my constant nightmare. But if I were stinking rich? No... I have no desire to own a Rolls Royce or any other fancy car for that matter, or a yacht, or a private jet. I don't want homes in half a dozen places. I'm not mad about champagne and I can't stand oysters, which not so very long ago were the poor man's meat, did you know that? "It's a werry remarkable circumstance, sir, that poverty and oysters always seem to go together" thus spoke Sam Weller. Folk in my part of the world dig over their gardens and unearth what were once cesspits and these cesspits contain layers and layers of oyster shells. I admit I do like caviar and I'm particularly partial to lobster which carries a bit of a price tag but even then you can have too much. I remember when I was in Liberia...' He would have been off on one of his stories had Holly not butted in.

'Never mind the money angle, Thornton, unless his money, as with Sir Roger evidently, is going to prove to be his undoing, Mister Maurice Chinnery gives the impression of being as randy as a tomcat but is more than likely impotent due to age, obesity, and too much alcohol. A philanderer nevertheless even if he does have difficulty in consummation. Quite revolting really. Employs a very dishy chauffeur though by the name of Albert, almost a spitting image of Cord Wainer.'

'That's all very well, Holly dear, but what exactly did this entertainment consist of? Details, girl, details. Did you learn anything?'

'Oh, I learnt a lot, all of it absolutely useless.'

'Really.'

'It would seem the members are all toxophilitic... '

'All?' Thornton laughed. 'Shouldn't they see a doctor? Maybe the place should be quarantined. '

'Of course, all. I'm not too sure about Maurice. Probably never held a bow in his life. He's there simply for the club atmosphere I think but, him aside, why else would they belong to an archery club? Quite fanatical some of them. Targets are set up in the grounds, but English weather being what it is, especially this time of year; there is also an indoor range set in a partly converted barn. The club was once part of a farm and is obviously rich though some of the members evidently aren't; middle class rather. It wasn't all Rolls, Bentleys, Jags and three litre Rovers in the car park but a couple of Fords, Vauxhalls, one or two real old bangers, so the membership is pretty mixed. And it isn't just the longbow they practice but the crossbow as well.'

'Ah, good, that's good.'

Holly shrugged. 'Well, which one do you want me to take up?'

'What?'

'I am, that is, Carmen Inez Hernandez rather, has been made an honorary member of the club while she is in London and any other time in the future she happens to visit.'

'An honorary member? Why an honorary member?'

'Because I do believe they will, sooner or later, try to get more out of me, out of Carmen that is, than just membership fees, which, true, are not exactly paltry, but on the other hand I don't believe they're sufficient to keep that place running. I visited Maid Marian.'

'Maid Marian?'

'The name given to the ladies. Pathetic isn't it? The men's changing rooms are...'

'Don't tell me don't tell me!... Triar Fuck... I mean Friar Tuck.' Thornton laughed uproariously at his joke. Holly sat stony-faced.

'Not quite as imaginative as that, Thornton. Robin Hood. Pretty obvious, huh? As I was saying, I excused myself to visit the maid of Sherwood Forest and deliberately left my handbag in the bar where the ponce could rummage through it to his heart's content, thus confirming my identity and the fact that I am mega mega rich beyond words. So, tell me, which do I go for, crossbow or longbow? I've already had sort of a go with the longbow and I was pretty dreadful I can tell you, but that was probably because old blubberguts was mauling me at the time under the pretext he was showing me how to go about it, how to shoot with a bow and arrow that is. Now if it had been Albert...'

'Yes, yes, the dishy chauffeur who reminds you of your one time fantasy playmate who, thankfully, will never darken our screens again. You would have been even worse. Trembling knees do not a good archer make. Well what if it had been Albert? Do you think he could be of use to us?'

'To me, definitely.'

'Holly! For information, a spy in the camp as it were.'

Holly shrugged. 'Maybe.'

'And I think I may have garnered a spy as well. Mike Aliff has a new friend, by name Annette Friedman Q.C. and...'

'Annette Friedman! How on earth did Mike Aliff cotton on to her? She is but definitely out of that skunk's league. Out of yours too I hasten to add so don't go getting any fancy ideas, you will only get hurt.'

'When are you going back?' Thornton sniffed, ego somewhat dented.

'As Carmen? Or as little old me?'

'Whichever.'

'Soon. I'm intrigued. Would you care for a drink?'

'I thought you would never ask.'

'Well just move away from the couch will you? In case you spill it.'

Holly's "soon" was, in fact, the very next day. She had hoped the Chinnery beast wouldn't be there so she could make acquaintances elsewhere or do some nosing about on her own but he, obviously from the smile that creased his ruddy cheeks as soon as he clocked her arrival, had been waiting on tenterhooks as the saying has it. He was obviously well and truly smitten almost to the point of openly panting with his tongue almost hanging out. Was it Holly's original fiery outburst or the gentle maidenly apology that followed it? Whichever, Cupid's arrow had gone well and truly home and what better location for it to do so than an archery club?

Holly parked the Jensen and sauntered across towards the clubhouse where he stood waiting with an itching groin by the main entrance. It's really sad, she thought, that he is going to be in for such a big disappointment. There was no sign of the Rolls and she wondered where Albert could be. Maybe Maurice was keeping him out of the way. He was, after all, thirty years or more younger than his employer: tall, slender of hip, fair of face and right up Holly's street. She couldn't help wondering if she too was in for a big disappointment. Why was love, well sexual attraction at first sight anyway, so often so contrary? Whoever loves who loves not at first sight and there were always itches destined never to be scratched. Romeo pined for Rosalind. The disdainful Rosalind couldn't give a fig for the rosy lad.

'Hello, there!' Maurice called out cheerfully, waving a podgy hand as she advanced on him. 'Hoped you'd be able to make it today. I've arranged a special session for you with our top coach, Steve Timpson, nice chap, you'll like him.' Why do people not only assume this but insist on saying it when more than likely the two meeting for the first time will loathe each other on sight?

'Ex-Olympic wallah don'tcha know? I left you a message at your hotel. Did you not get it? You're looking particularly charming, attractive today, if I may say so.' A nice compliment even if a little gauche and was the man at his age actually blushing?

It was rather an awkward moment. Holly wondered whether she should offer Maurice her hand or, worse, her cheek. Maybe a kiss on the cheek would negate the necessity of a reply about the message. Maurice on the other hand would have given a lot for more than a peck on the cheek so they stood there undecided until he turned away to open the door and usher her into the clubhouse, chortling, 'Come along then, old girl, let's get down to it as they say, haw haw haw!'

'I don't see your car,' Holly said brightly. It was a mistake. Why should she even notice the car wasn't there? Maurice was possibly in some matters, like human relationships for example, a bit on the dim side but in this instance, he wasn't slow in picking up her true meaning, "I don't see Albert." He felt a twinge of jealousy as he replied: 'Car's being serviced!' It was almost snapped out and there was acid in his voice. She wasn't slow to pick up on that one either. She excused herself by saying she needed to visit Maid Marion in order to change, she tapped her shoulder bag for emphasis, into more suitable clothes for target practice, and left him sulking in the bar.

*****

'Miss Friedman, there's a call for you from a Mister Thornton King, are you available?'

Annette as a rule never took personal calls in chambers but rules, as every lawyer knows, are made to be occasionally broken, which is why they are lawyers. There is an old saying, have lawyers for friends but never go to law, and never was a truer word spoken, but if that rule weren't consistently broken, lawyers would all be in Carey Street.

Neither could she get it into her secretary's head that usually she disliked the use of the word available; it had connotations. Though, in the case of Mr King she felt it was most apt and said yes, she was definitely available.

*****

Steve Timpson was on the short side, of stocky build with heavy jowls, strong hairy hands, somewhere in his late forties and tending to put on more than a little weight around the middle due to his penchant for black and tans, but he could still put an arrow exactly where it was meant to go and after a couple of demonstrations Holly was duly impressed. What is more, as Chinnery had prophesied, she did like him. He seemed a no-nonsense down to earth kind of fellow.

'There you go, gal! That's the way to do it, as Mister Punch would say. What do you reckon? Easy peasy, yes? Right, take the bow...'

Holly did as requested and stood looking at the weapon as though completely at a loss as to what to do next.

'Sideways on to the target then,' Steve instructed, placing an open hand on each hip to manoeuvre her into position, 'legs apart, comfortable like, that's it. No strain, no pain, to misquote.'

'Have you read *Zen And The Art Of Archery?*' Holly asked.

'What's that when it's at home then?'

'It's a book about archery, Buddhist. Japanese.'

'Can't say I know it. Funny people, those Japs. 'Ere, cop a hold of this.' He was holding out an arrow for her to take. She took it.

'You slot it in there as the actress said to the bishop.'

'Have you seen how the Japanese archers on horseback in Kurasawa's films hold their bows?'

'What?'

'Akira Kurasawa. Brilliant Japanese director. Rashomon? Seven Samurai?'

'Can't say as I have. Go for Westerns myself.'

'Well then, you must have seen The Magnificent Seven! Yul Brunner? And that rather dishy German boy, what was his name, Horst? Horst? Horst something I think. That was a Western based on the Seven Samurai.'

'Can't say as to how I recall it at all. Did I ever see that one? No, I don't think I did.'

'They hold the bow over their heads, like this.' She tried to demonstrate but an English longbow is not the same as a Japanese bow and she couldn't quite manage it.

'The theory is that at a certain point, a certain moment; you, the bow, the arrow and the target are all one and the same, like joined by an invisible thread or umbilical cord and so, when you let fly, the arrow simply has to hit the target. It can't do anything else. You can release it with your eyes shut and it will still be spot on.'

'Sounds bloody daft to me, if you don't mind me saying so. And we certainly won't be having any eyes-shut target practice here I can tell you that for starters. Accidents too easily happen. What? Now, come on, Miss Hernandez...'

'Carmen.'

'Miss Carmen. Let's be having you. Standing here shooting the breeze ain't shooting arrers, is it?'

'No, it ain't.' With no more ado, or further instruction from Steve, Holly raised the bow and seemingly in the most casual fashion drew her bowstring and let loose her arrow to hit the bulls-eye dead centre.

Slightly open-mouthed, Steve stared at it for a long while and then turned to look at her.

'Beginner's luck,' Holly said with a smile, and meant it. 'Now show me how to do it properly.'

*****

Thornton suggested they lunch at Simpson's or L'eminence Grise or even The Ivy but Annette said no, she could never make love on a full stomach, it gave her heartburn, so why didn't they eat Chinese? Half an hour after a meal you're hungry again. In Soho there are any number of excellent Chinese restaurants to choose from and afterwards, by the time the taxi had conveyed them to the Barbican and her apartment, that hunger would definitely be making itself felt. Fortunately she was not wanted in court and she had informed the office she was incommunicado for the rest of the day.

*****

'My spies tell me you were a regular hotshot yesterday.'

'Good coach,' Holly said.

'Told you you'd like him.'

'So you told me.'

'Hmn... I have a sneaky feeling you're not what you say you are, Miss Carmen Inez Hernandez. I think you're hiding something from me.'

'You're teasing.' Holly said, certainly hoping he was.

'No, I'm not. You're a real lady of mystery. Isn't there a song called Mysterious Lady?' He said it in what he fondly imagined to be a husky sexy voice but which sounded as though he really needed to see a throat specialist. 'I left more messages for you at your hotel and you never replied to one. I even thought of going around in person to find out why.'

'Wouldn't have done you much good. Haven't been there. Staying with friends over-night, in Kingston.'

'Oh, I see.'

Holly smiled. There was that jealousy again. 'I did say friends – plural. Time to go change if I'm to get in any practice before lunch. I'm so late today.'

'What's happened to the Jensen?'

'Gone back to its original owner. I think he needed it to go to the races.' She wondered what Maurice would have thought if he knew Rory had baulked a little over the rising cost of hire. Expenses didn't mean a bottomless pit hence Thornton's replacement. 'The car you see there...' She pointed to the Ford shooting brake, one of Harold Norris's less spectacular models that spent most of its time in his yard but which Thornton had hired, firstly for his own use as he said to visit his aged parents in darkest Shropshire and then for her to take over.... 'belongs to another friend.'

The car's number plates, both of which had been carefully obscured as much as possible with mud, most of it Shropshire mud, was a depressing sight.

'Who you stayed with last night.'

'What? Oh, yes. So I could pick up the car. She uses it to take her kids to school, which is why it looks a bit weary and worn. Kids and animals are rough on cars.'

This seemed to satisfy him. 'It's quite a come down from the Jensen isn't it?'

'More than you would suppose. It smells of junior peepee, orange peel, and wet Airedales. Do you have any children, Maurice?' This was the first time she had made mention of the fact that he might have a wife and family hidden away. He shook his head. 'Animals?' He shook his head again.

She was tempted to ask where the Rolls and Albert were but decided against it so turned to enter the clubhouse just as a prematurely old middle aged man and a young girl looking as though she was hardly into her teens came giggling out. This place was full of middle-aged men hankering after their lost youth. For a while she watched them as they headed laughing and joking for the woods that surrounded the club, she as sprightly as the nymphet she was, he almost tottering.

'Sir Hugo Ingle,' Maurice said, noticing Holly's interest. 'That's his transport over there.' He pointed to a sporty red Alfa Romeo with plates that read HUG 1. Holly shook her head in disbelief, vanity, vanity, all is vanity, as she disappeared in the direction of Maid Marion.

*****

The afternoon was developing in such a way it was everything Thornton could have wished for. He only hoped that she wasn't going to end it by suddenly pulling a gun on him as had happened on two previous occasions, once before actually getting down to the nitty-gritty, once after. He had managed to get out with a whole skin on both those occasions; he didn't know if it would be third time unlucky.

*****

'How long will you be staying in London?' He took another shlurp of his soup that made Holly's toes curl as she delicately sipped her own.

'A few more days.' She kept it deliberately vague. 'And then it's on to Monte.'

'Is it... ? Would it be... at all possible... I mean, could we meet somewhere other than here before you go?'

Hearts and flowers, Holly thought, hearts and flowers. This is

95

really painful. Out loud she said, 'I am sure that would be very nice, Maurice, but absolutely impossible.' She sipped the last of her soup and gently laid down the spoon. 'Hmn! That was so good,' she purred, 'delicious,' and it was the turn of his crabby toes to curl. 'You must have realised by now that, although I have trusted you with my true identity, I should be, in fact I am actually travelling incognito. It wouldn't do for me to be seen round and about, carousing in night clubs, dining at chic restaurants, that sort of thing, because I am sure that's what you must have in mind.' She laid her hand on his for a moment and withdrew it before he had time to realise and react. 'Having my picture taken and splashed all over the papers is a definite no-no. There are some very very nasty people out there in the big wide world of whom I am sure you are fully aware and for whom I would be a big cash prize, and I wanted this nostalgic trip to England to be as low key as possible without the constant necessity of having bodyguards around, if you get my meaning.'

He nodded disconsolately. 'We could make it a very low-key evening,' he said, more in hope than expectation. He glanced around to make sure there were no flapping ears and lowered his voice. 'We could make it a recherché dinner in my Chelsea flat and nobody need know you were there.' He knew this suggestion didn't stand a cat's chance in hell but he saw a candlelit table for two and made the pitch anyway.

'Let me think about it,' she said which almost lifted him off his chair. It hadn't been the definite "No way. José!" he was expecting and, looking at the ring on the fourth finger of his left hand, she hadn't as yet asked him outright that all-embracing question, "Where is your wife?"

They left the clubhouse side by side, he gently holding her elbow, which she felt she ought to allow, and started towards her car when Sir Hugo Ingle, without his Lolita, appeared and made for the Alfa Romeo on what appeared to be even more unsteady legs.

Maurice let go Holly's elbow and advanced on the obviously unwell gentleman. 'Hugo, old chap! What on earth's the matter? Here, let me help you.' He extended his hand to steady Sir Hugo but was shrugged off.

'I'm all right... I'm all right, damn it! It's nothing. Must get home. Have to get home.' He sagged against the car before wrenching open the door and flopping into the driving seat. 'Keys... Keys... Damn it, where are my keys?'

'The key is already in the ignition, Hugo, where you left it, and by the looks of you you really oughtn't to be driving. Let me get someone else to take you home.' Maurice sounded genuinely concerned. He turned to Holly. 'Talk to him, Carmen, He might listen to you.' But, before Holly could add her pleas to those of Maurice, the club steward, usually at this time a little the worse for wear, having been knocking back, as was his wont, any wine diners might have left on their tables after lunch, appeared at their side.

'Problem?'

'Oh, hello, Martin. It's Sir Hugo. He insists on dri... ' that was as far as he got as the reversing Alfa, scattering gravel, had them leaping backwards before it turned on squealing tyres and sped off up the track. They watched its not very reassuring progress.

'Oh, don't worry,' Martin said with a burp. 'He gets these turns I believe. He'll be all right as long as the cops don't stop him. Good chap, Sir Hugo.' With which he turned on his heels and made his own unsteady way back to the clubhouse.

Be all right? Holly thought. He looked more like being at death's door. And where might his little bit of fluff have got to she wondered? Holly looked around but there was no sign of anyone else.

'Right then,' she turned back to Maurice. 'I'll be on my way. Thank you so much for the delicious lunch.'

He opened the car door for her. 'Will I see you tomorrow?'

She smiled up at him. 'Of course. Must get in as much practice with the bow as I can before I move on don't you think?'

What was really going through his mind had nothing to do with bows and arrows as he slammed the car door and stepped back.

*****

She hadn't pulled a gun on him. She had pulled every other trick in the book but definitely no gun was involved. Thornton was exhausted. 'By goom, lass,' he said, for some reason adopting a Yorkshire accent though, apart from a brief excursion to the home of the Brontes, a pilgrimage seemingly in the coming years to be taken by all those Japanese, he had never been to Yorkshire, 'thou weren't

half eager.' Maybe there was no more succinct way of expressing it.
'What shall we do this evening?' she replied.
There was only one answer to that.

★★★★★

Holly hit the main road and drove a short distance down it, no way at all, in fact, until she saw another turning, a winding country lane, this time to her right. She motored slowly until, not too far along, she found a space to pull in almost wide enough to be called a lay-by, used evidently for local fly tipping but where she wouldn't be causing an obstruction and stopped the car.

It was beginning to grow dark. She opened the glove compartment and rummaged through Thornton's rubbish, it was amazing what he could accumulate in one day's driving, until she found the small torch he had informed her she would find there. She switched it on and off a couple of times to make sure it was working, it would be just like him to let the batteries run down or the bulb to have reached the end of its life, and got out of the car, opened the back door and reached in across the seat to where she had previously noticed Thornton, from that singular visit to the country, had left a greatcoat and his fisherman's hat. His fisherman's hat had been used once on a fishing expedition during which he had caught nothing but a chill, and any number of times when fishing was not involved as he had decided from that one and only fruitless occasion that fishing was for him a thoroughly boring occupation. Why he hadn't removed it from the car was anyone's guess but that was Thornton and she was glad of it.

Engulfed in the greatcoat, the collar turned up, and with the hat pulled well down, Holly made her way back to the main road, waited for one car to go by and then, making sure there was no more approaching traffic, swiftly crossed it and, a short distance back from the road, discovered the badly maintained barbed wire fence that bordered the club grounds. It was too easy she thought to find a place where she could slip through and enter the wood.

Unfortunately barbed wire though, no matter how badly maintained, always seems to have a secret life of its own and the occasional surprise in store as many a trespasser has discovered, and

98

the greatcoat was momentarily snagged in such a way that she had to squirm out of it in order to find the offending barb, release the coat, and make her escape. That had better not happen to hold her up if she were discovered on the way out. Carefully she released the coat and slipped it back on. There seemed to be no damage done, or not much anyway, and it was a pretty old garment, one of Thornton's favourites he didn't have the heart to throw away. Why do men do this, Holly wondered, keep garments until they're literally falling off their backs? Even women with little sense of style knew when something had outlived its usefulness and needed to be discarded, and that included men.

She advanced slowly into the wood and gathering darkness and she couldn't help but question what the hell she was doing there in the first place. So a man, Sir Hugo Ingle no less, multi-multi-millionaire but otherwise she felt sure of no particular interest, and his itty-bitty bint disappear into the woods. Later the man comes out alone, staggers to his car looking like death warmed up and drives off in a great state. So? It wouldn't be the first time, or the last; a little bit of hanky-panky back-fired or did for the old ticker. Why should it be in the least suspicious? Holly turned to look back towards the road. She wanted to make sure she knew in which direction she was heading. No light came from anywhere and, as long as she had some vision, she was reluctant to switch on the torch in case it attracted unwanted attention.

There was the smell of wet and decaying foliage in the air, which had turned decidedly chilly. Holly shivered, not just from the cold but because forests, particularly at night, are to the imaginative almost black magical places: a land of witches and hobgoblins where the trees; beautiful silver birch by day, majestic oaks, glorious chestnuts, beech, and larch become schizoid and take on horribly distorted grotesque shapes, and myth, legend, and superstition abound to put the wind up any normal red-blooded girl wandering about there on her own, even one as strong willed as Holly.

The ground beneath some of these giants was a veritable minefield of twitchy saplings, fallen logs of all shapes and sizes, some of which had been rotting for years, deep holes, steep inclines, slimy mossy stones, let alone creepy-crawlies no girl, or even gentlemen of a somewhat delicate disposition, should be asked to face in bright daylight let alone the dark. Her imagination started to work overtime. All it needed now to complete the panicky picture was for some animal to suddenly dart away from beneath her feet or for an owl to hoot and she would definitely need a clean pair of knickers. She was aware of the thumping of her heart and had an urgent desire to turn back the way she had come but instead took a deep breath and plunged on.

Plunged was the right word for it because her foot, on wet leaves lying there since the autumn, slid out from beneath her and she sat down with a thump before rolling down a steep incline and narrowly avoiding a shallow and rather smelly stream at the bottom that would have wet her through and through. Her first thought was not for any possible broken bones. She knew how to take a fall, even an unexpected one. She hadn't encountered any protruding rocks, branches, or rusted tin cans on the way and was fairly well cushioned in Thornton's coat. No, her first concern was for the coat. Thornton would never forgive her if it were totally trashed, even if this little adventure came up with the goods. Her second concern was for the torch. Was it still working? She withdrew it from the pocket in which she had placed it and, cupping her hand in front to lessen the light, switched it on and hurriedly switched it off. All was well, now to get her bearings. Well, she slipped down that bank to her right, so she had better step over the little stream and climb the opposite one, which was easier said than done. There was nowhere in the wet mud of the bank's surface for her shoes to get a grip and she was seriously beginning to wonder whether this little caper was really worth it. She turned to walk downstream on squelchy ground until she found an easier exit and she had no sooner made it than she went arse over tip again as her foot snagged on a surface root and she was sent sprawling.

Had holly not been made of sterner stuff it was at this point that she would have burst into tears, instead of which she merely sat up and took a number of deep breaths before checking the state of the torch once more. It was still in working order. Maybe it was telling her something. Instead of Alice in Wonderland being faced with objects saying eat me, drink me, etcetera, maybe this little torch was saying use me, for goodness sake, girl, before you break your pretty neck. She ignored the message; put the torch back in her pocket, got to her feet and moved on, much more carefully this time.

It was when she decided it was hopeless trying to discover anything in the dark and there was probably nothing suspicious in the wood, nothing she was going to see anyway, and was about to give it up as a dead loss that she came across an arrow imbedded between the roots of a tree. But what was so unusual about that near an archery club? Close to the arrow however she found, by the light of the torch she was using at last, nestling in the grass, a set of car keys with a Jaguar fob. She bent down to pick them up and, as she did so, another arrow imbedded itself quivering in the tree trunk right in front of her nose and Holly hit the dirt.

Cautiously the bowman advanced to the spot where he had seen the figure and the light from the torch, another arrow fitted to his bow and at the ready. But he found nothing. The quarry had vanished. He stood for a while listening but heard nothing except the noise of an occasional vehicle passing by on the road a short distance away before he continued moving to the edge of the wood and the fence in time to see a car head out from the country road opposite and speed away. It was too far away and now too dark to make out details though it looked like some make of estate car and there was nothing to link it in anyway with an intruder in the woods.

*****

'Rory, this is my friend, Holly. Holly, this is Aurora Pemberton, known to her friends as Rory.'

The girls shook hands and said their how do ye do's before they all sat down and Rory looked around for a waiter from whom to order drinks. Greenmeadows was a trendy bar near Covent Garden, a gathering place for the young set who thought the more money they forked out for less the trendier they were being. The place was packed and the three were surrounded by Hooray Henry's and their somewhat vapid, hysterically braying polones, as the doyen of fashion photographers, Adrian Spangle would have called them. And, talk of the devil, the little minx himself waltzed in, blowing kisses and smiles in all directions, the scent of Old Spice suddenly permeating the room and Thornton doing his best to hide behind Rory but to no avail. Adrian had spotted him and homed in like a

101

ballistic missile.

'Well well well! If it isn't Charlie Thorpe!' Adrian cried for the entire room to hear.

'Charlie Thorpe? Snap!' Rory and Holly stared at each other in surprise and then turned in unison to look at Thornton who was actually blushing, though there really was no need for him to do so. They waited.

'It's a long story,' Thornton said. 'Adrian, do you know Rory Pemberton?'

'Of course I do?' Adrian said, and, leaning towards her, pursed his lips a good six inches from either cheek and moved his head like a pecking hen.

'And Holly Day.'

'How d'ye do?'

'Adrian and I are such old old friends, aren't we?' Rory beamed.

'Not old friends you understand, Charlie, but old friends,' Adrian said. 'We'll only be old friends when we pass forty. Isn't that right, Rory dear? In the meantime we will remain thirty-nine and a half for at least another six or even seven years. It's not just death and taxes that are inevitable, birthdays are as well. They arrive with alarming frequency, at least once a year.'

Adrian was beginning to sound like sub Oscar Wilde, Thornton thought.

The man in question beamed at Rory and gave her a friendly punch on her bicep before turning back to Thornton. 'Well, Mister King Thorpe, Thorpe King, you are a very naughty boy, walking out on me like that, I must say. Was that the way to treat a generous host? I wasn't going to eat you, you know. Well, not literally anyway, maybe just a lick or two and nibble around the edges a bit and...'

Thornton thought he ought to put a stop to this immediately so indicated a spare chair and said, 'Adrian, would you care to join us?'

'No ta,' said Adrian, still sounding a bit miffed. 'I'm with friends.' Friends was heavily accentuated, meaning trustworthy people who wouldn't walk out the minute his back was turned or while he was busily sudsing himself in the shower preparatory he hoped to a lingering afternoon's lubricity. He waggled his fingers towards a table in the distance and three sets of fingers were waggled back then, ignoring Thornton and Holly but with a kiss blown towards

Rory, he pranced off in their direction. Both girls were now looking enquiringly at Thornton who shrugged and said:

'Like I said, it's a long story.'

'Wait a minute,' Holly said, 'Adrian Spangle. I remember now. Isn't he the photographer? The one you stole those incriminating pictures from?'

'Stole? Borrowed, if you don't mind. And they did help towards solving the Spitskaya case.'

'Yes, but you didn't tell me you had to fight for your honour in order to get them.'

'Yes I did.'

'You did?

'Don't you remember? I referred to him as the Adrian who tried to seduce me as opposed to the nice Doctor Adrian from Barts who stitched me up. I still have the scars, look.' He indicated his forehead where he had been coshed with the edge of a hard sample case and his finger where Adrian's dog Tiddly had bitten him. 'But it's time to order drinkies. What are we having?'

'Do you know what I truly truly fancy?' Rory asked, 'I fancy an Asti Spumanti. How about you?' She looked up at the waiter as though it were a fait accompli and brooked no argument. Neither Thornton nor Holly fancied Asti Spumanti above all else but as Rory held the purse strings and was to all intents and purposes their hostess they kept their mouths shut and the waiter went off to get it.

'So why did Adrian call you, what was it? Charlie? Charlie Thorpe?' Rory wanted to know.

'That,' Thornton said, 'is an even longer story and it can wait for another time. What Holly and I want to know from you now is, exactly how much do you know about The Bowmen Of Essex?'

'The Bowmen Of Essex?' Is it a book, a film, or a play?'

'Seriously, Rory, if you don't mind.'

'Sorry, never heard of them. Maybe it's a folksy English operetta? Butterworth? Or Parry. No, Parry was more churchy wasn't he? Maybe Roger Quilter? Ketelby! You know, like *In A Persian Market* or *In A Monastery Garden*. Got it! Edward German! Good old merry England stuff.'

Thornton was not amused. He sat giving Rory what he always referred to as his Basilisk stare. She was paying him good money to try and solve the mystery of her guardian's death and here she was behaving like a rather silly schoolgirl. What gives with this woman? Could it be that she was already drunk?

'I'm sorry,' she apologised. The Basilisk stare seemed to have had the desired effect. 'Its just that… well… I'm getting rather sick of the whole…'

'It's the archery club of which your uncle was a member.'

'Oh! Was he?' She shrugged.

'That was where he practised his archery.'

'No, I told you. He gave that up, oh, simply ages ago.'

'No, Rory, he did not. He may very well have stopped the actual physical thing of firing off arrows or crossbow bolts but he was still paying his membership dues. There is correspondence from the club in his desk drawer continuing almost up till the day he died. And, I may add, you yourself told me of the challenge match to which he was invited, not so very long ago. You still mean to tell me you know nothing about it?'

'Why should I? If my uncle ever thought I had been going through his desk he would have been absolutely furious.'

'He might still be alive.'

'Well…' She got a bit snappy, '…hindsight is all very well, Thornton, but I don't usually go poking my nose in where it's not wanted.'

'You're doing it right now or, at least Holly and I are doing it on your behalf, and I can assure you there are those who definitely don't want it. In fact I wouldn't be at all surprised if your own life weren't in considerable danger.'

'Don't try and frighten me, Thornton, because it won't work.'

'He's not trying to frighten you, Rory,' Holly butted in very softly 'He's telling you how it is. Someone out there has already had a go at me which means they don't appreciate people nosing around.'

'Do you know a Maurice Chinnery?'

Rory thought for a moment and then shook her head.

'Sir Hugo Ingle?'

'That mean old bastard! More money than he knows what to do with and he wouldn't give his granny ice in winter.'

'How well do you know him?'

'Not well at all actually. I only know we've tried to touch him for contributions to various charities and got absolutely nowhere. Ebenezer Scrooge before his Christmas conversion was the complete philanthropist in comparison to that one.'

'Hmn... I wonder why he would belong to a club like The Bowmen Of Essex.'

'It would have to be because they offer him something very special that he wouldn't get elsewhere, otherwise he would definitely begrudge every penny it cost him.'

'Like nymphets,' Holly chipped in.

'Quite possibly, if that's his thing,' Rory agreed. 'Ah, here comes the wine.'

'Do you think the girl could have been underage?' Thornton asked, turning to Holly. 'Who knows these days, it's quite possible. Twelve year olds look like nineteen year olds and behave like it. Childhood actually seems to be getting shorter and shorter.'

'In olden days a girl could be married at that age,' Rory remarked.

'True,' Holly agreed, 'but we don't happen to be living in olden days Nor are we living in third world countries were parents can sell their children for next to nothing for no other purpose than to satisfy the lust of perverted men and make money for their owners.'

'Right then,' Thornton said, 'I think, if it is true what we suspect, before we do anything else we had better have words with Sir Hugo Ingle.'

The waiter, having finally arrived at their table with the wine in its ice bucket, uncorked it with a quite unnecessary explosion, filled three glasses and slapped down a soggy bill on the table before leaving. Rory raised her glass.

'Cheers!' She said. 'Here's to a successful outcome to your enquiries.'

CHAPTER SIX

'Thank you for the loan of your identity,' Holly said. 'It has really proved most useful.'

'You've solved the case,' Carmen said, gushing slightly.

'Unfortunately not.' Holly slipped off her shoes and curled her feet beneath her.

'Oh, I hoped to hear lots and lots of the goriest details.'

'Well we know there is something truly weird going on but what it is exactly we've yet to discover. You haven't been sussed out by the paparazzi I hope.'

Carmen shook her head. 'No, much to my surprise because those guys can usually smell a victim a mile off, I am still incognito. I don't think there's any way they can know I'm here, that is unless one of my friends decides to unfortunately open her mouth. You know what some people are like; no matter how much you impress something on them it's blab, blab, blab, can't keep anything a secret for longer than ten minutes. "Don't tell anyone I told you this" they say "because it's meant to be a big big secret but guess what!"'

'Good, because I am going to need to be you for maybe another forty-eight hours or so.'

'There's no chance them, whoever they are, finding out you're not who you pretend to be?'

Holly crossed her fingers. 'So far, so good. I believe I've covered all my tracks. Famous last words. Oh, by the way, you're staying at the Hotel Diana.'

'Am I? And just where exactly is the Hotel Diana?'

'Bayswater. Cleveland Square. It's owned and run by Myrtle Cullen, Myrtle Greenberg as was. Delightful little creature she was as a girl with a voice like a foghorn. Thinks she's another Barbra Streisand. Married well, nice chap with pots of dough. I don't believe you ever knew her but she's in on our secret, had to be because you're staying in her hotel, and I don't think she's one to blab blab blab.' A slight note of anxiety crept into Holly's voice. 'Though you never can tell, can you? Thank you.' She stretched out her hand to accept her gin and It. 'Maybe if I promised her, that next time you visit, you really will stay with her and you won't be incognito so she can gets simply heaps of publicity that will definitely keep her mouth shut. Good idea?'

'Good idea. This guy you're working with...'

'Thornton?'

'Is that his name? Thornton...'

'King.'

'What's he like?'

Holly sat frowning for a moment and took a sip of her drink. 'What's he like?'

'Are you an item?'

'Good heavens, no! No, I don't mean that disparagingly,' she added hurriedly. 'Thornton's actually quite dishy in his own funny way.' Visions of Thornton in various situations flashed through her mind. 'Well, maybe cute is a better word to describe him. He has the air sometimes of a hungry homeless puppy that's not quite sure where its next bone is coming from or can remember where he buried the last one. Sexy? Hmn...' She pursed her lips, thinking hard. 'Oh, we're so like brother and sister it's hard for me to see him any other way. We're certainly not, as you put it, an item. I'm not sure he's ever looked on me as anything but one of his pals. Thornton never went to a public school but sometimes the way he behaves you would think he had. Does all that tell you anything?'

'Huh-huh.'

'Why did you want to know anyway?'

'Just curious. Maybe I'll get to meet him sometime.'

'Well, not this trip if that's what you're thinking. I do believe he's got what he fondly imagines is a secret lay holed up somewhere and she goes by the name of Annette Friedman Q.C.'

'What! Not the Annette Friedman?'

'You know her?'

'Know her! I'd say! If daddy has need of a firm of lawyers of international repute before whom everyone on the wrong side quails, whom else does he go to? Anybody who's anybody who matters uses Friedman Friedman and Co. The first Friedman by the way is Annette's daddy who is only a figurehead these days. All the power is hers. There's got to be more to Thornton than you think if he can pull a bird like that.'

'He first saw her with that sexual misfit and sociopath, Mike Aliff.'

'Who?'

'Someone you definitely do not want to meet. But maybe it wasn't what Thornton imagined it to be, but business. Oh, my God! I hope in the midst of satisfying his wild desires Thornton's not going to go blab blab blab!'

*****

Thornton was too exhausted to go blab blab blab. He lay on his back and all he wanted was to get up, trot to the bathroom, throw back his head and close his eyes under a long soothing shower, neither too hot nor too cold, but she wasn't going to let him go. One leg was crooked over his and her fingers were playing gently with the hair on his chest before they walked down to his pubics. He took hold of her wrist and moved her hand back to his chest.

'You make a great lover,' she said and tweaked one nipple twixt thumb and forefinger while she nibbled on the other, which made him squirm slightly. 'Hmn... I could eat you with a teaspoon,' she murmured, rolling the tip of her tongue in a small O.

'What an odd expression.'

'Swedish.'

'That explains it.'

She raised the sheet. 'And not too badly equipped either.'

'Thank you. I do believe you've seen it before.'

'What Shakespeare plays do these measurements represent: three inches, six inches, nine inches, twelve inches?'

'Is this the start of dirty talk? A bit arse about front wouldn't you say? That's supposed to come with the foreplay'

'Go on, let's see how good a detective you are, work it out.'

'What if I don't know my Shakespeare?

'Yes, you do. Of course you do.' She waited. He lay gazing at the ceiling. 'You're not even going to try?'

'No.' He turned his head to look at her. 'You tell me. What plays of Shakespeare do these measurements represent.?'

'Three inches: Much Ado About Nothing: six inches, A Midsummer Night's Dream: nine inches: As You Like It: twelve inches: Taming Of The Shrew.'

He thought about this for a moment. 'What about fifteen inches? There must be a few of those around otherwise hung like a horse wouldn't be an expression, would it?'

'How about Love's Labour's Lost?'

'How about All's Well That Ends Well? Hmn... You want to know something? That is a really feeble joke. Not even worthy of the fourth form that. Unbefitting the dignity of a Queen's Council and I can guess without a shadow of a doubt where you got it from. It sounds just like him. I bet he's told you the one about the dead horse as well. Anyway, I was always led to believe that size isn't really that important. It's what you do with it that matters.'

'You do very nicely. Are you as good a detective?'

'Well, if you must know, I'm actually a lousy detective. At the moment I seem to be earning my living under false pretences but no worries, so many people do these days.'

'You're not getting on with your current caper then?'

Thornton didn't really feel this was a subject to be discussed in bed after having indulged in what he felt was half the Kama Sutra so he dismissed it curtly with, 'I'm not.' He tried to move his leg. 'And I'm getting cramp,' he said as an excuse.

'Thornton, Thornton, you're not supposed to suffer from post coitus tristus. It's the mare and the woman who suffer that but I must be horribly abnormal because it has never affected me. I'm not just contented after a well-tuned orgasm; I'm positively bursting with joie de vivre.'

'I noticed.'

'If you're not getting on too well with your current investigations is there any way I can help?'

'You really do bounce from one thing to another, don't you? How could you possibly help?'

'Oh, I don't know. I could keep my ears open. It's amazing what one hears in the corridors of law courts and the corridors of power.

I could quiz Mike Aliff for a start.'

For an international lawyer of high repute this was a mistake she should never have made. She immediately sensed Thornton freeze and she started to cover up.

'I only mention Mike,' she hastily added, 'because, being where he is, he must know an awful lot of what's going on, don't you think?'

'Do you know what I think?' He managed at last to extricate himself from her leg and sat up. 'I think I would like a nice long shower and then where are we going to eat this evening?'

'I'm afraid we're not, darling. I promised to see Mike in The Wig And Gown.' She smiled up at him as he sat looking down at her. 'It's business,' she said.

'Well, in between business I think you should get your friend to tell you another lousy joke.'

He threw back the sheet, lowered his feet to the floor and without looking back marched off to the bathroom. Thornton had a nasty feeling that sooner or later this one would also pull a gun on him but he hoped not. Suddenly the apartment seemed to be over-heated and Annette Friedman not quite as attractive as he originally thought. She, on the other hand, watching him as he retired, thought he had the cutest bum she had ever seen. Why had she not thought to nibble on it with or without the aid of a teaspoon.

*****

Thornton and Holly sat in conference in Holly's flat. She didn't have all that much free time left, in fact was due back in the department in a couple of days so, if she was still to be of any assistance, they had to move fast.

Thornton was playing with the set of Jaguar keys she had given him.

'Could be quite innocent,' he remarked. 'Could have been dropped by just anybody but I'll keep them anyway. You never know.' He slipped them into his pocket. 'I suppose the best thing we can do now though is tackle Sir Hugo and see if we can get him to spill a few beans, and I suggest we do it right away.'

'You won't get within a mile of him.'

'You think not?'

'I know. What reason would two complete strangers have for wanting to talk to him considering the state I presume he's still in? Anyway, I have to also presume he keeps a pretty low profile at the best of times, do you know where he lives? How to get hold of him?'

'I do. Got the address from Rory, and the ex-directory telephone number.'

'Why does she have it?'

'Well you heard what she said, evidently she's tried to get the mean old bugger to cough up a few shekels for charity without any luck.'

'What else do you know about this man?'

'You mean apart from the fact that he's as mean as pigshit? Well... according to you it appears he likes pubescent or even prepubescent girls, which puts him well outside the law. If The Bowmen Of Essex provides him with this little outlet they, whoever they might be, have got him bang to rights haven't they? They could take him for all he's worth. Shall we try the phone first?'

'Help yourself,' Holly said, getting up and heading for the kitchen, 'I'll make some coffee.'

Thornton lifted the receiver and, taking a piece of paper from his jacket pocket, dialled Sir Hugo's number. He held on and watched Holly as she went about making the coffee. He held on as the coffee was made and she brought two cups through to the living area and put them on the table. He held on as she settled down on the couch, lifted her coffee cup, took a sip and waited. Finally he put down the phone and shrugged.

'Guess he's not answering,' he said.

'Obviously. He could be out of course. He could be in the bath. He could be wearing earplugs. He could be scared to death. He could be dead. That's more than likely the reason he won't answer.'

'Why hasn't he got servants? If he's that rich he should have servants.'

'Servants have to be paid.'

'Why doesn't he have an answering service?'

'Thornton, it's no use you asking me all these questions? I don't have any answers and, if it's answers we want and answers we have to get, then I suggest we finish our coffee and head for... where does he live?'

'South Ken. Well more Gloucester Road way.'

'Gloucester Road, and talk to the man, if we can get anywhere near him that is. I suggest we take a cab. West London is the happy home patch of the warthogs we're hunting. It would just be sod's law that one of them would see you and me in the car, recognise it and us, and start putting two and two together.'

Maurice Chinnery lay studying himself in his bath in his Chelsea hideaway and came to the obvious conclusion that he had really gone to seed passed no return. Even laying on his back and not subject to gravity his body was not a pretty sight, not even for its owner, and hadn't been for quite a while. Maybe he should take out a subscription to a gym but the thought of physical exercise was just too much of a turn off, which was why he never bothered to draw bowstring despite belonging to the club. There could be no turning back the clock. No amount of wishful thinking that he looked like his Adonis of a chauffeur could make the slightest difference to the ravages of time and his style of living. Why, he wondered, had he allowed Carmen Hernandez to get under his skin in the way she had? Did he really feel the need for one last great romantic love before they rolled his coffin into the flames? After all, he knew perfectly well that, should Carmen respond positively to his courting he would more than likely, no, he would definitely be unable to rise to the occasion. His mind would be telling him, you can't do it, old chum, not any more so why bother? Don't even try and the result would be total failure. One of the vicissitudes of growing old he supposed, like arthritis and shortage of breath and varicose veins. Maurice heaved a sigh and dreamed up a steamy scenario of a wonderful bucolic romantic sexual episode starring himself as shepherd and the divine Carmen Inez Hernandez as shepherdess. It was so vivid he managed finally to bring himself to a not very satisfactory climax of sorts by which time the water had turned cold. He used a big toe to turn on the hot tap and, when the temperature had been restored, fell asleep to wake up half an hour later with dead white horribly wrinkly fingers and toes.

They managed to hail a taxi prepared to take them half way across London and, for the most part, sat in silence as it made its way towards Gloucester Road. It wasn't until they past the Victoria and Albert Museum that Holly finally asked the question she had been dying to get off her chest all evening.

'So how are you getting on with Annette?' It seemed such a prim and proper way to put it that Thornton couldn't help but burst out laughing.

'Well, Holly, my dear, if you really want to know, we're at it like a pair of rabbits.'

'Oh,' was all she said, and then, after a pause, 'You will be careful won't you?'

Thornton didn't laugh at this. In fact he frowned, wondering just what Holly was getting at and what the hell it had to do with her anyway. She wasn't jealous by any chance, was she? By the time he thought of a riposte the taxi had stopped outside the address given and Holly had already opened the door and stepped out, waiting for him on the pavement.

Thornton got out and paid the driver who gave him a huge wink and said, 'Keep at it, guv, and more strength to your elbow.'

Now Thornton really was piqued. 'I don't fuck with my elbow,' he hissed, 'do you?'

'Pardon me!' said the taxi man and drove off. Touchy these toffs, he thought. Thornton turned back to where Holly was waiting. He was still inwardly fuming and Holly knew it. Oh. Boy! Was ever the wrong thing said and maybe a spot of explanation and possibly an apology was due to sooth the savage breast.

'Thornton, I...'

'Let's get on with it shall we?'

'No! We're not going to get on with anything while you're still in a mood. You're in no fit state to interview Sir Hugo and I might as well go home if you're going to insist on behaving like a big spoilt baby. All I meant by that remark was that, if Annette what's her name and Mike Aliff are as thick as thieves...'

'Who says they are?' He was still snappy and he had learnt Aliff was happy to tell her dirty jokes and she was happy to hear them, well, stupid jokes anyway. So? What on earth was he going on about? He wasn't kidding himself. He knew all along, as far as Annette Friedman was concerned this was just an interlude so why take it so much to heart?

'Take care, Thornton. She may not be all she makes herself out to be.'

'I'm already perfectly well aware of that thank you, now shall we get on?'

'No. Not until you've taken a deep breath, counted to ten and smiled at me. I apologise if I've committed a faux pas.'

Thornton did as he was bid and took a deep breath, well more of a deep sigh really, and then he actually smiled although he was still a bit quivery inside.

'Right,' Holly said, 'just how are we going to approach the unapproachable?'

'Step by step,' Thornton replied, 'starting with mounting the actual steps,' at which he did just that, with Holly close behind until they were standing outside the impressive front door. To one side there was the metal panel of an entry phone, slightly incongruous in its setting, although the building's period rendering did look as though it could do with more than just a lick of paint. So many of these large Kensington houses had been turned into bed-sitters because their owners could no longer afford their upkeep but this one, shabby though it might be, was still all of a piece and there was only one bell to press. Thornton pressed it.

'Maybe it would be better if he heard a woman's voice,' Holly suggested.

Thornton shrugged. 'Fine by me,' he said, and they waited. And they waited. Thornton pressed the bell again, keeping his finger on it for a long while. And they waited. He pressed the bell again and this time he kept his finger there until finally a voice came through with one word.

'Yes?'

'Good evening, Sir Hugo,' Holly started, 'my name is...'

'What do you want? If you're selling something you're wasting your time. I don't want anything! Go away! Go away!'

The phone went dead. Thornton pressed the bell a fourth time. 'It wouldn't surprise me if he pulled out the wires,' he said. 'Have you ever heard such downright panic?'

But Sir Hugo hadn't pulled out any wires. He was back on line.

'Who are you? What do you want?'

'We want to save your life,' Holly said, coming straight to the point.

There was a long silence while the surprised recipient of this remark thought about it and then, 'What on earth are you talking about? Save my life? I've never heard such ridiculous nonsense. How do I know you haven't come to take my life?'

Thornton and Holly turned to look at each other; two pairs of eyes opening very wide, and Thornton decided it was time he took a hand. 'Sir Hugo...'

At the sound of a male voice, Sir Hugo's own became almost a squeak. 'Who are you?' he enquired again. 'Go away, please go away, I don't want anything.' There was definitely the sound of a sob.

'This is pathetic,' Thornton whispered to Holly, and then back into the phone, 'Sir Hugo, My name is Thornton King and...'

The voice from the other end regained some of its strength. 'Never heard of you. Now leave me alone or I'll call the police.'

'Detective Inspector Thornton King.' This time Holly's eyes opened wide all on their own as she pulled a face like a Japanese Noh mask. There are heavy penalties for impersonating a police officer if the impersonator is found out and, right at that moment as if on cue, two Bobbies came strolling by at a leisurely pace, hands behind their backs in the manner of Prince Philip, to stop more or less outside the house.

'How do I know you're who you say you are?' the voice hissed. 'What do you want with me?'

'Only to ask you a few questions.'

'About what?'

Thornton was growing just a little impatient. 'Look, Sir Hugo, this is a matter of life and death and you know it, your life and death.'

Now there was a quite audible gasp through the answer phone.

'Are you going to let us in or do we have to break down the door?'

The two Bobbies seemed to have turned their attention to the house as though something very interesting might be going on or about to happen there. Holly tugged at Thornton's sleeve and cocked her head in their direction. Thornton glanced down into the street and then put his mouth close to the answer phone to speak softly.

'If you want proof, Sir Hugo, I am talking to Sir Hugo I take it, should have made sure of that right at the beginning shouldn't I?

If you care to look out of a window you will have the proof you need.' With which he bounced down the steps to confront the two policemen.

'Constable Roper!' he said, 'what a surprise. What are you doing around here? Shouldn't you be locking up villains in the West End?'

'Hello, Mr King! How are you then? Fancy seeing you here. Bit out of your patch this isn't it? Yes, you're right, out of mine as well. Been temporarily seconded to this manor. They do move me about don't they? "All grist to the mill" old fartface said. "Thought it would make a good change for you," he said. "They're a bit short staffed over there," he said. "Chelsea's playing at home tonight. Big important match. Too much football going on and too many hooligans on the streets. The West End's pretty quiet at the moment so go and troll around Earls Court," he said. Yes. That was his actual word, Mister King, "troll" he said. I ask you, he's been picking up a bit of the old palare. It's because he's always going on about perversion. Never stops. Got a right thing about it he has. "Pop into those gay pubs and give the buggers momentary heart attacks," he said. "Time you had a good look at perversion close up and en masse," he said. "It's not a pretty sight. It'll keep you on the straight and narrow in case, heaven forbid, you're ever tempted. Just because it's sort of legal now, one to one as it were, no one else around, doesn't mean I has to approve," he said. Oh, this is Constable Babcock by the way.' Roper indicated his sidekick.

'How do you do?' Thornton said. Babcock nodded, regarding Thornton suspiciously with a pale blue watery eye from either side of his helmet's peak.

'I don't know,' Roper moaned. 'Can't bloody stand Earls Court myself and it's not the gay pubs that get on my wick, if you'll pardon the expression. Kangaroo Valley they call it because it's full of bloody Australians. With a Bruce Bruce here and a Bruce Bruce there, here a Bruce, there a Bruce, everywhere a Bruce Bruce, and a whole lot of Sheilas as well of course, all guzzling Fosters like there's no tomorrow. Yes, well, all in all though it's been pretty quiet, dead as a bloody doornail in fact. All we've got for our trouble so far is aching feet. Isn't that right, Jes? No, that aint absolutely true. Jes took a right fancy to one of the Sheilas, didn't you, Jes? Boobs like dirigibles, isn't that right, Jes? She's promised him if he ever goes to Australia she'll teach him how to have it off on a surf board.' Constable Roper was grinning from ear to ear. Constable Babcock remained as impassive as ever.

'Sorry to hear about your own Sheila trouble,' Thornton said. 'Reg told me.' He glanced back towards the house and could see Sir Hugo's shape behind a ground floor window before the curtain was hastily drawn across.

'Oh, no, that's all settled innit? A lover's tiff is all it was. We've made it up. As a matter of fact I've been invited to visit her folks down the Principality soon as I get some time off.'

'There'll be a welcome in the valley, huh? I hope they keep it green for you.'

'You're a card, Mr King, you really are. They live in Swansea. Well, best get on then. Good night. Come on, Jes, let's see what we can find,' and they continued their leisurely stroll. Thornton returned to where Holly was still waiting. He pressed the bell once more and Sir Hugo came on the line.

'Satisfied?' Thornton said.

There was the sound of a click, the door opened and Thornton held it there for Holly to enter.

Sir Hugo, muffled up in an old-fashioned cardigan of khaki wool with holed elbows, and a heavy scarf that smelled vaguely of mouse droppings, the house evidently had no heating, was standing at what turned out to be the drawing room door waiting to usher them in. He retreated crab like as they advanced and, once in the drawing room he gestured towards a couple of chairs for them to sit; chairs that like the drapes and the rest of the furniture had once seen better days, and opened the proceedings by saying:

'Inspector Thornton... '

'Mister,' Thornton corrected him. 'I lied.'

'Oh, my God!' Sir Hugo sank into what was obviously his favourite chair from which the stuffing was protruding in an obscene fashion, some of which he started to fiddle with, and stared in horror at his night visitors. The only lighting in the room came from a single overhead bulb dangling on twisted brown flex and a brass lamp with tulip shade on the occasional table next to Sir Hugo's chair. Thornton noticed the light switch by the door was still the original protruding fluted brass, an antique piece from when the house was

117

converted from gas to electricity and the wiring evidently had never been touched since. The house itself was a virtual death trap. Sir Hugo was mute as he stared at his visitors. What had he let into his house? He knew so many stories about ruthless robbers who did unseemly and extremely painful things to their victims in the course of turning the joint over. Sir Hugo, apart from resenting every penny he had to spend, except on little girls, was an avid reader of thrillers borrowed from the local library most of which, once known as penny dreadfuls, would more accurately under a trades description act be described as science fiction. Not everyone can be a Mickey Spillane. He tried to speak but nothing would come although his mouth showed signs of trying to move.

'Please, Sir Hugo,' Holly said, 'calm yourself. I promise you we are not here to hurt you in any way, quite the opposite. We know you are in trouble and all we want is for you to tell us about it so we can help you.'

'Why...' he finally managed to gasp, 'why did you say you're a policeman if you aren't?'

'It was simply a ruse to get you to let us in,' Thornton said.

'But I saw you, through the window, I saw you talking to those two policeman. Or weren't they real either?'

'Oh, they were real all right. I just happened to be acquainted with one of them and I thought if you saw me talking to them...'

'Yes, yes! Well it worked, didn't it? But now that you're here, what...'

Suddenly, even though she had already addressed him directly, it was though he noticed Holly for the first time. He had hardly given her a glance before even while she was talking. She was at least fifteen years or more too old for his tastes, but now he gave her the hard stare.

'Don't I know you, young lady?'

'You've seen me around,' Holly replied.

'Around? Around where? Oh, yes, now I remember. You were lunching with that awful Chinnery creature. You're that South American heiress, the one who's worth billions.'

Holly raised an eyebrow. Carmen's worth was mounting by the day. In actual fact it more than likely was but not by the amount everyone was imagining. By the time this caper was over her fortune would be up in the trillions.

'You're the one who's joined the club.' he continued. 'Oh, my dear! Please, let me give you a friendly word of warning.' It's probably the only thing he would give, Thornton thought. 'If you know what's good for you, leave! Leave now. Don't ever go back there. That place is a nest of vipers and you will come to a great deal of harm. Listen to me, please!' And then another thought struck him. 'But why have you come to see me? You of all people? What have I to do with a South American heiress? At least I can be assured that you for one won't be after my money. Everybody else is of course. Always have been.' He turned an accusing look on Thornton.

'No,' Thornton said, 'I am not the slightest bit interested in your wealth I can assure you. It's your health I'm interested in. I am interested in what or who is threatening you. I'm interested…'

'Who told you I am being threatened? How do you know anything at all about what is going on?'

'I may not be a policeman but I am a private detective and I've been hired to investigate the death of Sir Roger Pemberton. You knew him?'

Sir Hugo shook his head. 'Afraid not,' he said. 'I don't really have much to do with other members of the club. I only go there occasionally when they've fixed up…' He brought himself up short and then continued with, 'I only know the Chinnery monster because he tried to flog me his ancient Rolls Royce. What would I want with his flaming Rolls? I'm trying to flog off my own car. It guzzles gas and costs a bloody fortune in every which way you can think of. I don't suppose you would be interested in buying it would you?'

'Out of my league,' Thornton said. 'How about you, Holly? Want to buy a motor?'

Holly shook her had.

'It was an aberration of course. I bought it secondhand, saw it in the dealer's window and thought it would be good for pulling the…' He sat for a moment mulling over his moment of weakness in spending so much money for so little return.

Thornton and Holly were silent too; both wondering how efficacious the car was in pulling the Lolitas of this world.

'I've advertised it in *Exchange and Mart* but I'm a bit chary of the replies I've had so far, particularly from unknowns who want to take it for a test drive, on their own! Would you believe it? Talk about chutzpah. Piss off! I tell them. I'm not as green as I'm cabbage looking. Anyway, I'm beginning to resent the money I spent on that ad. Should have just put a for sale notice behind the windscreen. Would have been just as effective. Chinnery tried to tell me his car would increase dramatically in value over the years. What years? I asked him. How many do you think I have left? No, you keep your car and you can benefit from its increase in value, it's of absolutely no use to me. I read about Sir Roger in the papers; I read them at my local library. I never buy newspapers. They're such a waste of money really, and I don't have a television. Do you see a television set? No you don't, do you? Bloody BBC! Taking all that money off us every year just to watch their bloody awful programmes. I read the coroner's verdict though and there was never any suggestion that he had been deliberately killed, Sir Roger I mean.'

'True, but we think the coroner's verdict was mistaken and I believe you can help us put things right and, at the same time, save yourself.'

'Save myself? Save myself from what? I have absolutely no idea what you're talking about.' He was now nervously trying to prod the stuffing back into his chair.

'We don't want to read in the papers, at the library or anywhere else, that you have suffered a similar fate.'

Holly rolled her eyes heavenwards. Thornton could sometimes be absolutely the most tactless person who ever walked.

It was at that moment the telephone rang and Sir Hugo actually screamed as, from leaning forward in his earnest entreaty to Holly and his waffling on about newspapers and cars and television licences and prodding his middle finger into the hole in his chair, he half lifted himself up and then fell back, his mouth dropped open, he dribbled copiously and his head lolled to one side as if his neck was broken.

'Holly, see what you can do!' Thornton urged and, as she moved over to see what she could do for Sir Hugo Ingle, Thornton lifted the phone and just said, 'Yes?' in his gruffest voice.

'Sir Hugo,' the caller said, 'complications have set in. A courting couple, trespassing of course, witnessed the incident but, as their wedding is imminent, they are prepared to forget the whole thing, for a price of course. It will be up to you to meet it. Too bad, isn't it? I think a meeting is called for where you will be given instructions on how to pay and how much.'

Thornton thought he recognised the voice but couldn't place it. Adopting what he hoped was a passable resemblance to Sir Hugo's he said, 'And where is this meeting to take place?'

There was a long silence at the other end and then a click as the receiver was replaced. Thornton had just made another mistake. He turned to look at Holly standing over Sir Hugo. She pursed her lips, shrugged, and slowly shook her head.

Someone was due to inherit a great deal of money that had done its miserly owner little if any good. If he were in a position to have his way he would most likely resent the expenses of his own funeral.

Thornton and Holly stood for a long while looking down at the late Sir Hugo Ingle and wondering what would be their best course of action in this tricky, uncalled for, and totally unexpected situation.

'We could just sidle out the door and disappear,' Thornton suggested.

'Come off it, Thornton,' she gave him a quick sideways look, 'I really don't think that would be very wise. Two policemen not only saw us here but one of them you actually know and spoke to. We are obviously the last people to see Sir Hugo alive. If we were to leave now without informing the police we would be, to put it in the vernacular, right up that proverbial creek without that damned paddle everyone's always talking about.'

'He could die minutes after we leave.'

'No. Besides, he obviously died of natural causes so what is there to worry about?'

'He drops dead because he hears the telephone ring and you call that natural?'

'Obviously a long time heart condition and with the state of tension he was in his elastic band went snap.'

'Yes, you're right. I heard of cases in Africa where a person would be told by the local witch doctor that they would die at a certain time and they did, right on the dot. Just keeled over and died. Sat there cross-legged on the mud floor of their huts, not looking at anything in particular, just gazing into the middle distance as though they were seeing the next world and waiting for it to happen. Isn't that weird? It's amazing what suggestion can do.'

Holly was singularly unimpressed. 'Call the police, Thornton. Dial emergency.'

'What are you going to do while I do that?'

'It's going to take you all night to call emergency services? Well, I tell you what, I'll just go find the bathroom. I'm in urgent need of it.' With which she turned on her well-turned heel and started to leave the room. At the door she turned back. 'You'll be bringing up Pavlov's dogs next.'

'Pavlov's dogs are old hat.'

'Old head you mean. Sometimes you do come up with some truly weird stuff, Thornton. And I suppose those who are about to die keep a beady eye on the clock or set the alarm so they know the exact moment when to keel over, huh?'

'Don't be silly. This is Africa we're talking about. Probably what the witch doctor said was, the time would be when the first rays of the rising sun struck the topmost branches of the thorny bush or something like that.'

'And the hyena laughs three times. Where on earth do you pick up all this weird shit?'

'Africa.'

'Naturally. The Dark Continent.' With which she left.

Thornton lifted the receiver and dialled. 'Weird,' he said as he waited for a response.

Sir Peter Wheeler was in the middle of his weekly bridge game and was within sight of making the grand slam he had contracted for and which had eluded him for so long when the phone rang and his lady wife, Penelope, Penny for short, who was also his partner and therefore dummy, put down her glass of chilled Chablis and taking up a handful of Macedonia nuts from a cut glass bowl, excused herself and went to answer it.

Sir Peter concentrated very hard. It was going to be a close-run thing as to whether or not he conquered this personal Everest that for months he had failed to climb. He blamed it on the cards. They just hadn't been falling his way and he simply couldn't remember when last he had a decent hand or one that his wife could respond to sensibly (which she seldom did) but tonight, tonight this was it, the big one, he could feel it in his water.

'It's for you, dear,' Penny said holding out the receiver towards him although she was a fair distance away and this particular phone did not have a long cord. She popped a couple of nuts into her mouth and crunched them on very strong teeth. One missed her mouth and slipped behind her blouse.

'Can't come now. I'm concentrating.' His eyes never left his hand as he pondered his next move.

'It's really terribly terribly urgent the man says, a matter of life and death.'

'Tell him I'll call back, God damn it!'

'He says there is no time. He must talk to you this instant.'

'Shit!' Sir Peter laid down a card and went to get the phone. 'What on earth are you doing, Penelope?'

'Trying to retrieve a nut.'

'Well go and do it somewhere else, your gyrations are obscene. The last time I saw something like that was in a brothel in Beirut.'

The Wheelers' opponents, having been reared very much Bethesda chapel, pulled disapproving faces toward each other.

'Yes?' Sir Peter yelled into the receiver. There was a silence in the room as he listened then, 'I'll see to it,' he snarled, slammed down the phone and returned to his place at the table.

'Where were we?'

'I'm just about to take your jack with my queen. You're one down I'm afraid. Lets see now, vulnerable and doubled...'

'Shit!' Sir Peter yelled again, making everyone jump. For the moment it was all he could think of to say. As a matter of fact he didn't even think of it, he just said it. Absolutely no point in playing the last two cards. He hadn't made it and it was his own stupid fault. 'That's what comes from being interrupted at a crucial point and losing your concentration,' he growled. 'Unfortunately, right at this moment, it would seem we're all rather vulnerable and that's a fact. What on earth possessed me to play that prat of a jack? I was fully aware the bloody queen was still out.'

'Oh that naughty queen of spades, she's such a bad bad girl. Tschaikowsky wrote...'

'And you can quit that infuriating Welsh lyricism, Herbert

Jenkins thank you very much. God, it's so bloody annoying!'

'Well, she certainly turned a trick for me though, did she not?'

If looks could kill Herbert Jenkins would have dropped dead on the spot. There was one helluva storm brewing and Penelope, who had stopped searching for the errant nut, decided to nip it in the bud (she was very fond of nipping in the bud, was constantly at it in fact) but unfortunately this time she tried it by saying the worst thing possible.

'You should have played the...'

'And you can shut up, Penelope Wheeler!' he yelled, almost turning purple in the face. 'Know it all Penelope! Geniarse Penelope! Just keep your bloody useless advice to yourself thank you very much. Who needs it?' Having had his outburst he calmed down enough to glance at his watch and say, 'Well I think we'd better call it a night.'

'Oh! We've time for one more rubber surely.'

Sir Peter ignored this. 'What do we owe you?' he asked and reached out for the score pad. 'My God! Brilliant Penelope and I could dine at The Ritz for that. Pay them, Penny. I'll be in my office. Got a couple of urgent phone calls to make. Good night all.'

'Same time next week?' Herbert called after him as he stomped off.

'Humph!' was the response and from a distance there was the sound of a door slamming.

'You should be thoroughly mortified, Herbert Jenkins. You should have let him have his slam. He won't be worth talking to and it will be at least a week before he's anything like a human being again.'

But Herbert Jenkins wasn't in the least mortified. He'd bested the bastard, thwarted his moment of triumph, stopped him at the last moment from planting his little flag on that peak and he grinned with delight, mentally accepting the congratulations of all the Idrises and Llewelyns throughout the course of Celtic history. The dragon was flying high breathing fire, the shade of Owen Glendower was positively glowing as Herbert and his mousy wife collected their meagre winnings. Dining at The Ritz? Come off it, at a penny a point it wouldn't buy one egg and chips at Fred's caff.

'Never you mind, lovely boy,' his wife smirked. 'You beat the old bugger and that's what matters.'

There was a ring at the front door and Thornton went to answer it. Roper and Jes Babcock were standing on the doorstep facing each other like a pair of bookends, or a wedding couple solemnly making their vows. They turned to face the now open door.

'Back again, Mr King,' was Roper's bright greeting, stating the obvious. Jes merely squinted from either side his helmet's peak. Thornton without a word stood back to let them in, closing the door after them.

'So what's all this about then?' Roper was obviously still in cheerful mood. 'Got a call on the old walkie-talkie from his nibs saying as to how there's been an incident and our local chief was to send us round to investigate seeing as to how his own men are all so busy clobbering football hooligans, so here we are then, two intrepid investigators.'

'In here,' Thornton said.

The boys in blue followed him to the drawing room and Roper stopped dead and turned deadly pale at the sight of death. In fact he stopped with such abruptness, the heel of his big black regulation boot came down heavily on Jesse's toes as he followed up close behind. For the next couple of minutes Jes hopped, limped, skipped, pirouetted, and generally made a meal of it though without uttering a sound. Thornton was beginning to wonder if he ever actually spoke. If he didn't, how could he issue a caution or say something like, "Bang to rights, me old mate!"

Roper was taking no notice and not going to apologise. He was standing stock still in the doorway having tuned a paler shade of pale. This was only his second brush with what Reg always referred to in his clichéd fashion as the grim reaper although one would suppose, by the manner in which it was said, that he, Reg Venables, was the sole originator of the phrase. The first time Roper had come face to face with death was at Heathrow Airport when he was ordered, for possible identification purposes, to show his incipient fiancé the corpse of a South African jewel thief, though nobody was actually aware at the time that that was what he was. As far as anybody knew, there being nothing on the body from which to identify him, not even an airline ticket, he was just a grizzled old

John Doe in a sweaty bush jacket who had died of a heart attack whilst straining on a toilet bowl in the gents' loo. Where had he come from? Where was he going? What was he doing at Heathrow in the first place? It was anybody's guess. Nor did Roper, who had been temporarily seconded to the airport, realise at the time that the delectable and slender if somewhat highly strung Blodwen Hughes was his incipient fiancé but, if gazing at each other over a corpse could be called love at first sight, that was what it was. Or was it merely sympathy, as she appeared to be of a disposition even more nervous than his own?

'No... no... nobody said a dickie to me about... about...' he whispered and, unable to say anymore, pointed a trembling finger at the body of Sir Hugo Ingle slumped grotesquely in his chair. The intrepid investigator certainly wasn't going to advance any further into the room. 'What happened?' he asked, and ran the tip of his pink tongue over dry lips.

'He died,' Holly said, thinking how cute the constable was.

'I can see that,' Roper replied, 'but how did he die? Why did he die?' He seemed mesmerised, unable to take his eyes off the corpse of Sir Hugo Ingle so long as he kept his distance, as though the body would suddenly leap out of the chair zombie like and send him screaming from the room.

'For the answer to that we will have to wait for an autopsy report but right now I would hazard a pretty shrewd guess it was heart failure, what else? There's a cabinet on his bathroom wall chocabloc full of medicines to keep a dickie heart ticking merrily away, only this time it was the big one and all those medicines were upstairs, out of the way and consequently useless. It was so sudden that, even if he had had anything to hand I doubt he would have been able to use it and no one was going to give him the kiss of life, not with all that dribbling going on.'

'Well, there's nothing we can do then is there? Except hang about till his nibs gets here.' And young Constable Roper, who would in all likelihood always be uncomfortable in the presence of death no matter how many corpses he would be forced to witness in the line of duty, went on to say, 'I'll wait out here then,' and indicated the hall. 'Maybe even right outside, could do with a drop of fresh air.' He had taken off his helmet and was wiping his forehead with his handkerchief. Constable Roper was feeling decidedly queasy. Constable Babcock still hadn't said a word. He had advanced into the room, still limping but mainly for effect, and at quite close range was regarding the lifeless form of Sir Hugo with some curiosity. Obviously made of sterner stuff than his colleague.

Thornton, who had been looking out the window, came to Roper's immediate rescue. 'Constable Roper,' he said. Roper, who was already halfway across the hall, stopped and turned back, his out of focus gaze concentrated on the ceiling. 'There's a car parked someway down the street on the opposite side and there is someone in it who I think is taking an inordinate interest in what is going on in this house. Do you think you ought to investigate?'

Roper nodded and raised an index finger. 'I'll do that,' he said with gratitude and promptly disappeared, taking deep breaths of the cold air as he stepped outside.

'How do you know there's someone in that car?' Holly enquired.

'Because the silly bugger's parked as near as damnit to a streetlight as he can get.'

'Probably the only space he could find,' Holly said, always the practical one.

'He's too far away though and still too much in shadow to see if it's anyone we know, but I clocked his silhouette behind the wheel. Roper will sort him out no doubt.'

'Well, if you can see him, then he can see you. Shouldn't you get away from the window?'

'I doubt he can see who it is from there. Yes, he can see my silhouette against the light but, just as I am too far away to recognise him, so he must be too far away to recognise me. I only knew it was Sir Hugo standing at the window earlier because it couldn't have been anyone else. Roper's going towards him now. Jesus! He's started the car and he's pulling out. Roper's standing there holding up his hand!'

'You sound like a Greek chorus.'

'Yes, and that was nearly a Greek tragedy. For a minute I thought...'

Roper, advancing on the car, suddenly found the car advancing on him and gathering speed. He had to stop playing at being a traffic cop as he leapt out of the way, flattening himself against another parked car as the suspect one sped by practically taking the skin off his nose. It all happened so fast he didn't even have time to note the car's number. It took a few moments for him to recover, enough to leave the car he had fallen against, and then more precious moments fled by as he tried to find his voice and use his walkie-talkie to report a case of extreme reckless driving with murderous intent, but by then the fugitive would have been well away and mingling with the heavy main road traffic. Roper staggered back towards the house. After a boring start he now felt he had had quite enough excitement for one night. He burst into the drawing room, all feelings of squeamishness momentarily banished by his own sudden brush with possibly severe or fatal injury. 'Did you see that?' he squawked. 'Did you see it? The bastard nearly knocked me down!'

'I saw it,' Thornton said. 'Did you get his number?'

'Did I hell!' Roper sank trembling into a chair in quite close proximity to the body and totally ignoring it. His heart was thumping so hard it was a wonder it didn't jump-start Sir Hugo's.

'Did you get the make of car?'

Roper shook his head. 'I could do with a drink,' he said.

'Not on duty.' They were the first words uttered by Constable Babcock.

'I brought you a nightcap,' Penny said, placing the glass of Chivas on Sir Peter's desk and kissing him on the top of his head. Neither the ostensibly affectionate gesture nor the whisky was likely to sweeten the old bugger's mood and he accepted both with bad grace.

'Sorry you didn't make your slam.' She stroked his shoulder but he shrugged her off. Physical exhibition of false sentiment was the last thing he wanted. He knew perfectly well, no matter her protestations, she was delighted he hadn't made his slam. Jealousy at the bridge table even between partners, particularly married ones, is a murderous unfathomable manifestation. It has sometimes led to the most acrimonious of divorces and is a phenomenon about which most psychiatrists would admit to knowing little if anything at all. How could the young Mister Vanderbilt know what a Pandora's box he was opening when he invented the game?

'Do you want to tell me what this is all about?'

He leaned back in his chair and delivered a long sigh, picked up his whisky and took what normally would have been an appreciative sip before looking up at her for the first time. He held out a hand, which she took, holding it with one hand and stroking his fingers with the other which only succeeded in increasing his irritability and made him immediately withdraw.

'For God's sake! Don't fidget, woman! You know I can't bear fidgeting.' She folded her arms so as to resist any further temptation to touch him. There was a moment during which he took another sip of his whisky before he went on. 'That stupid cretin Mike Aliff has, I believe, landed us well and truly in it. Our whole beautiful complex untraceable, or so we fondly imagined, plan, is unravelling at the seams thanks firstly to the accidental death of Sir Roger, secondly to his interfering ward, the monstrous mammoth Aurora who quite simply doesn't know what's good for her. Why can't she just accept the fact she's inheriting a whole heap of money and leave it at that? Why this ridiculous old-fashioned quest for what is euphemistically called justice or fairness when such a thing doesn't even exist? Thirdly, Aliff's ridiculous plan when she made enquiries, of recommending she hire a private detective by the name of Thornton King who, Mike, assured me, positively assured me in front of the whole board, is a total nincompoop who would never, I repeat, never solve anything more complicated than a five year old's eight piece jigsaw puzzle made out of plywood and showing a kitten with a ball of wool or, even simpler, A,B,C. Fourthly, it would appear something is happening or has already happened in the house of Sir Hugo Ingle, something which I believe complicates matters even further.'

'How do you know that?'

'That phone call was from Nikos. Said, when he called Sir Hugo's number, a stranger answered who didn't know the drill. Anyway...' He took another sip of whisky which, for once, he really wasn't enjoying, 'Nikos was more than a little worried, and so am I if it comes to that. I've sent that stupid sex besotted maniac Aliff along to keep an eye on things and report back. I hope he doesn't screw up yet again.'

Unbeknown to Sir Peter he already had.

'Well blow me down and bless my soul! Will you look who's

here? Thornton, my boy, you are, you are…' Reg clicked his fingers, 'what is the word I want for someone who is always turning up like a bad penny?'

'Ubiquitous,' Holly said.

'Hit it in one, Miss Day. Hit it in one. And where the uqwibitous Mr King is there too will be the uqwibitous Miss Day. I really like that word. Must remember it. Use it in my memoirs.'

'Do,' Holly said, 'and it's actually ubiquitous.'

'That's what I said. So exactly what is it the ubiquitous pair of you are doing here, Thornton?'

'Visiting. That is, we were visiting before… before…' He gestured towards the late Sir Hugo.

'And he is?'

'Sir Hugo Ingle.'

'Hmn.' Reg stroked his chin and surveyed the corpse watched by Detective Sergeant Ron Pocock who had entered the room with him: Pocock, Alcock, and the police photographer, Wilcox, which made for a lot of cock in one small room. Ron eyed Holly balefully. He remembered their previous encounter that could have got him into a great deal of trouble. He was lucky to escape with nothing more than a dressing down and being for a while the butt of many a jest in the station and he would be damned if he was ever going to interview the lady again. He'd call in sick first. He'd resign; forgo his pension. He'd emigrate!

'You knew the deceased well I take it.'

'A nodding acquaintance, no more than that,' Thornton replied.

'Yes, well, he won't be nodding with you anymore will he? What do you suppose happened?'

'I don't suppose anything, Reg. I'm not a doctor.'

'Are you not?' Reg had pursed his lips at the casual use of his Christian name. He was here on official police business and really ought to be addressed by his title. Now he raised his eyebrows in pretended surprise. 'Don't I recall in the not too distant past someone informing me quite categorically that you were a medical man?'

That was all a complete misunderstanding, you know that and, anyway, non-doctor that I am I would hazard a guess, and I doubt it will be gainsaid, that Sir Hugo has suffered a major coronary. It was very sudden.' He turned to Holly. 'Wasn't it?' She nodded in agreement.

'If you care to look in the bathroom cupboard upstairs, Inspector,' she said, 'you will find all the evidence you need as to the condition of Sir Hugo's heart which I am sure his doctor will confirm.'

'And what pray were you doing, Miss Day, peeping into someone else's bathroom cupboards?'

'I had to use the loo and I was curious.'

'Anyway, Reg...'

Inspector Venables turned his beady eye back to Thornton.

'... there has been some very funny business going on and I think you and I need to put our heads together for a bit of a confab.'

'Really. Concerning this gentleman? The late, what did you say his name was?'

'You know very well what his name was, though I will repeat it if you insist, Sir Hugo Ingle.'

'With whom you were on a nodding acquaintance.'

'Exactly.'

'You too, Miss Day, I take it you too were on a nodding acquaintance with the deceased.'

'Not really.'

'Then may I henquire as to exactly what the purpose of your visit this evening could have been? Because I am quite sure it wasn't merely a social call and I'm really interested. I mean, what were you talking about with this nodding acquaintance and someone you merely knew in passing as it were?'

'Look, Reg... '

Reg bridled visibly but Thornton, having no immediate reply as to what they talked about, had decided to take the bull by the horns.

'There's no need for an interrogation here,' he said. 'The man obviously died of natural causes which I have no doubt will be confirmed as soon as your doctor gets here, so you can forget about anything suspicious hanging over we two because it doesn't, so there. But I must talk to you about something... '

'All right, we'll leave it at that for the moment, shall we? Should anything unexpected turn up and I need to see you both again I know where to find you. Right? Right. See them out, Roper,' and he turned his back on them.

'You'll be sorry, Reg!' Thornton sang as they went. 'This could have been a big big case for you, the biggest you've ever investigated. It will be left to the city police now. You West-Enders won't get a look in which will be a shame. Wouldn't be surprised if it didn't lead to you being made Commissioner, Chief Constable at least, Order of Merit and all that sort of thing, but there you are, there's none so deaf as those who will not hear. Your memoirs are going to miss a whole chapter.'

And he was gone, leaving a somewhat bemused Reg pulling at his crotch and wondering if he had done the right thing in being so casually dismissive. Well, tomorrow was another day, as Scarlet would have said, he could always pick it up later if he felt so inclined.

He lifted a half open pack of duty free Lucky Strikes from his pocket. He brought his duty free allowance of pipe tobacco back from France and his wife Rita, who didn't smoke, purchased the Lucky Strikes for him. He'd experienced American cigarettes during the war when his parents were presented with them by visiting Yanks and he, as a nipper, would nick them from his dad's chest of drawers. At the duty free he was not tempted to buy any of that continental stuff that smelt like burning socks and set your throat on fire. He knocked a cigarette half out of the pack against the side of his other hand, pulled it out completely by raising the pack to his lips and lit it with his zippo. John Wayne could not have done it better or in more macho style but the doctor, who had just entered the room, looked at him with disgust and said, 'You really ought to cut that out you know, Reg. Not doing you a bit of good.'

God! Reg thought, another bloody health fascist. The day was fast approaching when tobacco would be totally outlawed.

'You'll end up looking like that,' the doc said, indicating the corpse of Sir Hugo Ingle, which he was just about to examine.

'I hope I'll look a lot better than that when I pop my clogs,' Reg said, blowing out a cloud of smoke and suppressing an urge to cough, 'and there's plenty in your profession smoke like bloody chimneys.'

'Don't I know it?' the doctor said, 'and more fool they.'

'It's a case then of don't do as I do, do as I say.' Reg cast an eye in Roper's direction. 'And what's the matter with you, lad?' he asked. 'You're looking decidedly seedy if I may say so. Been smoking too much as well have you?'

If it weren't for the fact that Constable Roper was officially engaged to that piece of Welsh fluff with the singsong voice he would still be having grave doubts about his subordinate's masculinity. 'Want the doc to take a look at you? Drop your trousers and cough, boy. We'll turn our backs.' Reg chuckled, obviously in jolly mood this evening, even in the presence of death.

'He was nearly run over.' It was Jes, breaking silence for the second time.

Venables turned to him. 'Oh?' And then back to Roper. 'How was it you were nearly run over?'

'There was this geyser sitting in his car down the road and obviously keeping a butcher's on what was going on in here,' Jes said.

'So I went to enquire as to his business,' Roper went on, 'but before I could get to him, he started up the motor, pulled out and nearly rammed into me. Quite deliberate it was. I could ha' been killed! And he could see my uniform,' he added plaintively. He had stood up to answer Reg's question and now, as the momentary recollection of his close shave with death was brought home to him, he swayed on rubbery legs.

'All right, lad, all right, take it easy.' Reg was suddenly all avuncular commiseration until Jes made the unfortunate decision of holding out a hand to steady him and his arm went around Roper's waist which immediately roused Reg's suspicions once more. Not two of them in his own force! Perish the thought. Maybe Earls Court was quite the wrong place to have sent them.

'All right, Babcock, you can let your friend go now. He'll be all right. Won't you, Roper?' His tone brooked no argument.

'Yes, sir,' Roper responded feebly, 'but I'd like to get a drink of water if I may.'

'Certainly, lad, certainly, off you go then.'

Roper tottered from the room and Reg was left frowning over the piece of news he had just received. Someone, rather than having to face being questioned by the police, was prepared to commit a nasty hit and run on a member of the force, someone who had been sitting in his car keeping a watch over this particular house. Was Thornton right after all? Was there a lot more to this than meets the eye? Would it have hurt just to listen to what the man had to say? He looked around for an ashtray but there was no sign of one. Sir Hugo was obviously not a smoker. Waste of money. Reg flicked his ash on the carpet that, threadbare as it was, was none the worse for it.

Holly and Thornton were making their way towards Gloucester Road tube station, hoping no one connected with their enquiries was anywhere around who might wonder at their being together in this particular neighbourhood, such a long way from Victoria Park and the city.

'Shall we stop for a nightcap?' Thornton asked as they passed *The Gloucester Arms* and he felt he really could do with a drink.

'Better not,' Holly replied. 'The sooner we're away from here the better. I only hope that nincompoop Venables or that bigger nincompoop Pocock don't spread the word that we were with Sir Hugo this evening. If they do our cover's gone for a burton and we might as well give the whole thing up as a bad job. Quick! There's a cab!'

Thornton stepped off the kerb and raised his hand. The taxi turned towards the pavement and slid to a stop. The driver, right arm casually draped over his steering wheel, leaned over to peer out the nearside window. Thornton leaned in a little to match the driver's movement, his fingers on the back door handle, Holly standing right beside him ready to climb in.

'The Barbican and then Victoria Park, Hackney,' Thornton said, starting to open the door.

'Sorry, guv. Just going off for my tea.'

There was a long moment during which Thornton did not move. Neither did the taxi driver who sat behind his wheel absolutely expressionless.

'Really?' Thornton stood up straight, closed the rear door and returned to his original leaning position. 'Now this is what I always do whenever a cabbie whose light is shining ever so brightly indicating he's for hire informs me he's just going off for his tea, I take his number and report him for refusing a fare when he has made it known he is definitely available. So would you like me to do that?' The driver stared at him. 'You do understand what I am saying. I have made myself quite clear.'

Without a word the cabby switched off his engine, gazed out of his windscreen for a moment as though deep in thought then opened his door, got out of the cab and sauntered around to the pavement to confront Thornton. This was one cabby who couldn't give a toss what Thornton did or threatened to do with recalcitrant taxi drivers. He was at least six foot five and built to match. There was the aura of a seedy gym about him such as is seen in old Hollywood movies where our hero, after a life of dissipation brought on by his girl friend doing the dirty on him is trying to rehabilitate himself and become once more a champion. There was no doubt the cabbie would have floored the intrepid detective with one blow of his very solid knuckles, doing considerable damage or, should he decide alternatively to put Thornton in a bear hug, breaking every rib in his body with consummate ease.

It was Holly who saved the day, stepping between the two men. Thornton had involuntarily backed off a step which gave her just enough room to do that and with her feet planted firmly apart, she faced the giant with, 'If you're not back in your cab by the time I've counted to five you won't be back in it until you come out of hospital, right? Right. One.' He didn't move. 'Two.' He moved. 'Three.' He was around the front. 'Four.' He opened his door. 'Five.' He slammed it shut and started the engine. He was still not going to take them to the East End of London though, it was way out of his patch, and he drove off leaving them standing there, only to stop thirty yards or so down the road to pick up another fare, at the same time giving them a vigorous twos-up as he set off once again.

'Damn it! I should have taken his number.' Thornton fumed.

Tea being obviously deferred for now, they watched the cab pulling away with its lucky passenger.

'Ah, well, thanks, Holly,' Thornton said. 'That could have been a very nasty moment.'

'Not could have, Thornton. Would have.'

'Yes. What would you have done if he'd called your bluff?'

'Bluff? What bluff? Would you like me to demonstrate?'

Without further ado she caught him by the collar of his shirt and twisted the knuckles of her forefingers inwards either side his Adam's apple, at the same time lifting a knee to gently prod his groin and, as he involuntarily moved his pelvis backwards so as to avoid any possible damage, she pretended to give him a head butt that would most certainly have broken his nose. Then she let go and stood back as he sputtered and croaked and fingered his neck.

'Damn it all, Holly you could have given me time to reply.'

It was at this moment that a sporty little bright red Morgan with a wide leather strap around its bonnet to show it was really a very butch little car despite its size, pulled up and a loud cheery voice said, 'Hello there, Mister Charlie Thorpe King! Hail and well met! Having a wee spot of bother then?'

'I wouldn't wear such a long scarf in an open top car if I were you, Adrian. You could do an Isadora Duncan.'

'Don't be absurd. She wasn't driving. She was sitting in the back camping herself silly. Can I give you a lift somewhere?'

'Well that's very kind of you, Adrian but firstly, just how do you squeeze more then two people in that thing?'

'Thing? Thing! I'll have you know, Mister Thornton King, this is a very expensive and exclusive hand assembled motor. None of your Mister Ford assembly line choose any colour as long as it's black for this baby. It is most definitely not - a - thing!' Adrian gave the dashboard an affectionate pat.

'Sorry, Adrian, I apologise if I've hurt its feelings but secondly, we're going to the East End where we happen to live so I think that may be just a mite out of your way. It most certainly was for that bloody taxi driver.'

'As a matter of fact, as luck would have it, this evening it's not out of my way at all. Word has got around via the grapevine and the jungle drums that there's a certain pub, where is it?' He fished in the breast pocket of the Hawaiian shirt he was wearing beneath his fleecy World War Two flying jacket for a slip of paper and looked at it in the glow of the street light. 'Mare Street, wherever that may be, that's supposedly full of the dishiest butchest omies this side of the River Euphrates; you know, plumbers and bricklayers and stevedores, things like that, and one and all of them TBH!' He switched off the engine so that he didn't have to shout though TBH had come out in a rather anticipatory scream. 'Of course there will be the usual hangers on and ever hopefuls (obviously this did not include him) as well as the muscle Marys and the leather queens and the forever wishfuls, poor things, but it so happens I was thinking of trolling over there to take a varda so hop in, one curled up in the back, sitting sideways knees under chin or legs dangling over the side whichever possie you prefer and clinging on for grim death, and one in the front next to me. That will more than likely be you Mister Charlie Thorpe King and I promise to concentrate on my driving and not to grope en route, ha ha ha!'

'Where in the back am I supposed to sit with my knees beneath my chin?'

'Oh, sorry! Custom job. I had it specially modified so I can stuff photographic gear down there and lock it away out of sight. Fortunately it's empty right now. Just lift that thingamajig that looks like a lid and slip in there like a sardine in oil.'

Holly and Thornton did as they were bid, Thornton almost disappearing into the front seat it was screwed so low to the chassis with not all that room for his long legs, and Holly with her knees as directed under her chin. Adrian, started up, slipped his sporty little monster into gear and roared off, almost causing whiplash in his passengers and a couple of cars approaching from behind to screech to a sudden halt.

'It's called *The Bargee's Arms*,' Adrian shouted above the noise of wind and traffic. 'Should have been called The Plumber's Balls really, or The Mechanic's Nuts, something like that, but there you are, no imagination, none at all, these innkeepers, though I'm informed mine host of this particular hostelry is a friend of Dorothy's and really should know better. They have a drag night every Wednesday I am told. Why Wednesday? Beats me. Maybe trade's slack in the middle of the week, but Wednesday it is. Really gross grotty queens, with blue jowls, five o'clock shadow no amount of close shaving or maquillage can camouflage, get up in screaming drag; the full amateurs, my dear, nante talent, no sense of style, no sense at all, and why is it always the ones with enormous hands and feet? And they mime quite hopelessly to Shirley Bassey records, throwing their arms all over the place and pulling faces, fings like that.' With "fings" he was evidently practicing his East End accent in readiness for his entry, although how anyone could possibly mistake Adrian Spangle for a plumber, bricklayer, or stevedore even in his ancient flying jacket was beyond imagination.

'I'm surprised at you,' Thornton chastised. 'I would have thought you'd be more charitable towards your sisters.'

'Sisters!' Adrian shrieked. 'Hark at 'er will you? Sisters! Well, get you, dear! Sisters indeed!' And he burst into gales of laughter, only stopping so that he could go on chattering away as they continued to head east. No one was going to get another word in edgewise so Thornton and Holly both sat back and took stock of where they were at with The Bowmen Of Essex.

CHAPTER SEVEN

'This will do nicely, thank you!' Holly shouted against the wind, having tapped Adrian on the shoulder to get his attention. The little car swerved to the pavement and came to a stop with a too heavy foot on the brake so that both passengers were precipitated towards the front, Holly sideways by only an inch or so as a couple of ribs hit metal, fortunately curved. She felt sure she was going to need her osteopath after this, certainly something for the heavy bruising and she hated to think what the trip had done to her hair. She was inwardly cursing that damned taxi and wishing she had put the boot in as, with Thornton's hand to assist her, she was eased out from the back of the Morgan in very unladylike fashion and stood on the pavement endeavouring to straighten up.

'Well, Adrian, many thanks for the lift. I must say Blackpool's helter-skelter's got nothing on you when it comes to a really thrilling ride and we didn't even have to pay for it.'

'Speak for yourself,' Holly growled, still feeling her bruises.

'I might as well drop off here too,' Thornton continued, 'Holly and I have things to talk about so we'll say good-night.'

'Look at that,' Adrian said, shaking his curly head and with a doleful look on his face as though yet another lover, who only wanted a one-night, stand had just deserted him. 'Will you just take a gander at that? Ugly, ugly, hideously ugly.'

Thornton and Holly both looked around but, apart from some sporadic night traffic, could see nothing they would remotely describe as ugly.

'What do you see that's so ugly?' Thornton asked, completely baffled.

'That! That!' Adrian shrieked, pointing to the high-rise block, pride of the City of London that housed both Holly's and Annette's apartments, two amongst many. Thornton and Holly were totally bemused as they turned to look at it. Had someone committed suicide by dropping from a high place and now, spattered and gory, lay spread-eagled on the sidewalk? They both turned back to look at Adrian.

'Don't you see it?' he asked, exasperation in his voice. 'Ugly ugly concrete: just look at it. We're covering the earth with concrete and it is sooooo ugly. We're chopping down rain forests and hedgerows with gay abandon and covering everything over with concrete as if there is no tomorrow and soon there will be no tomorrow. And just look at the result so far! Ugly ugly. Modern architecture, huh! How can any civilised creature see it and not weep?'

'I don't believe there were any hedgerows or rain forests right here in the middle of London to chop down in the first place, Adrian,' Holly remarked quite mildly. 'If here was previously a bomb site, which most probably it was, there would more than likely have been a bunch of nettles, maybe some brambles, perhaps even a buddleia or two, Black Knight more than likely, and look,' she made a sweeping gesture, 'now there are landscaped gardens and it's all laid out quite tastefully.'

'Tasteful? Tasteful?' Adrian queried with as much scorn in his voice as he could muster.

'Aren't we going just a wee bit over the top, Adrian?' Thornton asked in his usual clod hopping, though he would term it, forthright way.

'Am I? Am I?' Tones of exasperation were giving way to forceful attack. 'Look at that bleak hideous uninviting monotonous grey monstrosity they're building on the South Bank.'

'I don't believe we can see it from here,' Thornton said trying hard to keep a straight face. 'Ouch!' as Holly elbowed him in the ribs.

'How can any thespian worth his or her salt expect to be inspired, to give a performance, I mean a truly great definitive performance worthy of his or her talents, in that cold sterile atmosphere? Could Wolfitt have given his wonderful Lear there?' Adrian decided to give them an example of Wolfitt's Lear. He raised himself to sit on top of his seat, held the dead Cordelia in his arms and went 'Howl howl howl!' into the night.

An approaching couple hastened their footsteps and with anxious glances turned to enter the building. Once through the door they hurried on not daring to look back. Could this be a werewolf in the heart of old London?

'I saw him you know. Oh, yes. I was just a kid, sixpence up in the gods at the old King's Theatre, Hammersmith. Beautiful theatre that was, doesn't exist any more, they pulled it down years ago. I think it's a supermarket now. That's bloody progress for you. Gives my age away as well doesn't it? Now they're putting up things like that! Could Garrick play his Richard Three there? Could Irving play his Hamlet? '

'You saw Irving's Hamlet?' Thornton had the feeling they were going to be there all night if they allowed Adrian to rabbit on in this vein but Adrian ignored this.

'Could Mackie have indulged his pause, his long pause, and his grand pause? I doubt it.'

'A great many people seem to like modern architecture, Adrian.'

'Yes, Germans with their concrete block mentality. That place would have fitted in nicely with The Third Reich. Mussolini was the same, the bigger the blocks the better. It all went with the thrust of his jaw. Prince Charles now, he has artistic integrity, he has taste, refinement, he loathes modern architecture, simply loathes it!' Adrian was a great one for repeating himself for added emphasis.

'Oh, he's told you that personally, has he?'

'Well he could have done considering I was honoured to have taken his portrait once and we chatted away like old friends.'

'I never knew that,' Thornton said. 'That you took his picture I mean, not that you chatted away like old friends.'

'No, but it will one day be common knowledge, won't it? That he hates modern architecture. One day he won't be able to hold in his disgust any longer and I was one of the first in the know.'

'Well it's not all concrete you know, Adrian,' Holly was putting in her penny worth. 'There's lots of lovely glass as well in some modern buildings. Plain glass, tinted glass, reflective glass that gives off wonderful pictures of the passing scene, red double decker buses driving by, cloud formations scudding across the sky.' Poetic though her vision was she couldn't immediately think of anything else. 'You know,' she ended lamely.

'Nash died some years back, Adrian, and not everyone thinks a bijou mews cottage is the be all and end all of design or gracious living you know.'

'There's no need for sarcasm thank you, Charlie.'

'And, although I have to admit Frank Matcham did design some wonderful theatres as opposed to the one you so obviously loathe, and there are plenty of magnificent buildings on the continent, like La Fenice in Venice to name but three, red and gold and drop chandeliers have rather gone out of fashion don't you think?' Holly looked at him questioningly. 'Jolly well de trop as a matter of fact.'

'Merde alors!' Adrian replied, thus proving she wasn't the only one who could indulge in a bit of French one-upmanship. 'And so has the magic,' he sighed and then suddenly seemed to recover his buoyant spirits and with an evening of whatever to look forward to, 'Well, can't sit here chatting all night, fascinating though the conversation may be. Got a date with destiny and a bargee's pole. See you!' with which he put the car in gear and once more sped off, freaking out the drivers of another half dozen vehicles.

Thornton and Holly turned to face each other and burst out laughing.

'Well, you've got to admit, he is quite a character,' Thornton said weakly.

'Yes, and you still haven't filled me in with what went on that night in the bijou mews cottage. Fancy a nightcap?'

'Could do with it now I must admit.'

'Come on then.'

'Howl howl howl!' Thornton cried.

'Shut up, you idiot or you'll be arrested for disturbing the peace.'

*****

It was Rory's birthday and she was throwing a party for a few friends at The Prospect Of Whitby. She had wanted to invite Thornton but hadn't been able to get hold of him. It was a shame she wasn't exactly in a party mood, felt quite melancholy in fact as visions of her dear departed relative kept intruding into her thoughts to dampen her spirits, especially the vision of him sprawled backwards on their kitchen floor. But as the drinks were all on her, not only her friends were having a whale of a time, two or three gatecrashers had decided to join the shenanigans. She eyed them coldly but decided; as it was her birthday and birthdays only come around once a year, she would just let them get on with it? If they grew too boisterous with the intake of alcohol or overstepped the mark in ordering expensive drinks, she might throw a wobbler and possibly a punch or two, though the landlord wouldn't appreciate that so, for the moment, she sat alone at a table, kept quiet, and wondered how Thornton was getting on.

She had of course invited the McIvors but only Iris had shown up. Too bad but it was evidently a busy night and Jimmy was mini-cabbing, Iris had informed her as she handed over the McIvor's birthday present, a bottle of cheap perfume bought off a barrow in Shepherds Bush market, which Rory most certainly would never use.

Iris now sat in her best bib and tucker; a vision in a snazzy black number that looked as though it had come out of her mother's wardrobe, with buttons of jet and a once snowy white, now faintly yellowing fichu of broderie Anglais, great gear for a party. Mind you, looking at what some of the kids were wearing she wasn't all that out of place, any amount of it could have come from charity shops, second-hand market stalls, car boot, and jumble sales. Iris sat nursing her rum and black currant and eyeing purse-lipped and with obvious disdain the antics got up to by what was mostly the younger generation.

Rory invited the McIvors because she was a firm believer in the levelling of the classes, which was why one of her favourite charities was in aid of India's untouchables. Why should an accident of birth, caste, or wealth put a barrier between people who could be friends? If the French could go around yelling about equality and fraternity, even if they didn't actually practice what they preached (but then who does?) why couldn't the rest of the world? Rory sighed and lifted the glass of house red to her mouth. This wine definitely was not amabile.

Some of the Bruces and the Sheilas from Sydney, Melbourne and Adelaide via Earls Court had also discovered The Prospect Of Whitby and a group of them were outside braving the freezing night air, gazing at the river and chorusing billabong type songs. When they heard it was Rory's birthday they broke drunkenly into happy birthday to you, starting off much too high, as is usually the case, so that the men could never reach the top notes. Not that it really mattered it was so out of tune anyway, but it was a nice gesture and got them a free round of drinks.

While all this was going on Mike Aliff and Jimmy McIvor were sitting in Jimmy's new car, chain smoking and keeping an eye on the entrance to Thornton's block of flats. Every now and again Mike would look up at the darkened windows as if suddenly they might blaze forth with light but they remained stubbornly dark. They didn't talk much. Well they hardly had mutual grounds for conversation: an English ex-public school boy and Oxford graduate though not exactly with a first in history, working for Her Majesty's Secret Service, and a dour Scot from the Gorbals brought up in a family consistently on welfare and living on a diet of cigarettes and chips. One into rugby and cricket, the other into football.

The driver's window was open half an inch to act as a ventilator though, every now and again, it had to be wound down to its fullest extent for a few seconds to allow the build up of smoke to escape.

Thornton's office had been watched all day but there had been no sign of him and he certainly wasn't at home this evening.

'How long are we going to sit here?' Jimmy growled. 'We're out of fags,' and he lowered the window once more to toss out the screwed-up empty packet.

*****

'I wonder how Adrian's getting on,' Thornton said, for want of nothing better to say.

'Like the proverbial house on fire I would think. Here...' She handed Thornton a drink before seating herself with her own and raising her glass. 'Cheers!'

'Cheers!'

'Right, six impossible things before breakfast. What do we do next?'

'Well I hate to say this, Holly, but I think the only course of action open to us is for you to act as bait once more and hope this

144

time we land the fish.'

'Us, huh? Course of action open to us. Did I hear you aright?'

'Maybe you can get your Matthew…'

'Maurice.'

'Matthew, Marvin, Maurice, shmorris, to open up and let a few cats out of the bag.'

'Maybe Steve Timpson's the one to pump.'

'Who he?'

'Coach. Ex-Olympic Games. Didn't win anything, not even a bronze, but at least he was good enough to be part of the British team. British teams, athletes, never do seem to win very much come to think of it. It's the taking part that matters not the winning, huh? What shit! When last did a Brit win Wimbledon? Fred Perry was it? Back in the nineteen thirties? Anyway, I'll ask for a session with him and see where it gets me, okay? And while I am out there still pretending to be Carmen, what, sir, will you be up to if I may be so bold as to ask?'

'Probably doing a bit of snooping of my own.'

It was a statement so vague Holly rolled her eyes and took a goodly mouthful of her gin and Italian. 'Well, if I am going to make an early start, we'd best call it a night.' She got up and headed for the kitchen to rinse out her glass and leave it upside down on the drainer. 'You can have the sofa if you want. Save you having to trek home. There's a new toothbrush in the bathroom. Don't use mine. I love you dearly but not enough to let you use my toothbrush.'

'I've got a better idea. Can I use your phone?'

'I don't know whether or not you can but you certainly may. Just make sure you pull the door properly closed when you leave and I wish you joy of her. Good night.' With which she disappeared in the direction of her bedroom and shut the door.

Thornton got up, shifted over to the sofa and pulled the phone on the coffee table towards him. He dialled and waited but didn't have to wait long. The phone at the other end rang twice before the receiver was lifted and a husky voice said: 'Well, and about time too.'

'How did you know it was me?'

'Wishful thinking.'

'I'm not disturbing you?'

'Thornton you always disturb me, in the most delightful way.'

He was already beginning to feel a bit disturbed himself and wondered whether or not as foreplay he should try a bit of dirty talk on the phone before the real thing.

'Are you in bed?'

'No, but maybe I will be by the time you get here.'

'What are you doing now then; right this very minute?' Thornton had never indulged in sex talk on the telephone and, being a complete novice, this was meant to be her cue to start his balls rolling. It was a total failure.

'Talking to you on the telephone,' she said, 'what else?' He heard a chuckle at the other end. 'No, as a matter of fact,' she went on, 'I've been catching up on some legal work but I needed an excuse to stop. Where are you?'

'Closer than you think. If I had wings I would fly to you.'

'How romantic.'

'But as I am a mere mortal and have no feather or wax I will take an elevator down, a short walk across and an elevator up and be with you in a matter of minutes.'

'The door, as ever for you, will be open.' She put down the receiver.

Thornton did as he was ordered and made sure he closed Holly's door very carefully behind him. He heard the click of the lock but nevertheless gave it a good flat-handed shove to make sure. He took the lift down, walked his short walk, and took the lift up in Annette's block. He was about to knock on her door when he realised that, as good as her word, she had left it open. He walked in, closing it behind him.

If he had any ideas about hopping straight into bed or starting proceedings then and there with a frenzied disrobing and a bonk on the couch or even the floor ala a Hollywood director's fantasy, he was doomed to disappointment. True she had lit a couple of scented candles to give the room an aromatic romantic feel but she had also opened a bottle of champagne chilled to exactly the right temperature and two flutes were already on her coffee table, beaded to the brim and just waiting to be picked up and sampled. In fact, before he could even get close enough to gently kiss her, let alone search for her tonsils, she had a glass in one hand obviously meant for herself and was holding the other out towards him. He took it.

'To us,' she whispered, raising her glass, her eyes never leaving his face.

'To us,' he said, wishing he had spent more time on the telephone, and knocked it back much too fast. The result was that, within seconds, everything in the room had taken on the fluid quality of a Dali painting except that it wasn't a static picture in a frame but kept undulating alarmingly, and then the room did a three hundred and sixty degree turn before Thornton's nose hit the carpet.

She hadn't pulled a gun on him but she had pulled something just as lethal and much more sophisticated.

'It's time to call a mini-cab,' she said, smiling down at the prostrate form. 'Too bad, but business is business.' She lifted the phone and dialled. 'Come and collect,' she said, 'I have the goods for transport right here.'

*****

The party was over. Iris McIvor, still hatchet faced, if not more so after four or five or even more (she had lost count after the second) rum and blackcurrants, had said her good-nights and thank you to Rory and had been collected and whisked away by her Jimmy, for some reason looking very pleased with himself. The genuine friends, false friends, freebooters and gatecrashers, the Bruces and the Sheilas had all departed, heading up West. The pub was closed although there were still lights inside as the staff went about clearing away and cleaning up after a very busy night, before they could make their own footsore weary way home.

Rory had settled the quite hefty bill, an amount that would have lasted Thornton a couple of weeks quite comfortably without being in the least bit abstemious, and now she sat as she liked to do some nights, gazing at the river and meditating, thinking of past, present, and future. The evening, as far as she was concerned, had not been a success. Her mood had not allowed it and, still depressed, she wondered why she had even bothered. She also wondered why Jimmy hadn't come and then arrived all smiles to collect his wife. Couldn't he have taken one night off? And why Iris, after her original greetings, had kept her distance, getting steadily more sloshed on her favourite tipple. Obviously on pub nights and singsongs in their own local once a week Jimmy kept her on a tight rein so, unchecked as she was this evening, she had felt free to indulge. Rory looked down at the bottle of scent in her hand, unscrewed the cap, took a sniff, pulled a wry face, and dropped the bottle in the river. The tide was going out and below her a stretch of mud was showing under the wall, black and glistening in reflected light and already starting to reveal cans, bottles, broken toys, perambulators and other thoughtlessly discarded trash. She felt a small pang of guilt that she had added to it.

Did they really use to chain criminals down there she wondered, leaning right forward to inspect the wet stone, so that the incoming tide drowned them? Saved an executioner's fee if nothing else she supposed. She shuddered as she imagined the prisoners trying to hold their heads above the steadily rising water, hoping against hope a miracle would save them.

Old Father Thames had certainly seen a lot of history and a great deal of human folly in his many years as he just kept rolling along. He had seen the Romans come and go. He had seen Celts, Saxons, Normans, Hollanders, and Huguenots fleeing religious massacres, Jewish refugees fleeing persecution. He had seen the plagues and the great fire. He had seen the people rowed through Traitors Gate into The Tower with only the sound of the oars to break the stillness of the night, to suffer the thumbscrews and the exquisite tortures of the queen's Rackmaster that left them crippled or never to be seen again. He had witnessed the flowering of Elizabethan drama. Down at Deptford maybe he knew of the murder of Christopher Marlowe. He had flowed beneath London Bridge and seen the heads and the quarters rotting on spikes. He had been polluted to such an extent with offal and human excrement that nothing was left alive in his poisonous waters, but then there had been a start in cleaning him up somewhat so at least the fish were starting to come back.

He had seen the city of London grow out of all proportion. A dozen times or more in the fiercest winters he had frozen over to such an extent that Frost Fairs were held. Horse and carriage could safely pass over from one side to the other, market stalls were set up on the ice to sell all manner of goods, there was skating and sledging and boys played football and shooting at the mark. Tradition has it that Queen Elizabeth herself walked on the ice. Cleopatra's Needle had been raised and period museum warships were tethered to his banks. He passed by the Houses of Parliament and flowed beneath numerous bridges. He had moved majestically on through the Blitz his waters reflecting red from the fires, the glow illuminating the silhouette of Saint Paul's cathedral. How small, how insignificant is each individual's history, Rory thought, and she was wondering just what the point of this evening could have been and it was time to head for home when she heard a loud splash a little further upstream.

Rory, stone cold sober, which was just as well, got to her feet and went to investigate.

*****

Myrtle Cullen was busy fussing over her guests as they sat down to breakfast in the hotel's elegant dining room: curtains of shot silk with swagged pelmets and broad tiebacks: pink damask, Waterford crystal, Queen's Pattern cutlery, fresh flowers; when the bell sounded in reception. She firmly believed that, as proprietor of the Hotel Diana, it was up to her personally and at any hour of the day or night to see that every one of her guests was completely satisfied, especially considering the amount they were paying for their comfortable home away from home. There was of course the usual Continental breakfast available consisting of fresh fruit juice, brioche, croissant, preserves and coffee, but as her guests came from far and wide she could serve a kosher breakfast when wanted and even supply halal meat if required. Diabetics, vegetarians and even vegans were catered for though her personal taste ran to a substantial serving of good old-fashioned English bacon and eggs. She simply doted on bacon. She remember a bar Mitzvah party she once went to many years back that the local reporter, a cub of course who didn't know any better and who got a right bollocking when the complaints came flooding in, informed his paper's readers, ended with an egg and bacon breakfast. Her mother nearly fainted on the spot and her wig practically flew across the room when she read it, and her father forbade her to have anything more to do with that particular family, an order she secretly ignored.

It was all a load of old superstition really was her belief. Of course

149

the dietary laws in the heat of a virtually waterless landscape were logical once upon a time among other more practical considerations: like keeping goats, sheep, and camels is all very well but pigs in the desert? Animals that need cool and shade and plenty of water? To keep pigs would have been swinishly anti-social and, if you don't keep them to eat, what's the point of keeping them? The fact that a god was killed by a wild boar on Mount Lebanon and then was said to inhabit the body of the beast was merely another figment of man's overwrought mystic imagination and his attempt to explain purely natural phenomena, frightening though they may be, by supernatural means. But now, she assured herself, it was just tradition and she wasn't going to give up her love of bacon for the sake of tradition. Anyway, it didn't matter anymore. She was beyond the pale. She had married outside the faith and was no longer daughter, sister, cousin, or aunt. In many ways it was a great pity. There were still members of her orthodox Stamford Hill family she was very fond of but for them she simply no longer existed. She always had been the wilful child and they had always known she would come to no good.

Once parted from her family and married with her husband's money behind her, but before she took on the Hotel Diana for something to occupy herself, she had studied comparative religion at her redbrick university and the more she studied and the more she pondered, the more she realised what a load of old hocus-pocus it all was. Take fundamentalists for example, of which there are millions, particularly in the land of the free, who accept implicitly every word of the Bible; how can they possibly believe, considering the logistics required, that Noah and his ark is anything other than yet another myth? In the first place is there any mention in the Bible about the billion insects both flying and crawling that needed to be accommodated if they were to reproduce after the flood? Some were naturally accommodated of course, like fleas and ticks, and intestinal worms but it was a golden opportunity for God to get rid of some pretty obnoxious creep-crawlies like mosquitoes and locusts but he obviously had no intention of doing that. Maybe he needed them up his sleeve for a few future plagues. Secondly, old Noah and family might have been able to round up pairs of African animals, even from as far away as The Cape Of Good Hope, particularly if the hand of God was shooing them in the right direction; and they could have been collected from the east as well; tigers from India for example, pandas from China, maybe even orang-utans from Borneo, but how in hell's name did they get Kiwis from new Zealand and Kangaroos from Australia, let along Tasmanian Devils and Tiger Snakes? There was an awful lot of ocean to cross before the rains even started. And what about the South American fauna, possums for instance and giant anacondas? Animals coming from Chile would have had to make their way the full length of the continent all the way up to Panama, cross over into North America, continue further north into Canada, the Arctic Circle and then, those that hadn't died of exhaustion, dehydration frozen to death or been eaten on the way, then descended through Europe. Just how long would that journey take? Would they make it? Highly doubtful. What, for instance, if it were the giant anacondas that ate the possums on the way and stopped for a snooze, so missing the boat? Thirdly there was the problem of feeding once on board, particularly the carnivores of which there were a great many? How did old Noah manage it? Prepacked meat and tons and tons of fodder for the vegetarians and nuts and bananas for the apes? A modern container ship couldn't hold the amount required for forty days and forty nights let alone keep it from going off if not refrigerated. What stopped them from eating each other? That's what nature is all about, eat or be eaten. And just think of what came out the other end, the amount of waste all those creatures would have produced. By the time the boat was beached on Mount Ararat, if beached could be the right expression for parking on a mountain peak, it must by then have been an ex-floating cesspit. There simply would not have been enough hands or time to get rid of it all and one solitary pair of dung beetles and bluebottle flies, supposing they had made it, would have been totally inadequate. Yet there are people who still insist on believing that all that lives in this day and age are descended from that little old ark, the animals and the insects and the birds and, of course, Noah and family, all making their way back to their original habitat to start all over again.

It was the beautiful silk wall covering in the dining room with its highly colourful decoration of grinning stylised apes, and cockatoos in various poses amongst tropical greenery, flying with wings outstretched or roosting on branches, that had set her off along these trains of thought but the sound of another prolonged ring on the bell interrupted her musings. She excused herself with a smile from the folk seated at the nearest table, took a quick look around to make sure the waitresses in their nippy costumes, a gesture towards the long lost and lamented Lyons Corner Houses, were on the ball, and left for reception.

A rather large middle-aged gentleman with a florid complexion and giving the appearance of being either constipated or in an extremely bad mood was standing at her marble topped counter.

'Good morning,' Myrtle greeted him with a beaming smile only to receive a cold stare in exchange and then,

'Yes. I've come to see Miss Hernandez.'

'Who?'

'I thought you would say that. She's not registered here.' He lifted half the book off the counter to indicate he had been going through it and let it drop again as though it were something not quite nice. By this time Myrtle was around the other side and she pulled the book protectively towards her and slammed it shut.

'You should not have been looking at that,' she admonished him, her eyes like slits. 'That is private and confidential.'

'Miss Hernandez informed me that this is the hotel where she is staying while in London so, if she is not here, where can she be? Being who she is I fully realise her reasons for secrecy but is it possible you can inform me as to where I might find her?'

My goodness, Myrtle thought, doesn't he even stop to draw breath? Aloud she said, 'If you don't mind my saying so, sir, I do not appreciate your tone of voice. If you cannot address me in a polite manner I have no objections to your leaving right now. You mention her reason for secrecy and then you wonder why she isn't registered under her own name.' Myrtle was whispering, leaning forward and casting a look around to make sure no one else was within earshot and hoping to cover up the unfortunate glitch in her memory, and it was precisely at this moment that Holly breezed in through the street door.

'HOLLY!' Myrtle yelled.

Maurice, who had turned his head to see who had entered, now swivelled it a hundred and eighty degrees the other way.

'What did you say?'

'What?'

'I asked you what you just said.'

'When?'

'This very second, woman! This very second!'

'I would appreciate it, sir, if you did not address me as woman and, if you want me to repeat myself, I said golly. Satisfied?'

'Good morning, Carmen,' Maurice said and then turned once more to Myrtle. 'And just why, when Miss Hernandez appeared, did you feel the need to say golly?'

'Because I was not expecting her back until this evening so it was a surprise. I often say golly when I am taken by surprise, pleasant or unpleasant. I am surprised I didn't say golly when you first addressed me. I have some messages for you, Car-men. She proceeded to collect them from a pigeonhole and hand them over, at the same time giving Maurice a look that said all right? Satisfied now?

'I think I know who all these are from,' Holly said casting a slightly coquettish look in Maurice's direction. 'But what on earth are you doing here this hour of the morning?'

'I thought, if you're going to the club this morning, I'd offer you a lift. Save you having to drive.'

'That's very sweet of you, Maurice... Oh, by the way... Myrtle, this is Mister Maurice Chinnery... Maurice, Myrtle Cullen, proprietor of the hotel.'

'How do you do?' Maurice said. 'And apologies for being so abrupt with you to begin with, only isn't it the law that persons must register in hotels? But there you go, no harm done I suppose.'

'No harm done. Think no more of it,' Myrtle purred, so long as you don't call me woman again. Take a card.' She lifted one from its receptacle on the counter and handed it to him. He studied it at arms length.

'Strange coincidence, Carmen, that you should be staying in the Hotel Diana.'

'Oh? Why would that be?'

'Don't you know your mythology then? Diana, or Artemus to give her her Greek name, goddess of the hunt and a most disagreeable and vindictive lady. She didn't just hunt game, but anyone who displeased her was likely to end up on the sharp end of one of her arrows. Poor old Actaeon just happened to admire her whilst she was bathing and she took affront at being seen naked by a mortal, she was a virgin you know and such a prude, so turned him into a stag and shot him dead. There you go. I hope you don't turn out to be a latter day Diana who might take a pot shot at some poor old Actaeon.'

'Don't even say such things. Anyway, how do you know about Greek myths if you're not a literary bloke?'

'Myths aren't literature.'

'Fair enough, if that's what you think. As for the lift, Maurice, if you won't be too offended, I would rather make it under my own steam. That way I'm a free agent and not beholden to anyone for bringing me back.'

'Understood. Just thought... Right, well I'll be on my way then. See you there. A good morning to you, Mrs...' He glanced down at the card in his hand, 'Cullen,' turned and left the hotel.

They waited until sure he was really gone before Myrtle broke the silence.

'Oh. Holly, I'm so sorry!'

'Sorry?'

'I nearly spoiled everything. Just wasn't thinking. But it was all right in the end, wasn't it?'

'I'm sure. Even if he doubted you I do think he would believe anything I said.'

'Just as well you came strolling in like that. What are you doing here anyway?'

'Came to collect these,' Holly said, waving the notes in her hand, 'before his suspicions were really aroused.'

'I think he was pretty suspicious already, poking his nose into the register like that.'

'I'm surprised he hasn't thought of booking himself in for a couple of nights just to make sure and be near his Carmen.'

'He's got it that bad, has he?'

'He's besotted if you ask me and, if he tries to pull that trick, Myrtle, you know what to do.'

'Sure thing. Hotel's full.'

'On the other hand, should his chauffeur... Oh, skip it, just wishful thinking. Right, as the man said, I'll be off then.'

'How are you getting on with whatever it is you're doing?'

'Forty-eight hours at the very most, Myrtle and, if we haven't solved it by then, we'll just have to forget the whole damn thing. Ciao, baby!' And Holly was gone.

Thornton woke up with a splitting headache and a mouth that tasted like a drain, or was it his body that smelt like a drain. It was difficult to tell. He lifted a hand to his eyes and tried to press the pain from them with thumb and forefinger before sitting up and taking a look around. Where was he? The first attempt was a failure and, eyes closed, he flopped back on the pillows to remain there for a while before opening his eyes a second time. The curtains had not been properly drawn and, in what dim light came through the slit, he seemed to recognise the room as it came into focus.

He had been there before but it was not until he saw the King Charles spaniel sitting on the duvet between his legs and gazing at him with an unblinking stare that recognition struck. It appeared to Tiddlywinks at that moment that the visitor had come to his senses and was worth approaching for possibly a bit of a cuddle so he got up, stretched back legs one at a time, and moved his position to apply pressure to Thornton's crotch where he lay down again and wagged his tail. As Thornton's bladder was full to bursting this was the very last place Tiddly should have chosen and Thornton who desperately needed to get up and head for the bathroom wasn't quite sure what to do. He could give the beast a pat on the head or a scratch behind the ear but would it snap at his fingers again? Or he could throw back the duvet and immure the little bugger in its feathery folds. He decided a few judicious pats in order to cement a budding friendship could be the order of the day and proceeded to do just that. Tiddly on his part, in order to cement the budding friendship, gave the stroking hand a lick and to Thornton's immense relief, jumped off the bed and headed for the door. Thornton threw back the duvet and headed for the bathroom on very wobbly legs. He wasn't sure he could face the pictures and He stopped halfway there to look down at himself. Oh, my God! he thought. I'm stark bollock naked!

CHAPTER EIGHT

Holly stepped out of the hotel Diana and pulling up the collar of her coat on a clear and frosty morning headed for the station wagon. It had been completely cleared of Thornton's old greatcoat, fishing hat, and any other rubbish he had accumulated during his one day outing including pieces of trodden, torn and muddy pages from that day's *Times*, ice cream wrappers, Smarties tubs, empty bottles, wet-wipes and a handkerchief that was in desperate need of the laundry. Why were men such slobs, so oblivious to how gross some of their habits were? Mind you, men could retaliate by mentioning spilt powder, lipstick on cups and glasses, hair in the bathroom plugholes and smalls hanging up over the bath to dry. Whoever insists there is no difference between the sexes talks out of his and her respective hats. For proof just observe children in a swimming pool. Small girls shriek at the top of their voices even before anything like a good wetting happens or they've put a tentative toe in the water and they keep it up at great length; small boys do not shriek. They might yell every now and again but then they don't keep it up at any great length. Energy is needed for other things like teasing the girls or beating up on one another.

Holly arrived at the car and stared at the windscreen and the message left for her under the wiper. A ticket? A bloody parking ticket at this hour of a frosty morning? Good grief! She hadn't been gone more than ten minutes! Well maybe a little more but even so, what was London coming to? She reached out for it only to have it taken out of her hand and a voice, for which there was no adequate description except in a Mills And Boon novel, said

'The boss will take care of that.'

Holly almost gave vent to her own shriek, one befitting a preteen catching sight of her favourite pop star or all four Beatles at one go, and could have swooned on the spot if she didn't have such self-control. His smile was devastating. In taking the ticket his hand had actually touched hers. Touched it! If she were a blooming teenager she would swear never to wash her hand ever again. She leaned against the station wagon and wondered what would happen if she threw an arm around his neck and kissed him full on that gorgeous Cupid's bow mouth. Not only that but if she managed to get her tongue beyond the double barrier of his teeth. They were standing that close together it didn't seem such an impossibility. The fantasy was abruptly terminated by a loud and obviously impatient blast on the Rolls' horn (produced from the back seat by jabbing with the end of a shooting stick) that she noticed for the first time was parked a short distance away. She turned her head towards it and gave a weak wave as Albert, always alert to the main chance and finding Holly an extremely attractive prospect, whispered in the nearest ear,

'See you at the club, Miss.'

'Holly.' She whispered back.

'Miss Holly.'

And went back to his, or rather his boss's, motor.

Thornton had rinsed out his mouth, taken a quick shower, made a thorough mess of the bathroom and was back in bed with the duvet pulled well up when there was a polite knock on the door and Rory entered with a tray.

'Good morning! Tiddlywinks told me you were up,' she said.

'Oh, yes? Clever dog. How did he do that?'

'He came downstairs so as soon as I saw he'd left you I knew you were awake. How are you feeling?'

'Lousy.'

'Not in the least surprising seeing as to how you decided to go for a midnight swim in that poisonous old river and probably swallowed half of it. I'm actually surprised you're still alive. Luckily Adrian's trick last night happens to be a doctor, a very handsome one at that I may add. Wasn't that too lucky for words? And he took a good look at you.'

'I'm not surprised. I'm stark naked. Was I skinny-dipping?'

'No.'

'Then where are my clothes?'

'Drying. They went through the washing machine to get rid of the muck from the river and now they're drying. He decided, the doctor that is, you would do so long as we kept an eye on you so we put you to bed and took turns to keep watch. If you did swallow any filth from the river I think you must have vomited it all up on the way here. My car's a sodding mess. There is no way I am going to go anywhere near it. I'm surprised I managed to drive it here without hawking and making matters worse. Had all the windows wide open of course. It will have to be towed away and cleaned up before I can use it again and I won't envy those who have to do it. Sit up please this tray is getting heavy. Anyway, he's still here, the doctor, having breakfast downstairs so he'll probably look in again before he leaves.'

Thornton sat up, reached behind him, pulled out a pillow and placed it on his lap. She put the tray down on top of it. Thornton looked at it and decided scrambled egg on toast was not for him at that moment but he would certainly appreciate a cup of tea. Rory seated herself on the edge of the bed causing a sudden deep depression in the mattress that tilted so alarmingly Thornton had to quickly snatch at the tray to stop it toppling over. Keeping a firm grip on it with one hand and deciding the bed was not going to move any further he poured himself a cup of Earl Grey and said, 'And when you weren't taking turns in watching me, where did you all sleep?'

'I had the tiny guest room, pretty isn't it? and the boys slept downstairs, when they did sleep that is.'

'Boys?'

'All right then, fellas, guys, blokes, chaps, men, omies, whatever. The couch is convertible. It was jolly nice of Adrian to give you his bed I must say. I'm surprised though that Adrian hasn't taken to the futon. They seem to be so much in fashion these days. Aren't you going to eat your egg?'

'If you don't mind, no. My stomach is in no fit state.'

'Okay, I'll have it then. It's one of Adrian's specialities and he'll be ever so disappointed if the plate doesn't go back downstairs nice and clean.'

'As long as, between mouthfuls, you tell me the tale of Thornton King and Old Father Thames.'

'Well then...' She took her first forkful... 'it would seem whenever I sit on the river bank and think things over...' there was a pause to chew and swallow... 'something happens, like the night Sir Roger was killed and then, last night, you.' Another pause for another forkful. Thornton didn't think he could stand it and gently removed the plate from her hand and replaced it on the tray. She looked at it for a moment and then surrendered and went on. 'I was sitting there just lost in thought and what happened was I heard this splash, quite a loud splash, so I went to investigate and found you just about to float out to the estuary or the English Channel or somewhere like that. The tide was going out you see. I managed to haul you on to a slipway thank goodness, though it was quite a job. But there was no one else around so it was up to me and fortunately I found a boathook nearby. I'm afraid your jacket is a mess. I saw you were still breathing and rushed back to the Prospect for help. Fortunately some of the young staff were still there and they came running after I hammered on the door and heard "we're closed," yelled out a number of times. It wasn't until I shouted "emergency" that my call was answered. Anyway, to cut a long story short, they wanted to call an ambulance but, knowing what I know and not wanting anyone else to know it, I persuaded them to help me put you in my car. What to do next was the question. I don't know where you live so I couldn't take you home and, anyway, I didn't think that was too good an idea. I didn't think your being in the river was an accident and, if I took you home, who knows? Maybe there would be another attempt on your life. I have to admit it was a pretty amateurish attempt when you come to think of it, what with the tide going out and the water so low and they could at least have hung about to make sure you were well and truly on your way. But then I suppose they thought the best plan was to scarper before someone inadvertently came along.'

'Like you.'

'Like me. Going back to my place seemed just as dangerous if the McIvors had anything at all to do with your being in the water, and a hotel was also out of the question. Sure enough there would be someone on the night staff who would phone a pal in Fleet Street and say something fishy was going on and the next thing you know it would be all over the front page of *The Sun*. "Aurora Pemberton, niece to the late Sir Roger Pemberton, the scientist who died recently under suspicious circumstances, found in hotel room with unconscious man soaked from head to toe," or words to that effect.'

'A little literate for Sun readers wouldn't you say?'

'Also I would need help getting you out of the car and that's why I thought of Adrian. I wouldn't say he was exactly over the moon to see us but, little sweetheart that he is, he introduced me to his doctor friend, who is also called Adrian by the way, isn't that a coincidence?'

'Isn't it? He's not from Barts is he?'

'I do believe he is.'

'Well well well, small world. Who would have guessed?'

'Now what happened before I heard that splash I have no idea but I have a shrewd suspicion the McIvors did have something to do with it.'

'No,' Thornton took another sip of his tea. 'It was Annette, the bitch. She handed me a spiked drink in such a way I never for a moment thought it could be anything but a glass of pure chilled champagne lovingly handed to me, straight out of the bottle sitting there so innocently in its ice bucket. She was holding another glass for herself.' He shrugged. 'What could I have done even if I had had doubts? Spilt it accidentally on purpose I suppose and I wonder what would have happened then. Stabbed to death with an ice pick?'

He thought back to a night when a cute little vixen he had taken back to his flat, under the impression she had given him that he was saving her from the gravest danger, expected him to drink from a glass of spiked brandy and, when he didn't, pulled a gun on him. That little escapade could have ended in tragedy. Well, it did later but fortunately not for him. 'How did I get from Annette's apartment to end up in the Thames?'

'By mini-cab I would imagine.'

'Of course. Jimmy McIvor.'

'Hmn-Hmn. It's a pity it wasn't his car you puked all over. Anyway, he called in at the Prospect earlier to collect Iris, supposedly to take her home, so it must have been at least those two. I had the feeling she was behaving very strangely all evening but just put it down to the rum and blackcurrants. If anyone else was involved we don't know who it could have been, do we?'

'Maybe, maybe not. I think I can hazard a pretty shrewd guess though. Want to finish your eggs now?'

Rory pulled a face. 'No thank you, gone cold.'

'Okay, so what happens next?'

A familiar voice came from the doorway. Thornton turned to see both Adrians standing there, photographer Adrian with an arm around the medicine man's waist, Doctor Adrian with one arm casually on photographer Adrian's shoulder. They made a handsome pair.

'Next you get examined by my friend Adrian Rutherford, MD. FRCS. and other degrees too numerous to mention.' He pushed his new friend into the room. 'He's a specialist in anatomy... mine. How are you feeling Charlie?'

'Adrian, isn't it time you stopped calling me Charlie?'

'I don't know. I rather like you as a Charlie. You must be a bit of a Charlie, falling into the Thames in the middle of the night. What on earth were you up to? Did you fall or were you pushed?'

Thornton turned to the other Adrian and pulled a wry face. The other Adrian had meanwhile walked around the bed and taken Thornton's wrist to feel his pulse. He smiled, glancing at the scar on Thornton's forehead.

'Did a pretty neat sewing job there did I not? Another year or so you won't even notice it.' He looked at his watch, waited, nodded, and dropped the arm.

'You'll do, though it's a bloody miracle, that's all I can say. You didn't take anything last night did you?'

'Well of course I did but not on purpose. I was doped by a bloodsucking harpy from hell so don't ask me what it was.'

'Bloodsucking? Is that what you call it?' Adrian number one giggled.

'Whatever, it would no doubt have come out in an autopsy,' said Adrian number two. 'In fact if I had my kit with me we could take a blood sample now, take it to the hospital and find out what it was.'

'Forget it, Adrian. It's over.'

'Right then, must get weaving. I'm due at work half an hour ago. Hope there haven't been too many emergencies. Don't think so, my bleeper hasn't sounded off. Will you see me out, Adrian?'

'Of course, Adrian,' and the two Adrians started to go. At the door, medical Adrian turned back.

'Thank Rory for saving your life, Thornton.'

'Thank you for saving my life,' Thornton said.

*****

'This, my friends…'

There was a general stirring and shuffling around the table; the casting of anxious sideways glances, never before had the chairman addressed members of the board as "his friends." Something was seriously wrong.

'… constitutes the gravest situation this company has ever had to face and most of it unfortunately is down to one of our members who for the moment will remain anonymous but who has partly redeemed himself and remedied the situation somewhat by a process of liquidation.'

Sir Peter poured himself a glass of water from the carafe in front of him and took a sip while he waited for the brilliance of his pun to sink in. It didn't, except for Mike who looked around the table and smirked in a self-congratulatory way that was totally nauseous. No one noticed that either. Their attention was riveted on the glass of water Sir Peter was holding. Water? This was a new one as well. Before today no one had ever seen Sir Peter drink water at a board meeting. They waited as he raised the glass and took another mouthful.

'Gentlemen…' ah, that was more like it, tension eased somewhat. '… I regret I have to inform you that, although the company will carry on with business as usual along the lines of legitimate financial dealings…' general laughter, smiles all around, even Wee Willie managing a sort of sickly grimace that passed for a smile… 'and all that implies, our sideline money-spinner for the time being will have to be put on hold. That is, after we have made just one more transaction. I am fully aware this is tempting fate but, being a gambling man at heart, as are we all, I simply cannot resist the challenge. This last transaction will be an extremely large one, probably the largest we have ever made and will concern a certain South American heiress by the name of Carmen Hernandez.'

162

*****

Thornton put on his dry clothes. Each garment could have done with a good pressing and, as Rory had warned him, there was a large rip in his jacket but neither Rory nor Thornton were adept when it came to sewing or ironing. She used a valet service that was currently out of reach and there was no time, he felt, to send out his gear anyway. He was eager to get moving. Holly would by now, he was certain, be on her way to The Bowmen Of Essex Archery Club and he wasn't sure he shouldn't be hanging around keeping a brotherly eye on her. On the other hand she was the consummate professional and he really shouldn't worry too much. Perhaps, he thought, he ought to stay in town and rattle a few bars, shake a few trees, see what came tumbling down. He knew now more or less who the principals were in this little affair but exactly what lay behind it, what their hold was on certain people like Sir Roger, Sir Hugo, that he still didn't know. Hazarding shrewd guesses was one thing, acquiring desired proof another. He would make his way out to Epping later in the day and for that he would need a car so first a visit to Harold Norris was necessary but, carrying his breakfast tray in slightly trembling hands, after all it had been a pretty rough night one way or another, he wasn't going to get further than downstairs where Adrian and Rory were having a serious conversation over their morning coffee.

'Am I interrupting?' Thornton asked.

'Not at all,' Rory replied. 'We're just discussing what route to take as the best course of action.'

'The best course of action would be... Oh!...' He broke off. 'Where should I put this?'

'Here, I'll take it.' Adrian got to his feet, took the tray and headed for the galley.

'You didn't eat the lovely eggs I prepared especially for you,' he complained. 'Never mind, they will be a delicious treat for Tiddly.'

Thornton noticed Adrian was wearing very large furry bunny slippers and as he moved Tiddly tried to stomp and worry each foot in turn.

'Tiddly, will you stop that, damn it? You'll have me arse over tip and there goes your delicious eggies.'

Thornton wondered how Adrian didn't trip up over the ears. Out loud he said, 'I take it you two have already discussed the possible courses open to us?'

'There is only one plan of action, Thornton, and that is to lie doggo for a while. Isn't that the expression? They, whoever they may be, you haven't told me, think you are dead so no longer a problem but there could be niggling little doubts, especially if your body doesn't show up. But if you don't turn up at your office for a couple of days and you don't go near your flat they will definitely come to the conclusion their mission was accomplished. By now what's left of you is somewhere in the English Channel.'

'So you can stay here,' Adrian said, having put the plate of eggs down for Tiddly, left him to it, and returned to the room. One of the rabbit's ears had come off.

'Wouldn't that rather cramp your style?' Thornton asked.

'Not in the least, I won't be here, off to do a shoot in photogenic Bath. The baths and the beautiful Georgian architecture are a perfect elegant background for svelte models in the latest fashions to pose against, unlike some buildings I know.' He sniffed.

Adrian, I am sure that when it is finally finished and up and running the building you dread so much will be absolutely the most photogenic in the whole wide world and you can snap away in front of it for all you're worth. But, listen, if I am to stay here for a couple of days without going home, what do I do for a change of clothing? What do I do about this?' He indicated the rip in his jacket.

'I can take it with me when I go out and have it mended.'

'And clothes?'

'You can wear some of mine.'

'Come off it, Adrian, you don't really expect me to get into your kit do you? I could as easily rocket to the moon on a fart.' It was one of Thornton's favourite expressions. 'Sorry, Rory.'

Rory shrugged.

'Are you perhaps suggesting that what I wear is indecent?'

'Adrian, you wear your pants so tight that, except for the flares your skin is on the outside.'

'All right, Thornton,' Rory said, 'give me your measurements and I'll get you spares of everything. In the meantime though, you stay right here. You don't even poke your nose out the door.'

'What am I going to do with myself? I'll go crazy.'

'There's plenty to entertain you, Thornton. There's the telly, books, masses of magazines and records galore. You won't be bored. I would leave Tiddly with you for company except, if you're not to put your nose out the door, you won't be able to take him for walkies, so I'll take him down to Bath with me. I would have done that anyway. He loves the car. He stands up and looks out over the side so he gets the wind in his face. His vet tells me it's very bad for his eyes but what can one do?'

'Get him a pair of shades,' Thornton suggested.

'And I would be pleased to have someone in the house while I'm away, burglarinas you know and empty houses, so you would be doing me a favour. I won't cancel the milk.'

'It's by far the best thing at the moment, Thornton, and the only person you telephone is Holly. Don't call me in case Mrs McIvor answers. In a couple of day's time, before you go stir crazy,' Rory laughed at her use of the Americanism, 'you can start rattling those cages.'

Thornton shrugged and accepted he was a prisoner in a bijou mews cottage for the next two days. It could be worse.

Holly was deep in thought as she drove. Was there any chance she would be recognised as the snooper in the woods? She didn't think so, not wearing Thornton's greatcoat and hat. It would have been impossible to tell the sex of the intruder let alone get a good look at the face and it would more than likely be assumed it was a man. No, it was pretty certain she was quite safe, or so she assured herself. And the car? Too far away for recognition in the dark.

The white gates were wide open as she turned into the track and noticed for the first time just passed them on either side the large signs on white board which informed trespassers they would be prosecuted. Strange she never noticed them before. Could they have been put up this very morning? Was it possible a little jitteriness was setting in? She hoped so. It could be that today would be the day for all to be revealed.

Glancing in her rear view mirror she saw the Rolls pulling in right behind her and she smiled, a smile of expectation. It was fantasy time again. She knew Albert's eyes were on the occupant of the car in front, that is when he wasn't taking a quick look in his own rear view mirror to see how his boss was. His boss was in a filthy mood; there was no doubt about that. Albert looked away before Maurice could catch his eye.

The day had not started well. Even with the bathroom door shut he could hear her blubbering away and, when he went back into the bedroom, there she was propped up on a dozen satin covered pink pillows, face tear streaked and with a box of paper hankies on the bed in front of her and used ones crumpled up and lying all around. "Why are you going there again?" she demanded to know. "You're going there every single day. What's there that's so fascinating, so attractive? You've got a piece of skirt there, haven't you?" And then, before he could answer, "Don't lie to me, Maurice. You think I don't know all about your little Chelsea love nest? Men! You're all the same."

"How many men have you known that you can make a statement as bald as that?" he had sneered.

"You, only you," she wailed, taking up a handful of hankies that emptied the box. She tossed it aside and reached into the bedside cabinet for a fresh one, ripping it open. "I've been faithful to you all my life," she dabbed at her eyes, "and where has it got me?"

"You ungrateful cow! Just look around you. Look around and dare to ask that question again! Thank your lucky stars you want for nothing in this world."

"Only love and affection. Priceless priceless!" The howling reached a crescendo.

Maurice knew exactly what she was talking about. He wanted that too, oh, how badly he wanted it. He had slipped off his dressing gown and now faced his image in the cheval mirror rather than looking at it in the bath. Maybe those in a religious order who bathed wearing a full-length chemise so that they didn't look at themselves had the right idea. It was not a pretty site. The human body in all its manifestations is too often not a pretty sight. Even as a young man he was never going to be compared to a Praxiteles sculpture but now in late middle age as everything just sagged and wrinkled under the force of gravity, he often wondered, when God created man in His own image, which one was the replica of the template? He turned away from the mirror to look at Margaret still sitting up in bed and now sniffing rather than blubbering. She had almost exhausted herself.

"Look at me, Margaret," he said, "Look at me. Do you want love from this?" He knew he was not addressing his wife of so many years but a young woman who he would soon be seeing but for whom he could offer absolutely nothing. Why couldn't she have been from one of those South American shantytowns one was always reading or hearing about, dirt poor, ragged and starving, scavenging in city dumps so that, kneeling before her, he could lay down his riches in front of her bare feet? But it was more than possible, knowing who her father was and the ramifications of his business empire, she could have laid her riches at his very own gnarled old feet. He looked down at them, at calluses, corns, misshapen nails and bunions, shuddered, looked away and decided the sooner he covered his nakedness the better. Goethe was dead to rights when he said that pretty feet are a gift of nature. He went over to the linen press used as a wardrobe to select a shirt.

"I'm not talking about sex," she said. "I know you're well and truly passed that... "

Maurice closed his eyes and swayed a little. Did she have to rub it in? Just because he no longer coveted any desire for her did not mean he didn't have desire for... and yet, if push came to shove would he be able to manage it? Somehow he knew she was right. It was all pipe dreams. There really wasn't even any point in trying. He closed his ears to what she would say next because he had heard all this so many times.

"I wasted my youth for you, Maurice Chinnery. I wasted my youth, my figure and my beauty, yes, my beauty, bearing your bloody children, your ungrateful bloody children, and what have I got to show for it? Bloody stretch marks!" He couldn't get out of the house fast enough.

Holly parked, collected her bag from the back seat and waited for the Rolls to pull up alongside. Albert leapt out of the driver's seat and opened the back door for Maurice to clamber out, offering a helping hand that was ignored and all the while conscious that Holly's eyes were on him. At the first opportunity, that is when Maurice was bent almost double for a second or two getting out of the car and couldn't see it, he turned and smiled at her and she returned it with a smile lit up like a neon sign.

'Well, here we are again,' Maurice said with a false heartiness as he straightened up.

'Here we are indeed. Possibly for the last time,' she replied.

'Really? Why is that?'

'I told you, Maurice...' they started for the clubhouse, 'I'm off to Monte. It's all arranged and I am not going to rearrange it.'

Maurice stopped and took her arm to turn her towards him.

'Go now,' he said.

'What?'

'Go now. You've had some fun with your bow and arrows but it has absolutely nothing to do with your real life so go now. I really do not understand why you are here anyway. Good grief, Carmen, if you've become that much of an aficionado with your money you can set up a hundred archery clubs for yourself wherever you wanted, so what's so interesting about this one? Hey? This one you found by accident and which you seem to have become so particularly fond of. Is there something special for you here?' He couldn't help casting a glance beyond her to where Albert was standing gazing up at an empty sky.

For a long moment Holly stood staring at the man by her side. Was all her effort to come to nothing? Was she to be baulked at the last moment? His face told her nothing. In a way it was for the present moment a blank mask. What had caused him to suddenly come out with this suggestion? No, it was more than a suggestion, it was an urgent plea. Was it suspicion? Or was it a genuine feeling for her? She decided, as she became aware of the weight of her bag over her shoulder when they had been standing there for some time, that it was surely the latter. She laughed but it wasn't a mocking laugh. For the first time she felt truly sorry that this man was so besotted with her and she put out a hand to take his. He looked down, lifted the hand and brushed it gently with his lips. Albert, standing behind them, lowered his gaze from the empty sky and could hardly believe what he was witnessing.

'One more day,' Holly said, retrieving her hand. Strangely she had not been repulsed, the gesture having been so spontaneous and genuine. 'I really have enjoyed the experience, Maurice, so one more day to wind things up.' That has more than one meaning, she thought. 'Then, we can say good-bye.'

Now his face was no longer a blank mask. His features virtually crumbled under the finality of her statement.

Thornton had lasted no more than an hour before he went stir crazy and decided to break out from his comfortable prison. He had tried calling Holly a number of times although he knew it was pretty useless. She would be at the club or at least on her way there. Once outside the front door there was no turning back. Adrian had not left him a spare set of house keys. That was tempting fate.

Before setting off herself, Rory had called her garage and made arrangements for her car to be taken away and cleaned up. She explained in great detail the state it was in, apologised profusely and said she would give whoever was ordered to fetch it and do the dirty work an extra bonus for putting up with the stench which was pretty awful, the Thames mud by itself was bad enough, even with the windows wide open. She left the key under the driver's side mat and felt pretty sure that no car thief would even attempt to look for it or dream of stealing her car with the state it was in.

Adrian had stowed his camera equipment in the Morgan's special compartment and he and Tiddly were ready for the journey, Adrian in his faded, cracked leather, World War Two flying jacket and Tiddly in a special polo neck jersey of pale blue wool that covered his upper body and front legs against the cold and had Tiddly knitted in black down one side, and Winks down the other. Tres chic! He also wore a woolly bonnet, complete with pom-pom and tied under the chin to stop it blowing away, for when he wasn't curled up on the seat but sticking his head out the side savouring the wind. His bowl, water flask, and biscuits were all packed together with rubber bone and a couple of squeaky toys to keep him amused at journey's end. Thornton was tempted to ask Adrian if he had one or two squeaky toys as well but resisted the temptation.

Tiddly was in fact quite the little star as the girls all made such a fuss of him and he was in any number of shots if the occasion demanded it which Adrian made sure it did, there being extra payments for the dog's highly photogenic talent. In fact one photograph of Tiddly trying to stick his tongue up a model's nostril while she screwed up her face was a genuine prizewinner. Adrian had to airbrush some of the lower section of the picture.

Thornton watched as Adrian stood just inside the front door having one final check as to his appearance. He studied his face closely, first one side, then the other, then full front and patted himself under the chin with the back of his hand.

'My my my,' he murmured, 'time certainly has a way of catching up with one. Does my eek need a good going over with Ponds or does it not? Egg whites dried on the skin are very good for tightening up saggy bits under the eyes, did you know that, Charlie? It's like that naughty Mister Rabelais wrote in one of his disgusting but highly amusing books, the foreskin has the only wrinkles that please. Have you read any of that filthy French writer, Thornton? Don't. You will be most horribly shocked. Right off we go then. Got everything? I do believe so. There's masses of food in the kitchen and you know where the booze is kept so don't deny yourself. Now lock the door behind me, Thornton and don't be tempted to open to anyone, not the rather bona milkman, not the rather bona postman, and least of all not the big bad wolf whoever he may be. Tiddly and I...' Tiddly barked at the sound of his name wondering what the delay was in getting into the car, '... will be back in a couple of days.'

Tiddly, realising the time for departure had actually arrived, stood on his hind legs, his front paws pressed against Thornton and offered him a soggy eggy rabbit's ear as a good-bye present

Adrian opened the passenger door and Tiddly was in like a flash and then, around the other side, the man leapt athletically into the car and started her up. He gave a cheery wave to which Thornton responded. Tiddly gave a cheery bark and Thornton barked right back. Then, as the car pulled away over the cobbles, he closed the door, leaned against it and heaved a sigh. One thing you had to say about Adrian, he certainly took it out of you energy wise. He glanced down at the rabbit's ear held delicately between forefinger and thumb and took it through to the kitchen; intended to dump it in the bin but then had second thoughts and dropped it in the sink. Adrian might want to sew it on again.

Right the next thing was to decide what he was going to do with himself for the next couple of days. It was not at first an easy decision to make but as time dragged on, at least fifteen minutes of it as he wandered around the tiny cottage, he was more and more of the opinion there was only one thing for it and that was he ought to get the hell out of there.

He found himself in the studio from where he had once nicked one of Adrian's negatives. He doubted it had ever been missed but it had proved invaluable in the Spitskaya case. He switched on the overhead light and looked around. There didn't seem to be much on the go at the moment. Either that or Adrian had cleared the decks ready for his return and a busy developing session. The sinks and all the dishes were spotlessly clean and no negatives were hanging up to dry or in the drying cabinet. The place was pretty sterile by the look of it. He opened a cupboard and stood looking at half a dozen different cameras stored there. I wonder, he thought, if Adrian would mind my borrowing one of those for a day or two. He took the first one to hand, a Leica, out of the cupboard and looked elsewhere for film. Black and white negative was what he wanted. Can't use flash, he thought, so need something fairly fast. 800ASA might be a bit too grainy. Let's go for 400.

Next he needed some money. His wallet had obviously been swept away in the river and he was to all intents and purposes skint. He found some notes in a chest of drawers in the bedroom and slipped a tenner into his back pocket, had second thoughts and slipped in a second. Downstairs he left a note to tell Adrian what he had done and, should anything happen to him, to please claim compensation for camera and cash from Miss Aurora Pemberton, with which he left the house, slamming the door behind him. He hoped no burglar would pass by and notice the unclaimed milk bottles on the doorstep later or maybe Rory would take them in when she returned with his new clobber. No she wouldn't. She didn't have a key either.

'You want another car?' Harold was unable to conceal his surprise. 'On my life, Thornton, what are you up to, my boy? Three cars in as many days? What's happened to the Ford?' His eyes narrowed with suspicion.

'Nothing's happened to the Ford. Holly's using it.'

'She's not going to get into any trouble is she? You know I've got a soft spot for that girl.'

'God, I certainly hope not! Cross fingers, she'll probably bring the car back tomorrow.' He decided he wouldn't be cynical and believe

Harold's soft spot was as much, if not more, for the car than for Holly. 'In the meantime, what have you got for me?'

Harold waved a bony white hand towards the yard where half a dozen assorted vehicles were parked and then used the hand to draw his cashmere scarf closer around his throat.

'Take your choice,' he said. 'Business ain't so good at the moment.'

'You mean I'm your best customer?'

'You're my only customer.' Harold allowed himself a wry smile.

Thornton, who had been playing with some keys in his pocket, now withdrew and looked at them. Up to now he had quite forgotten about them.

'I'll take the Jaguar,' he said.

'Fine. Let's do the paperwork,' Harold headed for the office. 'Your client, whoever he or she might be, has more money than sense if you ask me but, business being what it is, let's be grateful for small mercies.'

Holly hadn't had any breakfast and thought it might be a good idea to visit the restaurant and put something in her stomach before doing anything else like changing and heading for the butts.

'Have you had breakfast, Maurice?' she asked. He nodded in the affirmative. 'Do you mind if I have some? I've been up quite a while and I'm starving. Haven't even had a chance to wet my whistle with a cup of coffee.'

He gave her a strange look as they seated themselves at a table and the steward, Martin, approached.

'Have I said something wrong?' Holly asked.

Maurice gave a little shrug. 'I was just thinking, it was a strange thing for a non-English person to say.'

'What was?'

'Wet my whistle. I take it, Carmen, your first language is Spanish?'

This was getting just a wee bit hairy and Holly knew that sooner or later someone would try to be smart and this would happen. She was getting careless. Was it because of what Maurice had said about leaving now that her mind wasn't totally focused? Her one hope had been that there was no one in the club who was remotely connected either with Spain or her lost colonies. She played for time, looking up at Martin now standing at their table.

'Buenos dias, Martin. Cómo está usted? Me gustaria un desayuno inglès.

Martin looked at her stony-faced. She turned to Maurice.

'Would you like to translate for me, Maurice? Considering I asked a simple question in my native tongue?'

She hoped her simple question, a phrase she had learned on a family holiday many years before and remembered for no reason other than it stuck in her head as some foreign words and phrases do, like ya vas lublu galubchik would have done the trick were she playing at being Russian.'

'Afraid I can't help,' Maurice said. 'Never was any good at languages. You'd better ask him in English.'

'What do you have for breakfast, Martin?' she asked.

'The kippers are a treat this morning, miss.'

'Good, then kippers I will have, lashings of toast and strong coffee to set me up for the day. Gracias.'

Thornton drove slowly passed the turn off and the white gates. Holly's directions were spot on. An ancient E Type Jag was parked close by, just off the main road. Further along he reached the country road opposite, the one Holly had told him about and turned off, driving up it only so far as she had previously to park his own Jaguar out of view. He got out, left the car unlocked and, taking the camera, walked back to the main road to take a look at the E Type parked there.

The car was vintage, a good ten years old with more mileage on the clock than was good for it but it had been well maintained and was obviously a love affaire for someone; polished until it gleamed and not a spot, dent, scratch or blemish of rust upon the bodywork. The interior was spotless, the seats immaculate under their sheepskin covers.

Having walked around the vehicle and given it a thorough inspection, Thornton was impressed. Whoever owned this car truly cherished it. Well, he thought, let us see if A goes into B and whether the engine is as good as the rest of it. He took the Jaguar key ring from his pocket, took a good look around to make sure he was unobserved, slid into the driving seat and, 'Surprise! Surprise!' he said out loud, 'the magic key fits.' The engine purred into life and, glancing in his wing mirror for any oncoming traffic of which there was none, Thornton pulled away and drove as far as the country road where he turned off once more and parked the second Jag next to the first. 'Talk to each other,' he said, 'it could be the start of a great affaire,' and walked back to the main road where, nicely concealed behind a clump of bushes, he would keep watch.

Breakfast was over. The kippers had been, as Martin had boasted, delicious and the table long since cleared. Now Maurice sat there impatiently drumming his fingers on the table and wondering what the hell Holly was up to. She had been in Maid Marian an awfully long time. "Just going to get changed," she had said. "Won't be a minute." He looked at his watch. What was she changing into, chain mail? Something obviously extremely difficult to put on he thought.

He would have been more than impatient had he known that she had already changed and was now with Albert in the process of billing and cooing like a pair of turtle doves through an open window on the other side of the building. It was only when she looked at her watch and realised how long the two of them had been at it that she reluctantly called an end to the tryst. Albert had asked how he could contact her away from the club and his employer. Should he call her at the Hotel Diana? He was aware that time was short, that she was only in England for a couple of days more. Surely they could, they must meet up before she left, and couldn't they keep in touch afterwards no matter what part of the globe she was trotting over?

Holly was on the horns of a dilemma. This was what came of pretending to be someone she wasn't. There was no way she could reveal her true identity, no way she could simply pass over her phone number and say "call me." Who was Albert attracted to? To her? Holly Day? Or to that fabulously rich South American heiress, Carmen Inez Hernandez? Was it a genuine attraction or could there be just a hint of gold digging, of fortune hunting here? If she closed the window now would it be the symbolic end of a beautiful relationship before it even had a chance to get started? She decided on a temporary withdrawal but left the window open.

Thornton too was growing impatient. There had been quite a large volume of traffic on the road but, after a while, one can grow bored with counting, identifying, looking at passing number plates and making up words and phrases from their lettering just to while away the time. It was like watching cheesy advertisements in the cinema before what he hoped was going to be the main attraction.

A couple of cars and a delivery truck had turned in through the white gates but there didn't seem to be anything suspicious about any of them. Nothing had come out. He was beginning to wonder if Holly had actually made it or whether he was wasting his time. After all, unless he actually ventured in and made a recce, an impossibility as he was supposed to be dead, he couldn't know for sure whether she was there or not. He was tempted to climb over the fence and approach the club through the woods as she had done but decided discretion was the better part and stayed where he was. The ground was wet and his feet were getting cold, and not only his feet. He turned up the collar of his jacket and dug his hands deep into his pockets. Whatever happened to his greatcoat? Did he leave it at Holly's? Was he wearing it when he went to Annette's? Maybe it was still drying at Adrian's together with his scarf, he really had no idea. He took his hands out of his pockets, rubbed them together and blew on them. A stake out is really the most boring occupation, especially outside on a winter's day.

Holly too was growing just a mite bored. There didn't seem much more Steve could actually teach her. He kept on telling her she was a natural and from hereon in it would be all practice, practice and more practice, not that she even needed that so much considering the placement of her arrows on the target as he looked at them with open admiration. This morning they seemed to be the only ones using the club's facilities, certainly as far as the grounds were concerned and, as they walked down towards the target, Holly was beginning to seriously wonder what the hell she was doing there. Thornton must have got hold of the wrong end of the stick if he thought The Bowmen Of Essex country style club had anything to do with the deaths of Sir Roger Pemberton and Sir Hugo Ingle. But then Sir Hugo's warning words before he died kept ringing in her head and suddenly another little bell tinkled as Steve said, 'Why don't we give up on target practice today and go hunting instead?'

Holly turned to him. 'Hunting? Where? And for what?'

'Right here in the wood and for rabbits. The wood is full of them.'

Holly objected. 'I'm not sure I want to go shooting at a harmless little rabbit,' she said.

'They're vermin, Miss Carmen. They breed like... well like rabbits and, if we don't control them they overrun the place.'

'Just how do you control them then?'

Steve patted her bow. 'A target is stationary and fairly large. Try your hand at something smaller and more or less constantly on the move. Come on, it will be fun. It's not like we're hunting some endangered species. Isn't that what they're called? Endangered? Come on, you know you want to give it a go.'

Holly's lower lip was set firmly behind her teeth, as she stood there undecided despite Steve's urging. Eventually, 'All right,' she said, 'let's give it a try.'

'Good. We'll go this way.' And he set off into the wood, Holly following dutifully behind. After a while she whispered to him. 'Shouldn't we be going more carefully, stalking or something? We seem to be making one hell of a racket and there isn't a bunny in sight. We're frightening them all away. That is, if there are any in the first pace which I am seriously beginning to doubt.'

'Oh, don't doubt it, Miss Carmen. There are rabbits here all right.' And then suddenly he stood stock still and, pointing to a clump of bushes, whispered, 'Look! There, right there.'

To Holly a patch of grey was a patch of grey; if it wasn't a rabbit then what was it? She took Steve's word for it and, following the direction of the pointed finger; she raised her bow, already fitted with an arrow and pulled back. Was it her imagination or had Steve simultaneously given her a little bump as she released the arrow? There was an agonised scream and a man, an arrow imbedded in his chest, lurched out of the bushes some distance away and dropped like a stone to disappear out of sight, probably rolling down one of those hollows Holly was already acquainted with.

She lowered her bow and for one horrendous moment stood shaking and absolutely stunned before Steve grabbed her by the arm and tried to hustle her away, but she would have none of it. She dropped the bow on the ground and tried to make a run for it in the direction of the fallen man but Steve grabbed a hold of her arm, desperately trying to stop her. Holly knew full well that, strong as he was, she could overpower him had she wished. Archery might be something new to her but the martial arts had long been a discipline assiduously practised as part of her profession. She stopped struggling because now she was thinking very fast. A rabbit is a few inches high, a man is five foot and more inches tall, there was absolutely no way her arrow could have brought anyone down, not even a midget, unless he was lying prone on the ground or was much closer to her before her arrow's trajectory descended almost to ground level to hit the nonexistent rabbit. She was conscious that Steve was tugging at her sleeve and talking to her with some urgency. She turned to look at him.

'What?'

'Come away, Miss Carmen, come away! You can't possibly be involved in this. This is really terrible! Terrible!'

'What are you talking about? There's a man over there who's been hit. He could still be alive. If he is we have to get him a doctor! Now! Come on!' She pretended again to head in the direction of the supposed casualty but once again she allowed herself to be prevented.

'Yes yes, I will see to it, I promise you!' He said, still desperately tugging at her arm. 'Please! Come back to the clubhouse and I will see to everything. Hunting accidents happen, they happen, but you needn't be involved. If the man has been killed there is nothing we can do. If he is only wounded, a few more minutes...'

'Could be the difference between life and death.' Holly was absolutely certain now there was no victim of an accident but she played along with the charade. She thought it was the worst mismanaged piece of stage management she had ever witnessed but it could have fooled someone a little on the fragile side whose nerves could be played upon and it obviously had a point. She was sure she would soon find out what it was; that is, Carmen Inez Hernandez would soon find out what it was.

Thornton was about to be rewarded for his patience. Luckily for him it had remained dry but he was now really feeling the chill of that winter's day almost to the point of having his teeth chattering, his lips turning blue and his ears turning bright red. He set to again to vigorously rub his hands together and blow on them before crossing his arms and shoving his hands under his armpits. If the ground hadn't been so soft he would have stamped his feet, as it was all that would happen was he would get his shoes covered in mud.

A man appeared at the edge of the woods on the club side and climbed through the barbed wire. Thornton, well camouflaged, watched as the man made it to the main road. It was Seymour Goodwin, the Uriah Heep look-alike from Fundraisers Limited but there was nothing Uriah Heepish about him at the moment. He was grinning from ear to ear and carrying what looked suspiciously like some sort of breastplate, possibly of leather, with half an arrow attached to it at a right angle. He stopped dead and stood at the side of the road, no longer beaming, but frowning mightily. He looked up and down in some confusion. Where was his car? WHERE WAS HIS CAR? Hadn't he parked his car right here? Panic set in; he started to run one way, stopped, turned back, looked the way he had come, walked back and stared down at the road as if by magic his car would suddenly materialise, in front of his very eyes, as Mister Askey would say.

'It's been stolen,' he whispered. 'My car has been stolen. What am I going to do?' He was ashen, trembling, on the verge of tears. He raised both arms sideways shoulder high and again looked up and down the road before dropping them to flap against his thighs in a gesture of hopelessness. It was impossible to believe. Where was his car? God damn it! Please! Where was his car? Who had stolen his motor? He looked at what he was holding. Best get rid of this, he thought, and threw the theatrical prop back over the fence and into the bushes but not before Thornton had been snapping away with the Leica. It was that damn set of keys he had lost, wasn't it? Someone had found them and waited for this chance and they had got away with it. Should he report the theft to the police? Yes, of course he should. He wanted his motor back, didn't he? Preferably in the same condition in which he had left it. Why was he parked there in the first place? That would be the first question the police would ask. Yes, why was he parked there, stretch of country road, nothing there, no reason to stop. He needed a pee! That was it. He was bursting so he stopped to have a pee. And in the few minutes he was standing there unzipped with his back to the road someone nipped into his car and drove off with it? They appeared like magic out of nowhere did they? Well, no. Being somewhat bashful he didn't want to pee in full view of any passing traffic that might have come along so he went further into the wood. If you stood with your back to the road, hands in front, people always knew what you were up to and had a little chuckle. Did he hear the car start up? No, he didn't hear the car start up. So he didn't turn around and see anything and he couldn't give a description of the thief? No he definitely couldn't give a description. Had he left the engine running? He couldn't remember. He wouldn't have thought so. Had he left the key in the ignition? He couldn't remember. Well, he had best report the incident to his insurers. By now his car was probably undergoing a personality change in a back street garage that, before the age of the internal combustion engine when vehicles were horse drawn, was a stable somewhere in London's East End. A sob arose and broke in Seymour Goodwin's throat as he set off down the road, occasionally looking back to see if a car was coming in which he could hitch a lift back to town or at least to the nearest point of public transport. He didn't dare go back to the club. Not if there was the slightest chance of her recognising him and he had better keep a wary eye out for her in case she now came driving by.

The first car to come by was a squad car. Seymour turned his head briefly to see about hitching a lift but then quickly turned back and continued on his way and the police car sped passed him. Good, Thornton thought, he's not going to report his stolen car to the police, not yet anyway. Guess there might just be a couple of hidden reasons for that.

Seymour's disconsolate figure disappeared around a bend and Thornton emerged from his leafy hiding place to return to his hired car. The beloved E-type would just have to stay where it was. The question now was, should he give Seymour a hint, or did he turn and drive the opposite way and keep his escape from drowning still a secret? What the hell! If he was going to rattle a few cages he might as well start now. He stowed the camera in the glove compartment, started the engine and reversed to begin his turning manoeuvre. He had left the key of the E Type in the ignition. Some villain might just be passing by and think all his birthdays had come at once.

Holly was seated in what she supposed was the administrative office of the club: at least it was a room she had never seen before;

spacious with wall to wall deep industrial quality carpet such as is used in hotels, cinemas, ships, places where a million grimy shoes will walk over them; a multi-coloured design in a small pattern to camouflage the dirt. A thousand pieces of sweet and sour pork could be dropped on it, trodden in and wiped away with hardly any noticeable marking. There were easy chairs in soft black leather, a large glass topped desk on which stood a number of executive toys and a copy of the club magazine, *The Quiver*. There was a framed poster for the nineteen thirty eight film *The Adventures Of Robin Hood* starring Errol Flynn, Basil Rathbone and the wonderful smooth smarmy Claude Raines, and photographs of various club members past and present indulging their love of archery or merely posing by targets. There was also, in the worst possible taste, one of Sir Roger Pemberton adorned with black crepe. She was managing to put up a reasonably decent performance of someone in deep shock, accepting with trembling hands the brandy and ginger ale she had requested and which Martin now held out to her. Steve stood close by and Maurice hovered like a clucking hen until none of them could stand it any longer.

'Mister Chinnery, for God's sake!' Steve hissed. 'Please go and wait in the bar. You're not wanted here.'

'No, I couldn't possibly do that.'

'Well sit down then, out of the way, and stop causing a distraction.'

'A distraction?' He squeaked. 'A distraction! After what has just happened? Are you mad? What is being done about... about... you know...' He waved an arm in the general direction of that part of the forest where the body was supposed to be lying.

'It's all being taken care of. Doctor Reid is out there now.' He turned to Holly, sipping her brandy and ginger ale, the glass still shaking in her hand but not enough to spill any, and taking in every word. Was Maurice in on this pantomime or was he an innocent bystander? It was impossible to know just who was involved, who was a part of the organisation.

'We have to report this accident,' she said. 'We must call the police.'

'No, no! That's the last thing we must do,' Martin jumped in quickly, a slight note of panic in his voice. 'Think of the scandal!'

'Scandal? What the hell are you talking about? A man is either dead or seriously injured and you are worried about a possible scandal?' She was playing her part up to the hilt.

'You don't think this could have the most terrible effect all round? It could ruin the club, ruin me, ruin you. Do you want to go to jail for manslaughter?'

'It was an accident, for goodness sake! There is a witness.' She pointed at Steve who shook his head violently meaning most probably that he would deny everything.

'Think of the effect it would have on your father, Miss Hernandez. No, no, leave everything to me. I promise you, I can fix it. You go back to your hotel... do you want someone to drive you?' Martin patted her on the shoulder. She squirmed beneath his fingers and shook her head.

'We will be in touch and let you know what the situation is. But don't, whatever you do, decide to make a run for it, I mean...' he added hastily, 'stick to your schedule. When are you due to leave, two days time is it? If you bring it forward for no ostensible reason and all this comes out it would look very suspicious, wouldn't look good at all if you made hasty rearrangements now would it? And don't for goodness sake call your father about this. It won't do a bit of good his knowing about it, quite the reverse I should imagine. You could have another casualty to your credit if he has say a weak heart.'

'My father is as strong as an ox but I suppose it is best he isn't informed about what's happened, not for the moment anyway.'

Holly was fully aware that, should Carmen Inez Hernandez make an immediate dash for another part of the world all this preparation and play-acting will have been for nothing. They needed at least one more day to wind up the plot but, with no actual means of keeping her there, like withholding a passport for instance, threat seemed the only alternative. Little did they know the real Carmen could already have left.

'Do you think he's dead?' Holly asked in a suddenly frightened little girl voice.

'We will know as soon as the Doctor gets back. In the meantime...'

'I'll wait for him,' she said.

'What?'

Holly was beginning to quietly enjoy this. Make them squirm a little she thought. She got up from her chair and moved over to the desk. Putting down her glass she ran her fingers over the telephone as though she might want to use it but picked up the magazine instead and started to thumb through it almost as if she were in a surgery waiting room.

'The doctor... I'll wait here for him and find out what...'

'No!' Martin and Steve shouted almost as one and she could sense their rising panic.

The magazine was proving most interesting, providing a great many names and some intriguing articles such as the debt the club owed to Sir Peter Wheeler for example for his continuing patronage and Holly was wondering if she would be able to take it with her when she left.

'Please. Miss Hernandez!' Martin said, 'Please do as we ask. Go back to your hotel, don't contact anyone or say anything about this and we will be in touch as soon as possible.' He turned to Maurice. 'Maurice, can't you talk some sense into her?'

'What makes you think she would listen to me? No, I don't want any part of this.' He pulled himself out of his chair and headed for the door. Holly looked after him not without some amazement. As a possible romantic sideline or maybe even a quick how's your father, she had been courted relentlessly; now as a possible liability, the man didn't want to know. How quickly emotions tumble about never to be the same again. In a way it was rather demeaning, insulting even and she couldn't deny she was a little hurt by his change of heart. Also there was the fact that it could be the end of her relationship with Albert before that sideline had even got warm.

'Maurice?'

He stopped but didn't turn around.

'Are you not going to help me?'

Then he continued on his way.

'Coward,' she said, just loud enough for him to hear before the door closed behind him.

Once outside, Maurice couldn't wait to summon Albert and make for his car. He thought it might be a long time before he returned to The Bowmen Of Essex. In fact he might even take a little trip abroad and enjoy the sun for a while. Albert opened the passenger door for his boss, closed it and moved around to the driver's, all the time looking at the clubhouse and wondering what had happened to Miss Holly. An impatient tapping on the window made him give up. He climbed in, slammed his door, and started the motor.

'Do I get an outside line from this?' Holly looked from one to the other and indicated the telephone. She would give them something more to think about.

'Who do you want to call?' Martin asked.

'The police of course.'

'I really do not think that would be wise, Miss Hernandez. You are obviously still suffering from shock, quite understandably, and you haven't yet let the seriousness of the situation sink in, thought of the consequences of dragging the police into this.'

'I don't intend to drag them in, Martin; I intend to invite them in. I may call you Martin may I not? No one has ever properly introduced us or told me your surname. But please answer my question, do I get an outside line from this phone, Martin?'

'Very well, if you insist, go right ahead but I, and Steve here, and anyone else who was around at the time will deny everything and, by the time the police arrive, it will be so arranged that there will be nothing for them to see. In which case, my dear Miss Hernandez, and please believe me we are doing this to protect you as well as ourselves and the reputation of the club, you will be taken for an hallucinating hysterical woman who has gone off the rails and, should that conclusion get out into the big wide world, I hate to think of the effect it would have on your family. The police do not appreciate being called out on a wild goose chase. So there is the telephone, go ahead, use it.' Martin seated himself in one of the easy chairs and looked steadily at Holly still standing by the desk, phone in hand. 'In the meantime, Steve will go and see what is happening.'

Steve dutifully left the room. Holly replaced the receiver on its cradle. Martin lifted himself out of his easy chair.

'Good. That is a sensible reaction and, what would be even more sensible now is for you to collect your things, get into your car and drive to your hotel. Stay there until you get the all clear from us because I am quite sure that is what it will be, the all clear. Shall we go?' Martin moved across the room to open the door and stood there holding it for her, a look not of triumph but certainly of satisfaction on his face. For some reason he made her think of Hitler doing his little dance of joy in Paris, a clip she had seen on television so many times. As she reached his side, 'Please don't worry, Miss Hernandez,' he said, 'everything will turn out just fine.'

Thornton reached the junction with the main road and stopped just as Maurice's Rolls, slowing momentarily in case of any oncoming traffic, swept out and turned in the direction taken by Seymour. Thornton followed, staying a fair distance behind. It was only seconds before they caught up with the lone trudging figure that turned, started to raise his thumb and then, obviously recognising the Rolls, frantically waved both arms for it to stop, but the Rolls swept on. Seymour stood practically in the middle of the road looking after it, completely at a loss as to why Maurice wouldn't stop for him. Thornton eased off the accelerator and gently applied the brake so as to widen the gap and give Seymour time to step to the side of the road and turn back to look his way, which he did, this time definitely raising his thumb. Thornton smiled and drove on. He looked in his rear view mirror. Seymour was standing motionless staring after the car. Thornton could have sworn his jaw was practically on his chest, if not the tarmac. He had kept a speed, which allowed Seymour a quick glance at his face so that there had to be an element of doubt and he was quite sure Seymour would think he was seeing things. Or was he? It had certainly given him something to think about apart from the disappearance of his beloved motor.

Holly collected her belongings from Maid Marion and left the clubhouse firmly believing she would never darken its doors again. She was so intent upon getting to her car without having to see, hear from, or talk to anyone she didn't notice a familiar figure in a corner of the bar but the familiar figure noticed her. It was Mike Aliff.

CHAPTER NINE

Thornton's first port of call was Adrian's mews to see if the milkman had been and to put his mind to rest by removing the evidence indicating an unoccupied house. He owed that to Adrian at least.

And the milkman had indeed called to which the presence of a pint bottle of gold top on the doorstep testified. Tiddly obviously liked his cream. Adrian, who was beginning to grow a wee bit nervous about his slightly expanding waistline and the fact that he could pinch his love handles between finger and thumb, probably skimmed it off the top for him. He had one of those little rubber and plastic pumps with which to do it, the kind you could buy from trendy kitchen stores packed with demonstrated gadgets that would have their short life of supposedly helping to make domestic life easier before their novelty wore off and they disappeared forever into a drawer or the back of a cupboard. You removed the cap and placed the bulb over the mouth of the bottle, depressed the rubber bulb, released it and the cream was sucked up the little plastic tube and into whatever container you had ready to receive it: very neat.

Thornton got out of the car leaving his door open and walked around to pick up the bottle of milk. He was on his way back when the front door of the cottage opposite opened and an apparition appeared there to first of all take in the car from front to back and then to stare at Thornton rather sternly. It had to be admitted the Jaguar wasn't exactly in pristine condition despite Harold's tender ministerings.

'Afternoon,' Thornton greeted the householder with a smile.

'Excuse me,' the apparition said, 'but just what do you think you are doing?'

'Doing?'

'Yes, indeed, that is what I said. What do you think you are doing? What is it you intend doing with that bottle of milk?'

There was a short sharp answer to that but not one Thornton felt he should use. He studied the man standing in his doorway. He was in every sense of the word a Belgravia quean, probably the owner of an exclusive art gallery or an antique shop Thornton thought, a member of the Arts Council maybe? Trustee of a museum? Friend of Covent Garden? If not something artistic then private banking possibly. Its blue striped shirt with the separate high white collar was definitely Jermyn street, its suit Saville Row and its shoes were from that bespoke shoemaker in Piccadilly who kept a boot in a glass tank of water in the display behind the window and whose name Thornton could never remember because he always stopped to look with keen interest at the boot that had been there forever. Presumably it was still totally watertight if somewhat mouldy and he was so fascinated he never thought to look at the name of the maker. He wouldn't have been able to afford the bespoke footwear anyway.

A wedding band on the left and a gold pinkie ring on the right bearing a family crest embellished the man's beautifully manicured hands, minor aristocracy no doubt, inheritor of a crumbling pile in the home counties somewhere, possibly sold on as finances dictated to a pop star, the Hari Krishnas or some billionaire guru supposedly from the Himalayas murmuring mantras to his credulous disciples.

Age wise he was probably in its middle fifties, medium height, very slender, clean-shaven, thinning blonde hair swept back. He was regarding Thornton with a look of sheer disdain. In fact it wasn't really looking at Thornton. It seemed to be looking at something about three inches above and a couple of feet beyond Thornton's head as though it simply couldn't bear to focus on the face it was addressing. Servants and lower orders it had been brought up to believe did not necessarily need to be looked at except in moments of disapproval.

'Do you have a fridge?' Thornton asked.

'I beg your pardon?' The eye level was brought down to the correct angle.

'I asked if you have a fridge because, if you do, you could put this in it for me. Save me the bother of lugging it half way across London all the way home.'

'And why, if I may so enquire, are you intending to lug... er take it... er home?'

'Because I promised Adrian I wouldn't leave it outside for any prospective burglar to see and realise there was nobody in. All right?'

'I see. Then you are, I take it, a friend of Mister Spangle.' Now there was no disguising the disdain in the man's voice. Quite obviously in his opinion Adrian Spangle, a commercial photographer of strange inclinations and dubious morality, lowered the whole tone of the mews and could it be that this man was of the same persuasion? He always maintained he could spot one a mile off but no distinctive signals were being given off here and he was slightly confused.

A little brown hen appeared behind him, nervously fingering a rope of amber beads that hung around her neck and down her rather flat chest.

'Is there something wrong, dear?'

'No, I wouldn't say there is anything wrong exactly. It's just that this man wants us to take this bottle of milk.'

'Take it? Take it where, dear?'

'Take it into the house, dear.'

'Oh, I see. Why?'

'To put in the fridge.'

'Our fridge?'

'Yes.'

'Who is he?'

'I have no idea? Who are you? I mean, what's your name?'

'Thorn...or...orpe... Charlie Thorpe.'

'Hmn... Well, Mister Thorpe, we will do you the favour this time but only this once you understand.'

'Twice,' Thornton said as he handed over the bottle, gingerly accepted by holding the neck with one hand and supporting the bottom with the other, a bit like a priest holding a chalice. He passed it on to the hen who accepted it in the same fashion.

'Twice? Now look here, my good fellow...'

'Tomorrow,' Thornton said, 'if you would be so kind. Adrian won't be back till late evening you see.'

'I see.' The man turned to his wife. 'I think we can manage that, can't we, my dear?'

'I'm sure we can, dear.'

'Very well Mr... er... Thorpe, we will take in tomorrow's delivery and put it in the fridge together with this one. Good day to you.' With which he stepped back and started to close the door but not before Thornton heard the hen whisper rather loudly, 'Do you think he's one of those, dear?' The door closed and he never heard the reply.

He stood for a moment completely dumbstruck before he climbed into the car and drove away. What had he just negotiated, an exchange of prisoners after a world war?

There was a discreet twitching of curtains as he made his noisy departure.

*****

Mike Aliff was having the mother and father of all anxiety attacks as he paced the club office watched by Martin and Steve, neither of them exactly figures of composure.

'I should have known,' Mike squealed, 'I should have known Thornton would get that bitch to do his dirty work for him. Oh, clever, very clever! While we're sorting him out, she's sorting you lot out. How was I to know she had a few days leave coming to her? She seems to have the knack of timing it so. Well, he's out of the picture now, but she isn't so what are we going to do about her? How on earth did she manage to take you all in, that's what I want to know? South American heiress! South American heiress if you please! Oh, God, I could weep,' He threw himself into the chair behind the desk and buried his face in his hands and, for a moment it looked as if he really was weeping but, after a few moments of these histrionics he pulled himself together, sat bolt upright and blew out with puffed cheeks a lungful of tar-tainted tobacco-scented air. With straight arms wide apart he placed both hands flat on the glass top and looked from one to the other. 'The question I repeat is, what do we do now?'

'I think we had better just get rid of her,' Martin ventured.

'Call off the whole caper,' Steve said.

'Hers wouldn't be the first body buried in this neck of the woods.'

'And everybody lies low for a while.'

'Are you both raving mad? What do you think Sir Peter's going to do when he hears about this?'

'We could lay the blame on Maurice.'

'What?'

'Well, he was the one brought her into the club and vouched for her. He took great care, he said to make sure she was who she said she was.'

'Yes? And how did he manage to do that?'

'She left her handbag in the bar with him when she went to visit Maid Marian the first time and he went through it.'

'Idiots! Dolts! Nincompoops! That's exactly what she intended him to do!'

'Well it wasn't us was it?' Martin resented being called idiot, dolt and nincompoop. 'It was Maurice, wasn't it?'

'Yes, but he passed the info along and you should have double-checked. Triple checked even!'

'And just how was we expected to do that?' Steve asked. 'Besides, he really had it bad for her and you know what they say, love is blind.'

'Well... like you say, we can drop the whole thing here and now and face the wrath of Sir Peter and the whole bloody board and worse, the wrath of that crazy oily Levantine who calls himself a Greek. He's no more a Greek than I am prince of the fucking pagodas. God, is nobody in this world who they say they are? I tell you what we can do, we can carry on as if Miss Holly Day were in truth this mysterious South American heiress and finish dealing the cards, stacked in our favour naturally.'

'There is one way to get her back,' Martin said. They both turned to look at him. 'Maurice Chinnery's chauffeur, Albert Finch.'

*****

Thornton drove into Harold's lot and parked the jaguar. As he got out he noticed the Ford shooting brake had been returned. Harold came out of his office with a look of relief on his face.

'Oh, finished with the motor then, Thornton?'

'No, Harold, you know perfectly well I've got it for another day. I see Holly's back.'

189

'Yes, drove in about an hour or so ago. She said if you showed up to tell you she's gone to the hotel.'

'The hotel? Oh! The hotel! Right. Thank you, Harold.'

'If you've got the car for one more day why have you driven it in here?'

'Can you think of a better place to park, Harold?'

'Not for free I can't, no.'

Thornton gave a wave and set off for the office. He might as well see what developments there had been in that direction if any.

There was nothing of importance in his letter box; no unexpected bills, no final demands, nothing from the bank or the Inland Revenue, only fliers on glossy paper for a chain of cheap jewellery stores, quick food outlets with special offers, and a mystic who promised she could foresee his future to the very minute. Clutching the whole lot in order to dispose of it in the office waste paper basket – the street outside really didn't need any more litter, practically the whole of a Brazilian rain forest was lying there as Adrian might have said – he mounted the narrow rickety stairs. He smiled thinking of Adrian and wondering whose nostril Tiddly was endeavouring to probe with his tongue right this minute. Of course the other embarrassing thing about this type of small dog, particularly poodles for some reason, maybe it was their French heritage, was its penchant for having a go at humping your leg in public when it took a great deal of shaking off or even a firm kick to deter the horny little beast.

He was halfway down the dingy corridor when he noticed the door to his office was slightly ajar. He stopped dead and seriously wondered whether he should go any further. After all, one attempt had been made on his life and he had no idea if anybody was in there waiting for him. He glanced back down the corridor to make sure no one was behind him and advanced cautiously, though hardly silently the floorboards were so squeaky under their worn linoleum, even treading close to the wall, and reaching the door, stood to one side as he gently pushed it further open.

'Come in, Thornton,' she said, 'don't stand on ceremony.'

At least that is what it sounded like as she spoke with a full mouth. She was sitting behind his desk – the chair hadn't given way and was actually accommodating her width – or somehow she had managed to squeeze herself into it - holding a bitten-into double cheeseburger in her hand and, in front of her on the desk, a box marked *Dunkin Donuts*. He noticed his battered old kettle on its tin tray on top of the filing cabinet was plugged in ready to boil for tea or coffee. If he didn't get to it fast enough to switch it off, the tray got splattered every time the kettle boiled over and ejaculated in great spurts.

'This,' she said, waving the burger and spraying a few blood red drops of ketchup about, 'is but totally disgusting as the actress said to the bishop.'

'Then why are you holding it in your hand.'

Rory took another bite.

'And, what is more, why are you putting it in your mouth? As the bishop said to the actress.'

'Thornton, I needed a quick carbohydrate fix.'

'May I point out to you, Rory, that not by any stretch of the imagination do cheese and minced beef fall under the category of 'carbohydrate but are protein and lipid.'

'Have you been dieting, Thornton?'

'Do I look as though I need to diet? There is not a spare ounce on my lean and manly frame.' He lifted his shirt front from his waistband and showed her his six-pack. She was duly impressed.

'Have you been going to the gym?'

'No, fortunately it's all in the genes,' he said, tucking in his shirt, 'my elderly dad's still as skinny as a rake and my mother in her younger days would have looked great on the catwalk. It's also because in my younger days I refused to eat my greens.'

'Greens don't make you fat. And how come you seem to know a bit about food then?'

'Holly.'

'That figures.'

'Of course it does.'

'All right then, would you like to finish it?' She held out the remains of the burger, 'and I'll go on to the doughnuts which most definitely are one hundred percent carb and there are six varieties and I don't care what they do to me, Thornton, I definitely need a sugar high.'

Thornton, who suddenly realised he had not eaten all day, felt his stomach suddenly lurch of its own accord and emit a long low rumble. He reached out for the remainder of the burger. These days he seemed to be into hand me down food. The kettle boiled. He pulled out the plug. For the moment eating was more important as he sat himself down opposite her in the client's chair. Not a word was said for a while as they both had their mouths too full and then Rory got up and replugged the kettle.

'Tea or coffee?' she asked.

'Oh, coffee, definitely coffee. You need your sugar fix, I need my caffeine.'

'In which case you should have chosen tea. I'm told tea actually has more caffeine than coffee though I don't know how true that is.'

'Serve up whatever you want as long as it's hot. Tell me,' he said, swallowing the last mouthful of cheese and bap, 'how did you get in? I know the lock is pretty feeble and even the most incompetent burglar wouldn't find it too difficult to break in but it is supposed to be some kind of a deterrent and I don't see any damage to the surround.'

'Are you suggesting I might have hurled my bulk against it? I might look like a Ukrainian discus thrower, Thornton, but I don't usually throw my weight round. The door was wide open,' she said, starting to spoon Nescafe granules into two mugs. 'Someone was here before me.'

'Well, good luck to them,' Thornton said, 'there really is nothing to take or anything of interest, except… hang on a minute.' He got up and moved around to his side of the desk, pulled open a drawer and shut it again.

'Well?' She had poured the boiling water over the granules and now placed the two mugs on the desk. 'You don't have any milk. Do you want sugar?' She proffered the tea-stained, partly used, and partly soggy because of the kettle's ejaculatory habit, *Tate and Lyle* bag, and replaced it on the tray when he shook his head.

'The only file missing is the one dealing with the Sir Roger Pemberton case. Guess, as they reckon to have knocked me off, they came in to see what I had left behind and took it to cover their tracks. It's not important now.'

'Remind me to get you some decent canisters for your tea and sugar and stuff,' and then, changing the subject. 'Where on earth have you been anyway? I knew you had disobeyed all our instruction when I kept phoning Adrian's house and got no reply. That is why I needed this,' as she started on her second doughnut. 'I was so worried about you.'

'That's very sweet of you, Aurora.'

'Rory.'

'Rory, but there was really no need.'

'There was every need, damn it! Should anything happen to you how would I ever bring my uncle's murderers to justice? And where, at this moment in time, might Holly be?'

'Holly is safe and sound, for the moment, and at the Hotel Diana.'

'This is such a lovely room,' Myrtle said, drawing the velvet curtains and lovingly smoothing them with the flat of her hands, revelling in the texture. She noted with satisfaction a maid had already switched on the bedside lamp, turned down the bed and laid a Viennese chocolate on the pillow. 'Do you like it?'

'It's divine,' Holly gushed, knowing she couldn't have thought of a better word to please her friend who smiled broadly in appreciation.

'I'm so glad. You're jolly lucky it was available for tonight. Usually at this time every year the sweetest old American couple occupy it. They're both well into their eighties and up to now still globe-trotting. They keep telling me I really ought to visit them for a change and see for myself the wonderful hostelries they have in the states. Their particular favourite, so they say, is in a place called Middletown, Virginia, and it's called The Wayside Inn. Evidently it was originally a coaching inn and is simply chocabloc with home and colonial antiques and serves the most wonderful food. If ever I manage to get away and go to America I will most definitely stay in The Wayside Inn.'

'So why aren't they here?' Holly asked.

'Last minute cancellation. Evidently his pacemaker caved in just as they were boarding the plane. Isnt that too sad?'

By this time she had crossed over to switch on the bathroom light and peek inside, making sure everything was exactly as it should be. It was of course: robes, enormous fleecy white towels, hand towels, soaps, face cloths, soft wipes, shampoo, conditioner, bath jell, shower jell, cologne; it was all there, the brand new toiletries all crying out, open and use me or take me away with you when you go which, of course, most people did no matter how wealthy they happened to be. Some even went further and took the toilet rolls. There's simply no fathoming some people.

'I'll leave you to it then. If there is anything you want, just ring. When you're ready come downstairs and we will have a long natter over cocktails and then some dinner, yes?'

Holly nodded. 'Lovely,' she said, 'I'm, ravenous, but first a shower and a change.' She had laid her suitcase on the long low slatted table next to the closet made specifically for that purpose and now opened the case. She had stopped off at her apartment on the way to the Diana to pack her own toiletries, night attire, and a suitable change of clothes with accessories.'

'Don't be long,' Myrtle cooed as she left, closing the door behind her.

Rory left the building first and took a good look around before poking her head back through the door and nodding for Thornton to come out. They had been sitting in his office in the dark for quite a while until Thornton finally decided to make a move no matter what Rory said about the danger of being seen and recognised. The lower half of Tottenham Court Road was packed with enthusiasts frequenting the Aladdin's cave of hi-fi and electronic stores or window shopping, looking for bargains behind the brightly lit plate glass. The delis in the side and back streets that carried out most of their trade during the day and the restaurants that thrived during the lunch hour were closed and dark. It wouldn't be long before the garbage men came around to dispose of the day's refuse of which there was any amount piled high.

'This way,' Rory said, 'I'm parked just round the corner. Was bloody lucky to find a space I can tell you.' She carried on talking as they scuttled along, heads well down, having the excuse of quite a strong breeze blowing in their faces and swirling the litter around their legs. 'You'll be pleased to know the car is beautifully clean. All last night's evidence gone. I gave the young man a handsome tip for having to do it. I'm sure he must have hated every second of it. It's definitely no fun cleaning up someone else's...' She couldn't actually bring herself to say the word. 'Don't you think it's absolutely wonderful how nurses and people like that can do it day after day? I do. Saints, that's what they are.'

Despite the wind and the cold, one of the working girls in a miniskirt and skimpy blouse had brought her Maltese terrier out to piddle against a lamppost. It decided to have a go at Thornton first, yapping and snapping at his ankles.

'Do you mind calling off your wolfhound, Carlotta?' Thornton said but there was now no need as the dog had already given up on the ankle attack and was now squatting in the gutter busy doing what it was meant to do in the first place.

They were about to move on when Carlotta looked at Rory and with a grin said, 'And what do we have here, Thornton? Two for the price of one?'

'Absolutely,' Rory said, 'and twice as good as you will ever be,' with which she took Thornton's arm and hustled him along leaving Carlotta busily trying to think of something to say. It would probably niggle her all night that she hadn't managed to come up with a suitable riposte.

In the car Rory said, 'Do you know all the girls around here, Thornton?'

'Not all. Just a couple who could be good for information.'

'That's your excuse and you're sticking to it.'

'That's my excuse and I'm sticking to it.'

CHAPTER TEN

Showered, shampooed, dressed in her best, looking and feeling like a million dollars, Holly entered the lounge and glanced about her. Her entrance was rather an anti-climax though in that the only person present was a young waiter standing by the door. Still he gave her an appraising eye, smiled, and greeted her with, 'Good evening, Miss Hernandez.'

Holly's look in return was more quizzical.

'No one is supposed to know my name,' she said.

'There's a message for you at reception. Would you like me to fetch it for you?'

'Thank you.'

'And I was asked...' He looked around to make sure no one else was present. '... to give you this in private. That's how I know who you are you see.' He held out a folded note that Holly took. The waiter then left to fetch the message from reception and Holly seated herself in the nearest chair to read her note.

Dear Miss Carmen. The boss says he is going to the club tomorrow. I hope I may see you there. If the shooting is out of doors the barn would be a good place to meet. That is if you want to. Hoping to see you tomorrow then. Yours faithfully, Albert Finch.

Shades of Lady Chatterley or Maurice even but in this case with opposite sexes. It wasn't the most poetic or romantic billet doux ever penned but it certainly pleased its recipient who smiled, folded it up and slipped it in her reticule just as the young waiter returned with a more formidable looking envelope.

'He left this as well, only like I said, this was at reception, not so, you know, private like. I will get you a drink, shall I, Miss Hernandez?'

'Yes, I'd like a gin and It please.'

196

'One gin and Italian coming up, and Mrs Cullen says she will be with you in two flicks of a lamb's tail. Those were her very words.'

Holly was beginning to get the impression the lad was starting to flirt with her. She watched his departing back until he disappeared and then tore open the envelope in her hand and read the message.

"You will be receiving a telephone call during the course of the evening. We will keep ringing until you are available to answer. Please listen to the message and take great care to follow the instructions given."

The note was on plain paper and unsigned. It was a little too bulky to stuff into a reticule and she was dammed if she was going up to her room to put it somewhere but she needed to keep it for evidence so, for the moment, simply left it on the table just as Myrtle appeared looking slightly out of place in a trouser suit of flowing silk with a design of giant red hibiscus flowers whose stamens were distinctly phallic.

'Now my dear,' she huffed, as she plumped down in a chair opposite Holly and looked around, 'have you ordered yourself a drink? Oh! And have you got your message? There was a message for you at reception.' She turned her head to see if there was anyone about who would collect it but Holly tapped the table indicating the envelope. 'Oh, you did get it. Did Ivan bring it? He's a dear lad. Irish you know. Now, where are we? Oh, here's Ivan with your drink. Ivan, dear, whatever Hol... Carmen's having, I'll have the same.'

Ivan, having placed Holly's drink on the table, gave her a smile that made her positively glow. Those violet Irish eyes beneath their black lashes were definitely smiling and then, with a slight bow and an almost imperceptible forward thrust of the pelvis, he withdrew to fulfil Myrtle's order. "Holly," Holly said to herself, "you are a slut. Don't even think about it. Remember, you're probably seeing Albert tomorrow and this one really is far far too young." Out loud she asked, 'What were you saying, Myrtle?'

'I was asking where we are at, you know, with the shhhhh?'

'Evidently we are expecting a telephone call this evening that will tell us all.' She tapped the envelope.

'And that is why you wanted to stay here tonight? In case of messages?'

'Huh huh.'

'May I see? I know I shouldn't but may I?'

'It only says more or less what I've told you but be my guest.'

Holly handed Myrtle the envelope. Myrtle looked about her in a manner she fondly imagined to be furtive to make sure no one was spying over her shoulder or with a hidden miniature camera ready to snap away and, having read the note, slipped it back in it envelope and laid it on the table.

'Gosh!' was all she could think of to say. This was better than reading detective novels. This was the real thing and she, or at least her hotel, was in the thick of things.

Ivan returned with Myrtle's drink on his tray and, placing it on the table, said, 'There is a telephone call for you Miss Hernandez. I've asked the caller to hold while you are paged.'

'Already so soon? This is it then,' Holly said. 'Let's go see what is in store for us, shall we?'

'I'll be waiting right here,' Myrtle whispered, almost unable to breathe.

Holly entered the phone booth in reception and lifted the receiver.

'Yes?'

'Miss Hernandez?'

'Of course.'

'Please listen very carefully to what I have to say.'

'Go ahead, I'm listening.'

'I have some very bad news for you. I am sorry to have to tell you the man you accidentally shot this afternoon died where he fell. The matter has not been reported to the police and the body has not been moved.'

'Who was the man?'

'What?'

'I asked you, who was the man?'

'Is that important?'

'Of course it's important.'

There was a pause while the person at the other end thought about this unexpected question or was he having a confab with his hand over the mouthpiece? He came back on line.

'Evidently he was an itinerant, a personage of no importance.'

'Not true,' Holly contradicted him, 'everyone is of some

importance.'

'Miss Hernandez I am not making this call to discuss morality or ethics with you. I am giving you the situation and making you an offer. When the police are informed of this accident you will be charged at least with manslaughter or, alternatively, we can put the whole thing to rest for a price. The question is are you prepared to pay the price before your whole privileged world collapses around you?'

'Are you a communist?'

'I beg your pardon?'

'I asked you if you are a communist.'

'No, I am not a communist. That was a bloody ridiculous question and stalling for time isn't going to help your situation.' He was fast losing his cool. Holly had a way of sometimes doing that to people.

'I only asked because of your mentioning privilege.'

'Miss Hernandez, please just answer the sixty four thousand dollar question, are you prepared to pay the price?'

'You haven't told me what the price is.'

'Two million United States dollars or its equivalent in whatever currency you are used to.'

The pause was now from Holly's side as she let out a low astonished whistle.

'That's a whole lot more than sixty four thousand isn't it?'

'You are being frivolous again. How can you be so frivolous when you are in such a desperate situation?'

His voice had risen half an octave. It sounded as though the caller was becoming more than just a little exasperated. He had never before had to deal with someone like Holly. Usually the person on the other end of the line was in a state of near incoherent panic and ready to agree to anything.

Holly wondered whether to add to his edginess by enquiring why, if she had shot this man some seven hours previously and the accident was common knowledge at the club, why had it not been reported to the police and emergency services seven hours earlier? It would need some explaining. But, as this was all a game, perhaps it wasn't the wisest course of action to take if it was up to her to close the trap.

Her brief silence made the man even more nervous. 'Miss

Hernandez?' he called.

'All right, then, give me instructions as to how I pay this exorbitant piece of blackmail?'

'Miss Hernandez please! Please do not use words like that. This is our way of trying our very best to help you. You should be grateful, not accusing us of... Anyway, to get to the point at last.'

'Do I have time to think about it?'

'No!'

'All right. How do I pay you?'

'Tomorrow morning you will come to the offices of a firm called Fundraisers Limited. The offices are in Foxton Street, E.C.4, having with you the means of paying the amount requested. Is that understood?'

'Fully, though it doesn't give me much time does it?'

'We know you are departing these shores in a couple of days; we don't have the luxury of unlimited time.'

My, my, Holly thought, this is one self-educated literary ponce. Departing these shores forsooth. Why couldn't he just say leaving the bloody country? He's one of those people who calls a rat catcher a rodent exterminator or a train driver a footplate operative. Out loud she said, 'There's no way of reducing the amount I suppose.'

'Miss Hernandez!' He was actually shouting now. 'Are you being flippant again? Please resist this temptation because I warn you...'

'All right all right, will you take a cheque?'

There was another short silence before he came back on the line.

'A cheque will be acceptable.'

'What time do you want me there?'

'Will eleven o'clock suit?'

'Perfectly.'

She wanted to add it would give her time for a lie-in but thought better of it. She could fool around with this bunch only so much even though she believed she had the better of them.

'Then I will say good night and please, Miss Hernandez, do not try to do anything foolish.'

There was a click as her caller replaced his receiver before she could say "Like what?"

Holly stood for a moment holding her receiver and then depressed the cradle, got a line and dialled another number. She wanted to bring Thornton up to date but there was no answer either from his office or his flat. She hoped she would have better luck with Carmen.

In the lounge Myrtle was hobnobbing with some of her guests who had arrived and settled down during Holly's absence but her mind wasn't on the polite exchanges of the day's happenings such as a visit to The Tower and a visit to Madam Tussaud's. When they're on your doorstep figuratively speaking, you don't really give them much thought. Half listening to her guests she kept her eye on the door waiting Holly's return. Ivan was accepting orders for drinks and Myrtle, having downed her gin and It, placed her glass on his tray as he passed and requested he bring her another. She excused herself from the couple she had been talking to and hurried back to her own table as Holly reappeared looking like the cat that got the cream. They sat down and Holly raised her glass.

'Well?' Myrtle, almost breathless, just couldn't wait. 'Well?'

'Would you mind if there were a third person for dinner?'

'Who? Who?'

'The legendary Miss Carmen Inez Hernandez.' Holly whispered.

'I'm going to meet her at last! Of course I don't mind. Why should I mind? I take it you've just called her. But didn't she have something on this evening? Girls like that don't usually sit around waiting for something to happen do they?'

'She had a date but it turned into a headache. Headaches can be so useful.'

'But what about, you know, the other… ?' Myrtle was tingling with expectation.

'That's why she's coming around. She's bringing a cheque worth a king's ransom. Cheers!'

'Cheers!' Myrtle responded, Ivan having brought her her gin.

Rory was seated at the kitchen table nursing a cup of tea when Iris McIvor schlepped in looking like death.

'Morning,' she croaked as she went to hang up her hat and coat.

'Morning,' Rory said. 'Haven't seen you for a day or so, did you enjoy the party?'

'Very nice, thank you. Yes, very nice.' She dragged her feet over to the Welsh dresser to collect a cup and saucer.

'You don't look all that well,' Rory remarked. 'Should you be here?'

'I'll be all right in a mo. To be honest, had a hard night at The Rose And Crown.'

'Rum and blackcurrants again? Was it a celebration?'

'Yes, in a way. Suppose you could call it that.'

'Well, before you pour yourself a tea,' Rory said, holding her cup with both hands in front of her mouth, 'we have a visitor in the guest bedroom,' she swallowed the last mouthful and looked into her cup as though she might find something there with which to tell her fortune but, as she used teabags, all she could see was an empty china cup, 'be a dear and take him a cup will you? Plenty of sugar.' She watched Iris as she made her way to the table, put the cup and saucer down and, without a word, pour the tea, add three heaped spoonfuls of sugar and depart for the guest bedroom. Rory smiled and waited.

The curtains being closed, the room was still fairly dark when Iris, having knocked on the door, waited a moment and, receiving no answer, entered. The guest, seemingly naked from what she could see of him, was lying with his back to her. She switched on the bedside lamp and was about to put down the cup and saucer when Thornton turned around.

'Good morning,' he said with a cheery smile.

Iris McIvor, for a nano-second, froze and then, from her momentarily semi-paralysed vocal cords emitted a clear soprano scream that should have shattered glass and shaken the building to its foundations. The cup and saucer went flying as she turned and fled the room on legs that had suddenly seemed to take on the characteristics of jelly but with still enough wobble to project her forwards.

Thornton sat up and looked at the mess on the bedspread.

'Well, I've heard about tea in bed but this is ridiculous,' he said. He found his watch on the bedside cabinet and squinted at it. Nine-thirty. He'd best get weaving. Holly could well be in the thick of things right this minute.

Rory had not moved from the table when Iris came flying into the kitchen as if all the demons from her personal hell were at her tail.

'It's that man!' She squealed. 'That man! He's here again! He's here to haunt me! He's here to drive me crazy!' All the while this hysterical outburst was going on she was hurriedly slipping into her coat.

'Are you leaving us?' Rory asked quietly, as though it were a normal everyday situation.

'I am leaving. Oh, yes! Oh, yes, I am most definitely leaving! I wouldn't stay here another minute, not if you was to pay me a thousand pounds.' She had slapped on her hat and was now busily fastening up the large wooden buttons on her ancient coat. Rory noticed one was only half a button. 'Can I have my money for the week now?'

'No,' Rory said, 'I haven't been to the bank. 'You could of course wait if you like.'

'Not on your bleeding Nellie! And why do you have to go to the bank? You always keep money in the house.' She cast an anxious glance towards the door from which at any moment she feared Thornton would appear, possibly naked and that would be too much for a woman brought up in the strictest Calvinist tradition even if she had lapsed quite considerably.

'Well today I'm afraid you're out of luck Iris McIvor. There is no money in the flat.'

Iris's eyes narrowed. Why had Rory called her by her full name? She hadn't done that since her very first interview, after which it was Mrs McIvor and then just Iris, but never again Iris McIvor until this moment.

'All right,' she whispered with as much venom as she could muster considering the state she was in, 'you can keep your stinking money and a fat lot of good may it do you.'

'At last we show ourself in our true colours,' Rory said, and laid a couple of notes on the table.

Iris hesitated for a second then moved swiftly to snatch up the notes before turning and fleeing through the back door to make her way down the fire escape just as Thornton, in one of Sir Roger's much too small for him dressing gowns, appeared carrying the cup and saucer.

'Hi! How're you feeling? Sleep well?'

'Like the proverbial log but I'll feel better after a nice hot cup of tea. The one Iris brought me ended up soaking the bedclothes. Sorry about that.' He put the cup and saucer in the sink and Rory got up to fetch another from the Welsh dresser as Thornton sat down at the table. For a while he watched as she poured.

'Milk?'

'Huh-huh.'

'Sugar?'

'No thanks.'

'There you go.'

'Ta.'

For a while there was silence as Thornton savoured his tea, then he put down his cup and said, 'Well, was that a normal reaction or was it the reaction of a guilty person? I won't mention the reaction of a certain Scottish king at a dinner party when a ghost appeared because that's supposed to be terribly bad luck and today I think we're going to need all the good luck we can get.'

'Guilty I would say, without question.'

'Hmn-Hmn. And where might the good lady be now?'

'Gone. Thataways,' as she indicated the fire escape. 'And she won't be back. In fact I wouldn't be at all surprised if they abandon everything in London and head back across the border. Where would they go from? Euston? Kings Cross? Or would they go in their brand new car? Maybe we should inform the police to keep a lookout for them.'

'Why? We don't know they actually... well, let me rephrase that, we do know but we can't prove what they got up to so, for now, they're free to take to their heels. If only Reg had listened to me... '

'Reg?'

'Chief Inspector Venables.'

'Oh, him.'

'Yes, him. Well, never mind. Do you have any food in the flat? I'm absolutely starving. How about some breakfast?'

Rory got to her feet. 'I'll have a look, see what there is.'

'When you open the pantry door, stand to one side.'

'Don't be silly. Lightning doesn't strike the same place twice.'

'Famous last words.'

He noticed though that she did as he suggested and stood well to one side.

'What'd I tell you?' she said, laughing, he couldn't help but think with relief.

'Rory...'

'What?'

'How lucky for me they dumped me where they did, and how lucky you were where you were at the time. There is such a thing as fate you know. Did I thank you for saving my life?'

'You did. I wonder how Adrian's shoot went. He should be back home by now.'

'I hope his neighbours remembered to take in the second bottle of milk. Do you think they handed it back wearing rubber gloves? Wouldn't surprise me.'

'Corn flakes do?'

'Delicious. I read somewhere, couldn't have been The Reader's Digest, that the original Mr Kellogg, the inventor of cornflakes, made his contribution to our culinary delights in an effort to stop the youth of America from masturbating. Goodness only knows why he imagined corn flakes would have that effect. Do you think it could be true?'

'Sounds pretty far-fetched to me.'

'Yes, and it obviously hasn't worked.'

As she waited for her cab, Holly was in what she referred to as her working outfit just in case she had to, as the Americans say, "kick some ass!"– Soft black leather jacket and trousers, and boots that were practical and comfy but with pointed toes and sharp heels. The Commonwealth Bank of Virginia (Roanoke branch) cheque for two million United States dollars payable to an account held by Fundraisers in the Cayman Islands was safely deposited in a money belt. The cheque was unsigned.

First port of call was Adrian's cottage. She still had no idea where Thornton was and it could be he was there. Adrian was ex-directory and she didn't have his number, besides which she wanted him to photograph the cheque and keep the evidence together with the note announcing the telephone call.

The cab pulled up at the end of the mews, Holly got out, paid the man and walked to Adrian's front door. Her one and only previous visit here she remembered was the evening she followed a suspected murderess all the way from Soho to this very mews before losing her. She had a vision of the girl's middle aged victim slumped over a table in L'eminence Grise with his face in his cream dessert. It was one of a number of murders in what became known as The Spitskaya Affair. She rang the bell. There was the sound of excited yapping from inside and a twitching of lace curtains from across the way. Funny, Holly said to herself, I thought it was only the middle and lower classes that twitched curtains. Her musing was interrupted by the opening of Adrian's door and Tiddly sniffing around her ankles before he wandered off a few feet to cock his leg against a neighbour's jardinière.'

'Yes?' Adrian barked and then, as the penny dropped, 'My word! It's you! But you're so butch!'

'Only to look at.'

'Lovely to look at. Where did you get that gorgeous leather? Oh, just feel it, it's so sexy? I think I could be on the turn.'

'Can I come in before your neighbour...' She jerked back her head to indicate the house opposite '... pulls her curtains off their rods.'

'What? Oh, don't mind her. She isn't half a right nosey bitch.' He peered around Holly's shoulder, took his fingers off her arm where he had been feeling the leather, waved them in the air and yelled, 'Cooee!' and the curtain stopped twitching. 'Come on in, come on in. It's Holly isn't it?'

'That's right. I don't suppose Thornton is here is he?'

'No he is not. That naughty boy! Against all admonition from both Rory Pemberton and myself, he did a runner once more. Seems to me he makes a habit of it. Anyway I haven't seen him since but he was good enough to get her across the way to take the milk in for me, which I am sure she didn't do with good grace. So, would you care for a cup of coffee? Oh, hang on, where's Tiddly?'

Adrian went back outside to find Tiddly sitting on the doorstep and a furious next-door neighbour glowering at him.

'Now look here, Mister S-S-Spangle, this just isn't on you know. If that animal of yours relieves himself on my jardinière once more I will really have to d-d-do something about it like c-c-c-call the RSPCA and have him taken away.'

'He's only following the call of nature.'

'Well I would prefer it if he f-f-f-followed it elsewhere. Is that understood?'

'P-p-perfectly.'

The man returned to his house, slamming the door very loudly. Adrian gave a silent twos-up and prodded Tiddly with his foot for them both to re-enter the house. He took a quick glance across the road and the curtains stopped twitching.

'My god, what a lot of old pussies I have as neighbours,' he said to Holly. 'I would hate for something really dreadful to happen in this mews. They'd all throw their skirts over their heads and faint clean away just like the Rabelais story about the old lady and the lion... Oh, no! You don't really want to hear that one.'

'I'd love to hear it, Adrian but I'm afraid there's not much time.'

'Some other time then. Where were we? Oh, yes, Thornton. Sorry, can't help.'

'Well never mind. He will turn up when least expected I suppose. There is something else you can do for me though.'

'Oh? And what may that be?'

Holly removed the cheque from her money belt and held it out for Adrian to take.

'Photograph this for me please and keep the negative safe, together with this.' She handed over the note in its envelope.

'Talking of notes, Thornton borrowed twenty quid and my Leica. I don't mind about the twenty quid but I do hope he's careful with the camera; it's one of my favourites. I tell everyone it belonged to Leni Riefenstahl' Adrian stopped talking to look at the cheque and almost freaked out.

'Two million dollars!'

'Don't worry; it's actually not even worth the paper it's printed on. As you can see it is unsigned and Miss Carmen Inez Hernandez whose account it is drawn on will never sign it.'

'Then what's the purpose of the exercise if one may be so bold as to ask?'

'It's a mousetrap, isn't it? Only we have high hopes that it's going to catch quite a few very big rats.'

Thornton tried calling Holly's flat and got no reply. He called

Harold but Harold hadn't seen her that morning and the car was still in the lot. He called the Hotel Diana to be told Miss Hernandez had already left. Unfortunately it wasn't Myrtle who answered the phone or Thornton could have got the information he wanted.

He went back into the kitchen where Rory, in hat and coat, was just stuffing some papers into her briefcase before setting off for a scheduled meeting regarding charity to yet another third world country in the midst of a brutal civil war where, as usual it was mainly civilians, particularly women and children, who were suffering.

'What's the plan of action, Thornton? Did you manage to raise Holly?'

He shook his head.

'Well, can I drop you off somewhere. I mean, stay here if you like but if you have plans…' She trailed off.

'I have plans,' he said.

CHAPTER ELEVEN

Annette Friedman Q.C. fiddled with her papers for a few moments. There really was no need for her to do it. She new exactly what she was going to say, what questions needed to be asked in her cross-examination, from which direction her attack would come, but this short delay heightened the sense of drama as the man in the dock waited, sweated, and looked and indeed felt as sick as a parrot, as she believed with a certain amount of sadistic satisfaction he had every right to be.

It wouldn't do to delay for too long though, as Mister Justice Stampley, crotchety with extreme age and the fact that after a lifetime of indulgence, he was now incapable of raising anything other than his blood pressure, was prone to becoming extremely agitated and she knew what he was like when his short fuse was lit, having suffered the lashing of his tongue on more than one occasion in the days of her inexperienced youth. It certainly wouldn't look good for him to have a go at her now. This case was of great importance both to Friedman And Friedman and particularly to herself and she had every intention of doing it full justice, in other words, a thorough demolition job.

The dark panelled courtroom, its Gothic windows with occasional palely coloured diamond panes set high in the wall facing the street from where the muffled sound of traffic penetrated the building, was small and packed, not just with the legal teams, officers of the court, jury, and newspaper hounds scenting blood, but a number of spectators crowded in the public gallery on hard benches sitting uncomfortably hip to hip.

Annette sensed she had played her delaying card long enough and was ready to launch her assault. This was her triumphal moment when the victory to be won was in her brilliant hands. Her team were gazing at her with something not short of adoration. She looked up, holding her papers in one hand, and surveyed her audience because, to her, that was what the people in that courtroom were, her audience. There is not all that much difference between events taking place in courts of law and events taking place on theatrical stages. Think how many films have been produced on the trials of Oscar Wilde and that gasp making moment when asked by an earlier Q.C. by the name of Carson if he had kissed a certain boy and he replied, "Oh, no, he was much too ugly," and, too late, realised the courtroom was not the time or place for an ultra smart mouth. And now a gasp making moment was about to take place in this particular court as Annette, surveying those intense faces all concentrating on her, thought she saw one smiling face in particular that just should not have been there. Her heart missed a beat. The room seemed suddenly to be suffocating. There was a humming in her ears. Her papers fluttered to the floor as she clutched at her head and swayed against the table and men rushed to her aid to help her from the room as Mister Stampley, who had actually dozed off for a moment, woke with a start, huffing and puffing and wanting to know what on earth had happened. A clerk whispered to him.

'Oh, dear, oh, dear!' The old codger growled, looking around his courtroom, 'I sincerely hope my learned friend will soon recover. This case has dragged on quite long enough.' What he really meant was that, despite his air cushion placed so carefully on the bench beneath the coat of arms with its heraldic beasts and motto of Dieu Et Mon Droit his piles were complaining bitterly and he was fully conscious of their complaints because he was totally bored with the proceedings. He crooked a finger towards one of Annette's juniors who advanced on the bench. Mister Stampley leaned forward and in a voice that was meant to be a question simply for the lawyer alone but which the whole court heard quite clearly, he asked, 'The lady isn't pregnant is she?'

'I don't believe she is, my lord.'

'Oh.'

So there wasn't even a whiff of scandal to enliven the proceedings. He decided he had been a judge far too long. It really was high time he retired but for now a recess was in order and as "All rise" was called, he stood up very gingerly. He would hate to blow a fuse at this point because the court had been suddenly reduced to dead silence and, cheeks clamped as firmly together as his ancient gluteus muscles could manage, he departed humped backed and stiff-legged. Immediately the noise in the room was horrendous as Annette's team gathered up their stuff preparatory to moving out, reporters dashed away, and virtually everyone had some comment to make about this untoward event.

Holly glanced at the brass plate bearing the Fundraiser legend and waited for someone to answer her imperious ring. It wasn't too long before Seymour opened the door to her.

'Good morning,' Holly said. 'I am… '

But without a word Seymour, a picture of dejection, stepped back and to one side to allow her in before closing the door after a quick glance up and down the narrow street. Seymour was a very much-subdued animal since losing his beloved Jaguar. He spoke not a word as he led her through reception to the door of Nikos's office and rapped on it before opening it, indicating with a gesture for her to enter, and then turning away again. Holly was sure he must have suffered the bereavement of at least the closest person in his life. Well perhaps he had but here she was ready to continue the game as Nikos Filodopoulis eased himself out of his chair and, smiling at his visitor, held his hand out to indicate the one opposite.

'So, Miss Hernandez, we meet at last. I'm so sorry we never got a chance to bump into each other at the club but, not being into archery myself, I seldom go there, only for business meetings you understand, or for a bit of socialising, wining and dining that sort of thing. Thank you for coming. My name is Nikos Filodopoulis. I presume you have the necessary with you and everything is shipshape and Bristol fashion?' He resumed his seat.

Holly fished in her money belt and handed over the cheque before she sat down.

'Thank you,' Nikos said. 'Everything aboveboard? There will be no complications I trust. Please excuse my use of nautical terms but we Greeks are a seafaring nation just like the British, are we not?' Nikos suffered seasickness just looking at waves let alone being on them. He would have been sick boating on the Serpentine.

He had resumed his seat and now opened the cheque that had

been handed to him folded in half and looked at it for a long time.

'Two million United States Dollars,' he said as though hardly able to believe it, 'a not inconsiderable sum of money, Miss Hernandez. That tramp died not knowing how much loot his miserable carcase would generate.'

'You have a macabre way of putting things if you don't mind my saying so. Loot? Blood money is what I would call it. And carcase? Have you no respect for the dead? How do you think I feel having been responsible for what has happened?'

'You have too soft a heart. I am led to believe that in South America there are death squads that go around murdering little children, is this true? If it is true then why are you so upset about the death of one smelly drunken old tramp? Because that is what he was you know.'

Nikos sniffed and gave his chair a vigorous swivel so that it turned a complete circle and then, facing Holly again, he held out the cheque in both hands.

'However, like I say, in dying he has produced this, which is of absolutely no use to us as it bears no signature. Why is that?'

'Well of course it's unsigned,' Holly said, unflinchingly meeting his gaze, 'I filled it in for the amount you asked for but left it to sign here in front of you. You would want to be absolutely certain the signature is genuine wouldn't you?

'Of course we would, Miss Day, of course we would,' he purred as he handed back the cheque and Holly, taking it, was about to ask for the use of his gold fountain pen with which to sign when the penny dropped.

For what seemed an age she sat looking at the cheque in her hands and then up at Nikos. How on earth had they rumbled her? Well there was only one way to find out and that was to ask which was exactly what she did. So it was Mike Aliff was it who fingered her? Of all people it had to be him. What dreadful bad luck to be spotted at the last moment. So what now? Nikos Filodopoulis she decided was a pushover, as was the runt who showed her in. Somehow her thoughts seemed to transfer themselves to Nikos because he shook his head and said, 'I don't think it's worth you trying anything stupid, Miss Day, your sporting coach, Mister Timpson is waiting outside together with Martin to escort you to The Bowmen Of Essex where it will be decided what is to be done with you.'

But Holly wasn't having it. She stood up, kicking back her chair and lunged across the desk where she was brought up short by a snub nose revolver in inch from her own snub nose.

Nikos laughed. 'You're squinting down the barrel from the wrong end, Miss Day,' he chortled.

Myrtle Cullen was a worried woman. She stood behind the reception desk and drummed her fingers on the marble, every now and again glancing at her watch. She should have heard from Holly simply ages ago but there had been no word and the bawdy hand of time was well passed the prick of noon as one of Shakespeare's immortal characters might have said. What could have happened? If only she could get in touch with Thornton but she had absolutely no idea where he could be. She had looked up his number in the telephone directory and called his office but the phone was dead. She would leave it a while longer, she wasn't quite sure how much longer and then, if there were still no sign of Holly, she would call the police.

Sir Peter and Nikos the Greek were in The Wig And Gown enjoying a quiet conversation over their Stilton and an excellent vintage port when Nikos happened to glance towards the street door as it opened for a moment and then closed again. His knife was half way to his mouth when it stopped and he visibly paled. He dropped the knife which fortunately did not shatter his plate but he stood up in such a hurry he knocked over his glass sending a blood red stain streaming across the table and forcing Sir Peter to shove back his chair and hurriedly rise, wiping himself down with his napkin and uttering very loud curses that brought the pub to a standstill.

A barman hurried over to clean up the mess. On shaky legs Nikos made for the door, pushed it open with no thought as to who might be on the other side, a young lawyer in fact who was nimble enough to jump back out of the way as the corpulent figure dashed out and stood looking up and down the busy street for the man he thought he had seen, but of that man there was no sign. He returned to the table, passing the scowling young man he had almost barged into but ignoring him completely.

'I would have thought an apology might have been in order,' the young man bleated.

Now Nikos turned on him. 'What?'

'You heard me. I said…'

'You want an apology? Here's your apology!' and Nikos raised a threatening fist. He had just been startled out of his wits by an apparition and was in no mood for being told to apologise to a smarmy little creep of a lawyer, a lawyer's clerk even.

'Go on then!' The young man said. 'Go on! Hit me! Hit me! Do! I'll have you for assault. I could already have you for assault. We can always add with intent to commit GBH.'

'Steady now, steady,' a calm voice intervened as Sir Peter moved over to virtually place himself between them.

'And who might you be?' The young man asked becoming more and more belligerent.

'Sir Peter Wheeler. Who might you be?' The young man did not like the look on Sir Peter's face. There was a silence before the older man continued, turning to look at Nikos. 'I feel sure that, had any damage been done, my friend here would have immediately apologised but, as it is,' he turned back to the young man, 'why don't we all just forget it happened, yes?'

There was something in Sir Peter's voice as well that warned the young man he was treading on dangerous ground if he insisted on continuing his uppity stance so he merely nodded. Like a losing stag giving in with as good a grace as he could muster, he turned his back on the pair, and made his way to the bar.

The bar's habitués, who had been agog from the moment Nikos dropped his knife, realised the possible fracas was not going to take place and the pub for a moment returned to being a fairly calm and pleasant watering hole. That is, until the young man in a voice loud enough for all to hear broke his news.

'You'll never guess what's just happened.' He paused until he was quite sure he had everyone's attention. 'Annette Friedman has just collapsed in court. Had to be carted out.'

The result of this announcement was hubbub as Sir Peter and Nikos returned to their table and sat down to hopefully finish their meal. At least that was Sir Peter's idea. He was particularly fond of really ripe Stilton and he wasn't going to lose out just because mayhem seemed to have erupted this day in The Wig And Gown.

For a moment he eyed the young lawyer who was now the centre of attention and then turned to his companion.

'And what was all that about may one ask?'

'What? Annette Friedman? How would I know?'

'No, your sudden rise and exit.'

'I saw Thornton King.'

Sir Peter stared at him. This time it was his arm held suspended in mid-air, not holding a knife but a portion of Stilton that crumbled in his hand and fell back messily, distributed equally between the table and his lap. Using his napkin he started to wipe away the mess before it could look as though it was he who had an accident.

'Thornton King is dead,' he said in his boardroom voice that brooked no argument.

'I tell you I saw him there, large as life. He stood at the door for a second. He was smiling. And then he disappeared. That's when I went to look for him.'

'You saw him again when you went outside?'

'No.'

'Hmn.' He stopped jabbing at his trousers with the napkin. Things were not improving down there. 'I wonder if the sudden appearance of this dreaded spectre was the reason for Annette's indisposition.'

'Could be. Could be. I swear to you, Sir Peter. He was there!'

'All right, he was there. As I have no belief in an afterlife or in things such as ghosts and, as I know with what you have drunk at lunch that you are not pissed out of your mind and simply seeing things... wait a moment though... could it have been a doppelganger do you suppose? A double? Someone who is the spitting image of our man? That's a possibility.'

'No. There is no point in fooling ourselves. Thornton King is alive and obviously ready to kick butt.'

'Oh, God! I do so hate these vulgar American expressions.' He helped himself to another portion of cheese. 'Why does everybody use them? What is happening to the English language? Well, I suppose then it is up to us to kick butt before we give Mister King the chance to kick ours.'

'All very well, but how do we find him now? After what's happened he's going to be like the scarlet pimpernel. We'll seek him here, we'll... '

'Yes, yes, all right, all right. That's enough of that. God! If I'm not putting up with whimsical Welshmen at my bridge table I'm putting up with lyrical Greeks at my lunch table.'

'Where is he then?'

Thornton was in fact no more than two hundred yards away trying to find a telephone that hadn't been vandalised, used as a public convenience or was still in working order, and one that had a telephone directory intact. Attempt number five proved to be the one but it was already in use by a young lady in a mini-skirt and sporting a beehive bleached hairdo and fingernails of assorted colours as though she couldn't make up her mind which she preferred. Chewing gum in between words she evidently intended to stay there a long time as, by her tone, she was obviously billing and cooing and there was a pile of coins on top of the box. Why couldn't she use the office phone like any normal person, Thornton thought. He waited, growing more and more impatient. Made faces through the glass. She turned her back on him. He walked around to the other side and held up his left arm to tap on his watch. She turned her back again. He had had enough. He flung open the door and hissed:

'Just how long are you going to be on that phone?'

'Piss off!' she said and tried to pull the door closed but he wasn't having it.

'Look, woman!' he snarled, in his most menacing manner, wrenching the door open and almost pulling her out of the box with it, 'if you're not off that phone in one minute I'm going to carve you up so bad you'll wish you'd never been born. Get it?'

She stared at him wide-eyed before turning away and addressing the phone for the last time.

'Gotta go,' she squeaked, 'call ya later.' She put down the phone, hurriedly scooped up her coins and edged passed Thornton sideways to make her escape.

It wasn't until he had lifted the receiver off its cradle that Thornton realised he had no coins. He pressed the B button in the hope that some might fall out but without any luck. Were there any on the floor? He took a quick look but again drew a blank. He could have beaten his head against the back of the booth instead of which he noticed reflected in the little mirror that the young lady was standing some distance away talking animatedly to a policeman and pointing towards the telephone booth. In a moment when they were looking at each other rather than in his direction he slipped out of the booth and moved away to mingle with the pedestrians enjoying their lunchtime freedom. A man entered the phone booth and was startled, just as he was about to dial, to receive a tap on the shoulder from the stern faced upholder of the law as curious passers by stopped to watch.

Thornton could break a note by purchasing something and so get coins with his change, but what would he purchase? He didn't smoke so cigarettes were out and nobody would be pleased to change a tenner for a bar of chocolate. There was a branch of Barclays close by but, what with the lunchtime queues, it would take forever to even get to a teller so he decided rather to head back to the office where he could make his call in peace. No, he couldn't. He had forgotten to pay the bill despite final demands and being flush with Rory's cheque, and his phone had been cut off. He could make the call from Harold's office. No he couldn't. Harold was out and the office was closed and locked. He could make the call from Carlotta's. No he couldn't. She was busy with a client and bound hand and foot. Her maid was out doing the shopping. It seemed everybody and everything was tied up one way or another and the only answer he got to his ring at the door was the dog yapping in the dim recesses of the house.

Time was passing and he was growing desperate. He decided to hail a cab and head for the Hotel Diana. He had no idea where Holly could be.

The car pulled into the club car park and Steve got out of the driving seat to open the nearside passenger door and jerk his head to indicate Holly should get out. Even with her hands tied behind her back Holly would have made an attempt to escape were it not for the fact that Martin was quick to follow her out of the car and the gun was once more pushed rather brutally against her side. Given just half a chance she would get this bastard for that but it seemed, as they marched her toward the clubhouse, one on either side, that she might never get that chance. She looked around but could see no sign of Maurice's car. That surprised her. Albert said they would definitely be there but maybe he meant later in the day.

They passed a couple of members, bows in hand, exiting the club laughing and chatting who gave no indication they thought there might be something wrong with the way the men had Holly between them, in fact hardly gave them more than a passing nod, and Holly gave no indication she was in any kind of trouble. She could have pretended to stumble, thus attracting their attention but who knows who could be trusted here? Who all were in the conspiracy?

In Oscar Wilde's time when he was sent down to serve his term of hard labour any number of English gentlemen thought it prudent to take the next packet to France and disappear for a while either there or further afield in Italy or Greece and, if this little racket came to light and the perpetrators brought to justice, Holly thought, there could very well be a similar sort of hasty exodus.

No one else passed them as she was bundled through the building and into the office where, to her astonishment, Mike Aliff was waiting, seated calmly in the chair behind the desk and smiling.

'Well well well, and what do we have here? If it isn't my dear friend and colleague, Miss Holly Day, soon I am afraid to be of blessed memory.' He got up and walked around to the front of the desk to sit back on it in nonchalant fashion, a gesture meant to say that at last he had Holly where he wanted her, well, almost. 'What do you think, gentlemen? Should we have some fun with Miss Day before we finish her off?'

'No,' Steve said. 'Let's just get it over with nice and quick.'

'Hmn... All right, if that's the way you want it.' He sounded most disappointed. 'But first a few questions just to satisfy my curiosity.'

'In that case,' Holly said, 'can I have my hands back please? They're running out of blood and I am afraid gangrene or something equally as nasty will set in. Not, I suppose that it really matters if I am soon to be deceased but take it as a last request.'

'Oh, Holly, Holly, Holly.' Mike metronomed an admonishing finger, 'you just cannot resist it, can you? Do you think I was born yesterday?'

'Three hulking great men, one with a gun, and probably more men outside and you're afraid to untie my hands? Do me a favour, please!'

'All right, even though it's against my better judgment.' Mike nodded to Steve who stepped forward somewhat reluctantly and started to undo the knotted cord.

'Now tell me,' Mike continued, 'does this Carmen Hernandez really exist? Or is she a fabrication schemed up in your own devious little brain?'

'Oh, she exists all right and she was quite willing to enter into the spirit of things and allow me to impersonate her.'

Holly's wrists were now free and she rubbed first one and then the other, restoring the circulation.

'Does she know why?'

'No. I deliberately kept her in ignorance.'

'Yet she was willing to give you a cheque for two million dollars.'

'Unsigned and useless.'

'But surely her curiosity would have got the better of her?'

Holly shrugged. 'If it did, and maybe it did, she was still in the dark and obviously now will stay that way.'

'And where at this moment might your friend Thornton be?' This was said with such a knowing smile, Holly had the feeling Mike already knew, or thought he knew, where Thornton was.

Again she gave a shrug. 'Actually I haven't a clue,' she said.

Thornton handed the cabbie a note to keep him pacified, told him, to wait and almost ran into the Hotel Diana. Myrtle was still behind the reception desk and looked up somewhat startled at his entry.

'Are you Mrs Cullen?'

'Ye-es?'

'My name's Thornton King and...'

'Oh! You're Thornton?'

'Where is Holly?'

'Holly?'

'Mrs Cullen...'

'Myrtle.'

'Myrtle. I must know where Holly is. She could be in the greatest danger. There's no time for pleasantries, just tell me if you know.'

'She left this for you.' Myrtle fished under the counter and came up with the copy of *The Quiver*. Scribbled at the top of the front page was Fundraisers Limited.

'Thank you.'

Myrtle called after him as he turned to dash out again.

'Mister King!'

'Thornton.'

'Thornton. You left your magazine.'

'Keep it safe.' And he was gone.

'Foxton Street, the City,' he snapped, and jumped into the cab. The cabby flicked his cigarette stub out the widow, put his cab in gear and they set off. It was going to be one of the most nerve-racking journeys of Thornton's life. At that time of day traffic was at its heaviest and, by the time they reached Foxton Street, he would be beside himself with anxiety. He had got Holly into this. If she was in trouble it was up to him to get her out, if he wasn't already too late.

'Well, the bad news I have for you, Holly,' the smile on Mike Aliff's face broadened, 'is that your friend Thornton King is dead.

Holly stared at him but said nothing.

'The good news I have for you, is that it won't be long now before you join him.' He really seemed to be relishing the situation.

For a moment Holly's stare was one of incredulity and then she burst out laughing.

Mike's smile turned into a frown. 'You find that amusing?'

'You look a right ponce, you really do, and you sound like the author of bad crime fiction. Who wrote your lines for you?'

'Most amusing, yes, most amusing, but whatever I look like and however I sound, I am the one who is going to survive and survive quite handsomely I might say. The department may miss you for a short while Miss Day but you will soon be replaced. You are not unique. Fortunately there are plenty more where you came from.'

'That is the crassest thing I have ever heard,' Holly said.

'Right, I reckon it's time to move.'

The telephone rang.

'Wait a moment.' He went around to the back of the desk and lifted the receiver. 'Yes?' There was a pause. 'It's Mike Aliff.' Another pause during which it was noticeable Mike's knees suddenly gave way as the great survivor turned ashen and sat down with a thump.

'It can't be true,' he whispered, 'it can't be true.'

He swivelled the chair around so that he could listen without having to face Holly and his companions while, sick to his stomach, he digested this piece of unwelcome news, and Holly seized her chance. She took a step towards the desk and lifted a glass paper weight the size of a cricket ball and five times heavier, turned and, in one swift movement, let fly. It hit Martin slap bang in the middle of his forehead. The gun in his hand went off and Steve let out a howl as the bullet hit his shoulder sending him staggering back. Martin was already on the floor, out cold.

Mike turned back to face the room just in time to see Holly make a dash for the door and fling it open only to be brought up short by the bulk of Maurice Chinnery standing there, a bulk large enough to stop her and not be bowled over.

Showing an agility belying his years, Mike was across the room and had Holly by the arms to pull her back while Maurice was still thinking of stepping aside and apologising. Unfortunately, in pulling Holly back, Mike wasn't watching where he put his feet and the next thing he knew he was falling backwards, his heels having been suddenly stopped by Martin's prostrate form. He went down with Holly on top of him and enough force to take the wind right out of his sails. She rolled off and would have headed once more for the door except that Steve had recovered enough to have picked up the gun and now held it pointed in her direction. Holly was still on all fours as she looked down the barrel. With one hand menacing Holly with the gun, albeit not too steadily, and the other over the flesh wound in his shoulder, no more than a nick really though the amount of blood being spilt made it look truly dramatic, Steve slammed the door shut with a hefty back kick.

'I could have been killed!' He yelled. 'Look at me, look at me! I'm fucking bleeding to death!'

'Let me take a look,' Holly volunteered, getting to her feet.

'Don't you bloody come near me! You're a flaming menace, you are!'

'Suit yourself.' She turned to see Mike had got to his feet and she gave a little shrug as she realised, for the moment at least, the game was up.

Thornton rang the bell and waited. It would seem at the moment the offices of Fundraisers Limited were empty of personnel. What was he to do? He stepped back to look up at windows as though they might tell him something and, at that moment the door opened and was being hastily closed again when Thornton yelled,

'I know where your car is!'

The door started to open again and, before Seymour Goodwin could change his mind and close it once more, Thornton shoulder barged his way in sending Seymour flying.

Hearing the ruckus, Nikos quickly retired to behind his desk and drew his gun and, as Thornton burst into the office, he was brought up short at sight of it. He should have known better.

'It is you.' Nikos said. 'I knew I wasn't mistaken.'

Seymour had entered the room behind Thornton.

'Where's my car?' he asked.

'Where is Holly?' Thornton shouted in return.

Holly was back in her chair. Mike rolled Martin over onto his back in order to survey the damage. There was a cut, a widening bruise and a fair sized egg on the man's forehead but he groaned and seemed to be coming around. Steve, meanwhile, still menacing Holly with the gun, had managed to get a handkerchief from his pocket and was holding it against his wound, stanching the blood. The nick was beginning to sting and he didn't appreciate that one little bit. He glared at Holly as if he could kill her which he was hoping to do fairly shortly anyway.

There was a timid knock on the door.

'Not now!' Mike yelled and went to answer the phone ringing once again.

'Yes?'

'Mike?'

'Who else?'

'This is Nikos. I have some very interesting news for you.'

'It had better be something good because I don't think I could take any more bad news right now.'

'Oh, it is, it is. You will never guess who I have here in my office.'

'Oh, please tell me it's true. Please tell me it's who I think it is.'

'It is! It is!' Nikos was almost squeaking with excitement. 'And, guess what. He wants to know where Miss Holly Day is. Isn't that interesting? Shall I tell him or shall I put him on to you?'

'I have a better idea, why don't you just bring him to where she is and we can kill two birds with one stone?'

'Fine. We will do that, amesos, that is Greek for immediately.'

'No, Nikos! Don't say that!' When a Greek says immediately he doesn't necessarily mean this moment. Amesos could mean next week.

And, before the phone went dead, Mike heard a plaintiff voice crying,

'Where's my car then?'

CHAPTER TWELVE

Nikos's car, as befitted a highflying executive, was a silver Bentley, the acme of very expensive smooth running luxury, and Thornton, apparently completely relaxed, lounged in the back with the car's owner at his side while Seymour drove, heading east for Epping. The offices of Fundraisers Limited would be closed for the rest of the day. Seymour still did not know where his own beloved Jaguar was but he was determined to get the location out of Thornton before it was too late and wondering how best to go about getting it. Maybe he ought to start trying right now. 'So, Mister King,' turning his head slightly to the left and talking over his shoulder while keeping half an eye on the road and half an eye on the rear view mirror, 'you say you know where my car is?'

'Stop going on about your bloody car,' Nikos growled. 'We'll find it sooner or later.'

That was what Seymour was afraid of, that it would be later rather than sooner, too late more than likely. He was so distracted by this thought that he drove without due care and attention and had to screech to a stop at a zebra crossing just as an old lady with a walking stick and busily inspecting a basketful of groceries instead of watching where she was going and looking out for oncoming traffic was stepping halfway across. A tin of pineapple chunks she had in her hand flew in the air and made a large dent in the Bentley's bonnet before bouncing off and Nikos was beside himself with rage.

'Malaka!' He yelled. 'Gamo to! Can't you watch what you're doing?'

The old girl stood quivering with shock in the middle of the road while a couple of good Samaritans coming to her aid started to pick up her spilled groceries; but the squeal of the Bentley's tyres had unfortunately alerted a policeman standing nearby and he now approached the car which, unable to move because of the little drama being played out on the crossing, was beginning to hold up the traffic.

'Pull into the side over there please, sir, when the way is clear.' The bobby indicated the far side of the zebra crossing.

The first Samaritan now took hold of the old lady's arm; the second carried her replenished basket as they made it to the pavement. Seymour, his heart palpitating, eased ahead to park the Bentley where ordered, looking straight ahead and ignoring the vicious reactions of the old girl and her new friends (by the looks of them both members of The Workers Revolutionary Party) one now stepping into the road behind the car to retrieve the undented tin of pineapple. In his rear view mirror Seymour could see the cop studying the Bentley's tyre marks and he could only hope the outcome wouldn't be too serious though he realised he was certainly in deep shit, not necessarily with the law but most certainly with Nikos Filodopoulis.

Having taken his time to examine the brake marks and waved on the stopped traffic; the policeman now slowly approached the Bentley. He was going to thoroughly enjoy this. It had been a very dull day so far and, whoever this posh git was in the car, he was going to give him as hard a time as he could. First of all he examined the back tyres, giving one a kick for no reason at all, then he walked around to the front and examined those. He might have known they would all have a good tread. Owners of Bentleys do not allow their cars to run unserviced or on worn tyres.

Getting no joy from that and there was no point in asking about the brakes, they were obviously in good working order, the cop moved to the driver's window and held out his hand.

'Your driving licence please, sir.'

Seymour cleared his throat. His mouth was bone dry and he was finding it difficult to speak but eventually he said, 'I'm afraid I don't have it with me, constable. It's... it's in my car you see.'

'In your car... I see... This car then...' He took a step back to survey the Bentley as if seeing it for the first time '... belongs to?'

'Eine thikó mou.' For some unfathomable reason Nikos obviously thought if he let the cop know he was of foreign extraction it might make matters easier. The cop was suitably unimpressed. 'This car belongs to me.' Nikos said. 'Well not me exactly, the company, it's a company car.'

'And your name, sir?'

'Nikos Filodopoulis. The papers are in the glove compartment, everything is in apple pie order.' Nautical terms seemed to have temporarily deserted him.

'Is that right?' The cop was still singularly unimpressed. He peered passed Nikos and looked hard at Thornton. It seemed he was more than likely thinking he had stopped a right load of East End villains here.

'And who might you be, sir?'

'Thornton King.' Thornton said it as though the policeman would immediately recognise the name but the man's face remained a blank.

'And you are?'

'Oh, I'm just a passenger here,' Thornton said with a smile.

'Indeed. A passenger to where if I may ask?'

Thornton thought for a moment. He couldn't very well say to possibly his imminent death at the hands of bow and crossbowmen but he could tell part of the truth. 'Well constable,' he announced, 'we're on our way to The Bowmen Of Essex. Perhaps you know it?'

'Can't say that I'm familiar with it, sir.' He looked back at Nikos. 'If it's a pub I hope you won't allow your driver to indulge in too much alcohol. He's in enough trouble as it is.'

'It's a club,' Thornton said, 'an archery club. Surely you must know it.'

'No, sir, I don't.' The cop was most emphatic

'Near Epping?' Thornton gesticulated with his left hand in a circular motion as if that would activate some dormant memory in the bobby's mind.

Nikos was growing more and more worried. Thornton was up to something and he didn't like it. Hidden by folded arms he was holding his gun against Thornton's ribs and he now gave them quite a hard jab.

'Ouch!' Thornton went. 'Don't do that.'

'What did he do?'

'Pushed his gun into my ribs. It hurt.'

The cop stared at Thornton for a long moment and then said very sternly, 'If you think this situation calls for humour, Mister... King was it? You are very much mistaken.'

'I'm not joking. Show the man your gun, Nikos.'

Nikos grinned up at the policeman with the look of a naughty child caught playing with himself and raised both hands to show they were empty. Thornton lifted the gun off the seat and transferred it under cover of his right arm to his left hand.

The policeman, for the moment at a loss as to how to continue, decided to return his attention to Seymour sweating with nerves, possibly easier meat. Nikos turned to glower at Thornton who smiled sweetly back.

'You say your licence is in your car, sir, so where might your car be at the moment?'

'I don't know.'

The silence this time was even longer as the cop stared at Seymour. Was everyone here taking the Mick or what?

'And just what do you mean by you don't know?'

'Exactly that, officer. I don't know where it is because it's been stolen.'

'Stolen? When?'

'Recently.'

'And how long ago is recently?'

'Like... er... yesterday.'

'You reported it of course.'

'Er... no... not yet... been meaning to but... '

'You realise you have to present your licence at your nearest police station in the next twenty four hours and just how are you going to do that if it is in your car and your car has been stolen and you have no idea where it is? From where was it stolen?'

'Close to the club.'

'The one you're going to at the moment.'

'Yes.'

'Step out of the car please.'

Seymour opened his door and stepped out. The cop led him a short way from the Bentley, out of earshot of the other two and, taking out his notebook, started his questioning. The old lady and her two new friends whose ears were practically twitching had to be shooed away but not before they felt they ought to put in their pennyworth.

'If you need witnesses…' the young man began, his female companion nodding encouragement.

'Thank you, sir, thank you. If you wouldn't mind waiting over there'.

But the young socialists had no intention of hanging around being that inconvenienced, it was either instantaneous or not at all and, leaving the old lady looking somewhat bemused, off they trotted at a fairly brisk pace.

Nikos and Thornton sat in silence for a while, a silence finally broken by the fuming Greek.

'Well,' he hissed, 'aren't you going to make a break for it? Now's your chance.'

'Certainly not,' Thornton said. 'I'm staying right where I am and when Seymour's finished getting the third degree, we will continue on our merry way to where I hope to rescue a damsel in distress. I must admit I never thought I would be armed for the occasion but there you are, luck just happened to come my way in the shape of a little old lady with a basket of groceries.'

'You won't get away with it,' Nikos said. 'The odds are too great.'

'We'll see about that.'

The policeman closed and pocketed his notebook and an ashen-faced and slightly wobbly Seymour returned to the car, got in and placed quivering hands on the steering wheel.

The copper looked again in the back window.

'Where's this gun then?' he asked with a wry smile.

Thornton and Nikos pointed to each other and said in unison,
'He's got it!'

Thornton and the cop laughed. Nikos did not.

'By the way,' Thornton said, 'do you know my friend Inspector Venables at Central?'

'Not personally, no. Heard of him though. Wasn't he the guy that solved all those murders last year?'

'That's him!' Thornton cut in hurriedly, squirming a little inside. 'Maybe you could do me a favour.'

'Oh, yes? And what might that be?'

'I was supposed to meet him this afternoon but something else has come up. Do you think you could have him informed that I am at the archery club called The Bowmen Of Essex and, if he could manage it, I would like to see him there? As soon as he can make it,' he added for emphasis.

'I think I can do that. And I hope the rest of your journey... ' He stepped back again to look at Seymour who looked straight ahead. His hands had stopped shaking. '... is without incident. On your way then.'

Seymour, all at sixes and sevens, put the car into gear and pulled out but he forgot to look in his mirror and there was a blast from a horn behind him as he quickly swerved back and applied his brakes. The policeman stood on the pavement and shook his head.

'I should have taken him in,' he said to himself, 'he's a bloody menace.'

Reg couldn't feel the side of his mouth. He had impressed on the Rumanian butcher that if she didn't give him an injection this session he was going to get out of the chair there and then and head for home. Now it felt as if she had given him enough to put an elephant out of its misery having a tusk removed. He was endeavouring to sip delicately and sideways at a cup of tea with frozen lips and a tongue that felt three times its normal size and consisted of vulcanised rubber when constable Roper holding a scrap of paper appeared at the door

'There's been a weird message from Thornton King, sir, via the station at Billericay.'

'They've arrested him,' Reg said gleefully, 'on what charge?'

'No, it's evidently a personal message for you.'

'Yes? What's the boy been up to now?' He made another attempt to take a sip of tea but most of it landed on his desk. He took out a handkerchief to mop up some sodden papers.

'The message reads,' Roper squinted at the piece of paper, 'Can't meet you as planned. Am at The Bowmen Of Essex. See you there.'

'Has he gone stark raving mad? What meeting? And what's this Bowmen Of Essex when it's at home?'

'Search me,' Roper said with a shrug. 'Shall I make enquiries?'

'No. I have no idea what all this is about but I am not going to trundle all the way out to Essex to find out.' Another splash of tea hit the desktop. The handkerchief came into use a second time. 'Tell the

Essex lot to send a squad car round to whatever this bowmen thingy is and find out what Thornton's up to. No good or I'm a monkey's uncle.'

'Righto!' And Roper turned to go.

'Roper?'

He turned back.

'See if you can find me a straw will you?'

The Bentley, suffering no further mishap, turned into the track leading to the clubhouse. Seymour was fuming. Not only had he lost his car but the copper, he felt sure, was going to throw the book at him, starting with driving without due care and attention or worse, failure to produce his licence, withholding information from the police, in fact anything he could dream up, but it was all as nothing compared to what could happen now.

Nikos had decided the odds were in his favour once they reached The Bowmen Of Essex so he might as well just sit back and relax, if that were possible. It wasn't possible, firstly because he too was fuming, at Seymour and the damage to the Bentley and, secondly, because Thornton had made it obvious to the police that something not quite kosher was going on. Or had he? The copper could have taken his badinage about the gun as being that of a stupid joker trying to be amusing.

Thornton was on edge, wondering just how he was going to go about rescuing Holly. He still had the gun gripped in his left hand and transferred it to his right to facilitate opening his door. Nikos thought for a moment of grabbing it but should it go off in the struggle there would definitely be more damage to the Bentley, like possibly a hole in the roof and that would have to be explained at the garage when it went in for repairs.

Once out of the car, Thornton looked around to see if anyone was about but the place seemed strangely deserted. He waggled the gun to indicate Nikos should also leave but Nikos had other ideas. He would stay exactly where he was. What could Thornton do about it? Thornton showed him what he could do about it. He took aim at the front offside wheel and pulled the trigger. Nikos still didn't move. Thornton gave the rear tyre the same treatment and then walked around to Nikos's side and opened the door.

Seymour was already out of the car and skulking by the bonnet not sure of what he should do or what Thornton would do next. He made certain he stood well clear of the wheel.

'Do you want to know where your car is?' Thornton asked. It was a totally unnecessary question. Seymour nodded. 'Go back to the main road, turn left until you see a road to your right and you'll find your car a couple of hundred yards along. The key's in the ignition.'

'Don't listen to him!' Nikos screamed. 'Stay here!' But Seymour was already on his way.

'One down, how many to go?' Thornton asked and, grabbing Nikos by the lapel of his jacket, hauled him from the car. Then, with one hand on his collar and the other holding the gun in the small of his back, he marched him towards the clubhouse. He wasn't exactly sanguine about the situation. There had been two gunshots and not a soul had appeared to find out what was going on. That could only be described as a wholly unnatural situation.

Thornton knew there was no way he was going to use the gun on a human target. No matter how justifiable he felt it might be, he was not one for killing and also he had no intention of going to jail for life on a manslaughter charge or even for a shorter period on a charge of unlawful use of a firearm but Nikos was not to know that.

He pushed his captive forward to open the door of the clubhouse and they entered to emptiness and an eerie silence.

'It's the bloody Marie Celeste,' Thornton whispered. 'Where is everybody?' He looked around and decided to head for the kitchen where he might possibly be able to get rid of Nikos. He was right; there was a walk-in storeroom that locked from the outside.

'In you go, Nikos old lad,' he said, then, 'Two down,' as he locked the door. He stood for a moment looking around before he tried the restaurant which was empty, the office, which was empty, Robin Hood men's changing room and toilets, all empty; the Maid Marian, ditto. The building was totally deserted. But this was ridiculous, there were cars in the car park, someone must be around. He went outside and looked around. The last place to try was the barn.

Caution deserted him as he entered and saw Holly gagged and bound to a pillar beneath what was once the hayloft.

'Holly!'

She tried desperately with her eyes and shake of her head to warn him but it was no use. A hand covered his face. There was the sweet smell of chloroform as the gun clattered to the floor and for a few seconds he lifted his hands and struggled, but gradually he gave way and slid gracefully to the ground in someone's arms, catherine wheels and bright sparkling lights and off-key sounds of a carousel going round and round in his head.

It wasn't long before Thornton came too, bound to the second pillar holding up the floor of the hayloft. It started with him seemingly hearing his name repeated, 'Thornton, Thornton, Thornton,' and a couple of slaps across the face. 'Can you hear me? Thornton, wake up!' He woke up and looked at the grinning face of Mike Aliff in front of him.

'There you are then,' Mike said, stepping back.

'There are then what?' Thornton burbled, still in something of a mist.

'You were very foolish to interfere, Thornton. All this is way out of your league, my old china. You too, Holly Day. I can't believe I have finally got you both to rights. You've always looked down on me as if I were the scum of the earth and now it's time to face your come uppence and we, the company, will carry on before, going from strength to strength, as though nothing has happened.'

'Somehow I don't think so,' Thornton said. He made a sort of Maori type challenging gesture with his tongue between his teeth such as the All Black rugby team use at the beginning of their matches but this wasn't a challenge it was merely that his mouth tasted awful. 'We now have evidence that will send the lot of you to jail for a very long time.'

'That is why you are still breathing, Thornton and why I haven't finished you both off. I want to know exactly what you do know and what this evidence is you mention so glibly.'

'Find out,' Thornton said.

'All right, if that's the way you want to play it.'

He marched off a fair distance, grinning at Martin and Steve who Thornton noticed now for the first time.

'We're going to play a little game, Thornton,' Mike said, 'And I am really going to enjoy it. When I was at school, junior school I hasten to add, we did a play based on William Tell and I was Tell.

Can you imagine me in wrinkled tights? Of course then the crossbow bolt that split the apple was a trick one but now I am going to fire one for real and the apple will be on your head, my son.'

Martin stepped up to Thornton and, grinning from ear to ear, placed an apple on his head.

'Don't bother to try shaking it off,' Mike advised. 'I am going to take aim at its position whether it is there or not.'

'He's mad,' Holly said, 'stark raving mad. I always thought he was.'

'Your turn next Miss Day, when I've polished off your friend here.'

Steve handed Mike a crossbow and loaded it. Mike raised it to supposedly take aim at the apple although Thornton realised the aim was too low and it was all in Mike's mind a game of sweet revenge and the ending of an episode.

'The apple is a much abused fruit,' Thornton said. 'There was the apple in the Garden of Eden that started the rot. The poisoned apple given to Snow White, Paris and the siege of Troy and now this.'

'Are you some kind of clown?' Mike snarled, 'or is this meant to be a sort of delaying tactic which I am here to tell you, simply won't work.' He raised the crossbow and took aim again.

'It already has,' Thornton replied, 'and I don't believe I was ever meant to be a latter day Saint Sebastian.' He was struggling against his bonds and wondering if he could manoeuvre enough to avoid the deadly missile. But he had no need to worry. At the precise moment that Mike released the bolt he was thrown by a perfect rugby tackle from behind, an All Black couldn't have executed it better, as Albert had him around the knees and they both hit the ground. Thornton, who had shut his eyes in anticipation of the inevitable, now opened them and looked down at his feet to see two halves of the apple lying there and, looking up, the bolt imbedded in the wood just above his head.

It was virtually a repetition of what happened to Sir Roger Pemberton only in Thornton's case it meant life, not death.

Albert hauled Mike Aliff to his feet just as two squad cars, sirens blaring, drew up in the car park and Steve and Martin tried to make a run for it.

Holly gazed at Albert. 'My hero,' she gushed.

EPILOGUE

'I'm so glad you're safe, Carmen,' Maurice said.

'Not Carmen. My name is Holly.

'Whoever you are, I did try to warn you, did I not?'

'You did. How come you arrived in the nick of time and what caused your change of heart?'

They were sitting in the bar. There were police swarming all over the place and Maurice knew there was little time before the paddy wagons arrived and he, together with the others, including Nikos Filodopoulis released from the storeroom, would be carted off. He wondered how many of the board might have already fled.

'Call it an epiphany,' he said. 'Albert... '

Albert, who was standing nearby, stepped forward.

'Sir?'

'It seems unlikely I will be needing the car again today. Please drive Car... Miss Holly and....'

'Thornton, Thornton King.'

'Mister king...'

'Thornton.'

'Thornton, to wherever they wish to go.'

Albert nodded his head and winked at Holly who winked back.

'Good-bye, my dear,' Maurice said. 'I am actually very glad to have met you even if you are not who you said you were.'

Holly took his hand and kissed his cheek and Maurice with a smile turned away to take his turn with the Essex police. At least he would be free of a nagging wife for a while.

'Reg really lost out on this one,' Thornton said to no one in particular. 'He wouldn't listen to me. Could have made chief constable banging this little lot up. Ah, well, he always did think he knows best. Anyone care for half a granny smith?'

*****

Thornton reached out and had his wrist metaphorically slapped.

'Not yet, Thornton,' Rory said, 'First of all I have something for you and she handed him a cheque for one thousand five hundred pounds and, in a jeweller's box, a diamond beautifully cut and sparkling on its bed of midnight blue velvet.

'Thank you,' he said. What more was there to say?

'No no,' she replied. 'It is I who must thank you. Thank you for being the best private eye on the block. Now, why don't you help yourself to a delicious cucumber sandwich? And shall I pour?'

'Please do,' he said.